I0594911

KEEPER
OF MY HEART

BOOK TWO
THE IMMORTAL KEEPERS

HM HODGSON

Copyright © 2021 by HM Hodgson

All rights reserved.

No part of this book may be reproduced in any form or by any electronic or mechanical means, including information storage and retrieval systems, without written permission from the author, except for the use of brief quotations in a book review.

This book is a work of fiction. Names, characters, places and incidents, other than those clearly in the public domain, are fictitious and any resemblance to actual events, locales or persons—living or dead—is coincidental and not intended by the author/s.

First edition 2021.

Ebook ISBN 978-0-6451286-5-9

Print ISBN 978-0-6451286-6-6

Edited by Sarah Proulx Calfee, Three Little Words Editing

https://threelittlewordsediting.com

Proofread by Jo Speirs, Nurturing Words

https://www.nurturingwords.com.au

Front cover by Amanda Pillar from Smoking Hot Covers

https://www.smokinghotcovers.com

Inside cover design by Jacqueline Hayley with Marina Farcic

https://jacquelinehayley.com

✾ Created with Vellum

For my family. Love you.

1

———

"What the fuck?" Nate Jones said as he spun the steering wheel of his unmarked police car into the Mountain View Road strip mall.

His headlights picked up a gleaming trail of shattered glass all the way to a jagged hole in the window of the cafe, the last business in the row of the normally neatly maintained shopfronts.

Nate's hands clenched into fists. No one messed with his town. His people.

He cut the engine and headlights, his magic allowing him to see even in the dark surroundings. He eased into the predawn winter air, briskly rubbing his hands. The tang of wattle and eucalyptus carried to him on the sharp breeze.

Shit, it was cold. And quiet.

These shops wouldn't open for hours yet, and this early on a Friday morning, the only action was blocks away over on Main Street. Not that the action was much, given Warragul was a country town, and it was bloody early.

A scraping sound echoed behind him.

Nate spun, and pain punched through his skull, a sharp crack renting the quiet. Something thudded to the ground.

He pushed hard through his core, managed to hold his balance, glimpsed a man rushing at him, fists raised.

Nate pushed out with his magic—a complicated, delicate sleeping spell raced from his lips—at the same time as he raised his fists. Ducking the incoming blow, he sent a hard, fast jab at the man. His fist connected at the same time as his spell.

The man dropped to Nate's feet, still but for the rise and fall of his chest with each breath. He was maybe midtwenties. Not a local. His eyes were open but unfocused, and he blinked slowly, sleepily. No longer a threat.

A high-pitched ringing echoed through Nate's ears, and he gingerly ran a hand over the back of his head. Nothing wet. But it hurt. Bloody hell, did it hurt.

Wincing, he shook his stinging knuckles, then grabbed his phone and called the station.

"Yeah, Kat. It's Nate. Can you head over to the Mountain View Road shops? I accidentally stopped a break and enter on my way in. Nah, I'm okay. Yeah, yeah. Laugh it out. But the guy got a lucky drop on me, so now *he* needs a pickup, and I don't want to leave the shop for anyone else to walk in and take what they want."

Nate hung up to the sound of Kat's ongoing laughter.

But he didn't mind. He was more relieved that his spell and fist had handled the situation together. Cohesion between his magic and human reactions was important—a lack of balance could impact either or both. Not good for a cop.

He went to check on his attacker when the ringing in his ears grew louder.

Maybe that's why the connection happened. Hell knows, he'd been keeping it at bay for years now. But there, in the empty car park, buffeted by the icy breeze, a wind-whipped knock echoed at the door to his mind.

Even with his attention diverted, he didn't risk answering the rap-rap-rap. But his focus was off because he left the mental door ajar.

And then the wind pushed through. And the World Tree entered his mind. It was the softest mental touch he'd ever experienced. Yet totally overwhelming. Thousands of years of wisdom, of experiences, filled his consciousness. Suddenly, the Tree filled his vision, a waning moon at its back.

A sharp chill racked Nate's skin right before the moon disappeared and the World Tree caught fire. It burned and burned till its incredible trunk, branches, and leaves were nothing but ash.

The cries of hundreds, thousands—millions—of people echoed through him as their world was lost.

Over the ashes, a figure, shrouded in a black hooded cloak, stepped down from an altar of mangled bleached bones.

Even as the ashes reached up in hesitant fingers to grasp at the cloak for help, the figure crushed them under a blood-red boot.

The image changed.

The World Tree stood as it was today. Its mighty branches swiveled like arms, reached out toward him, its leaves bent their tips in beckoning waves. The wind echoed his name as it whistled through the leaves.

Nathaniel.

It wanted him. Wanted him to become a Keeper.

The clock had just struck nine o'clock when Sim Morris charged through the hotel's wide lobby and veered into the public bar.

Frank stood behind the counter, serving a mix of late-breakfast coffees and early start beers to three regular customers, all sitting on the high stools at the bar. She said a quick hello to her regulars and gave a fast wave to Frank as she sailed past.

The regulars called out, "Hi."

"Welcome back," Frank said as he dried a glass with a white cloth almost the same color as his hair. "Time for a coffee?"

Oh man, she'd kill for a cup of coffee. "Thanks, but no can do," Sim said. "I've got to get to the accountant."

"No worries. And Nate stopped by while you were out. Said something about having a hearing this morning, and he'll come back later."

A surge of warmth flooded her belly, but Sim resolutely ignored it. She tightened her bag over her shoulder.

Detective Irresistible, with his rumpled blond hair, piercing blue eyes, and dimples—*dimples!*—was off-limits, even if her body was having a hard time accepting that order. Nate was a friend, had been from the moment she'd come to the country town of Warragul in Gippsland,

Victoria, a year ago. And that was where she was keeping him.

"Got it. Thanks, Frank."

She forced Nate from her mind, ducked through the connecting door into the commercial kitchen.

"All good, Stu?" she asked her short-order cook and all-round kitchen hand.

Stuart looked over the stainless-steel counter and gave her a thumbs-up. He had his wireless headphones in as he cleaned up the breakfast equipment. She gave him a thumbs-up back and kept going through the kitchen to the next connecting door and into her office. She dropped her purse onto the desk and picked up her phone.

Damn it. What had started as a good day had officially taken a wrong turn. She was late. She hated being late. The impulse to just sit, okay, grab a coffee and *then* sit, hit her hard.

But there was no time for that. Sim straightened her shoulders, pulled on her braid. Okay, her hair was still tied back. She was good to go.

She dialed her accountant's office.

"Good morning, Ellison and Tyndall; how may I help?" said a man's cool and professional voice.

"Hi, Gary, this is Sim Morris from the Grand Hotel in Warragul. I have a meeting with Ms. Ellison at nine, but I'm running a bit late. I have to grab my paperwork, then I'll drive right over."

"Well, Miss. Morris, as it's just gone nine, and Ms. Ellison has another appointment at nine forty-five, you'll have to reschedule."

Sim winced, but she'd dealt with plenty of hard-asses in

her time in hospitality. "Not a problem. Let me know when she can see me next, and I'll be there."

Minutes later, Sim ignored the urge to crash the phone back on the desk. Damn it. She'd specifically put this morning aside to get her bookwork up to date, and she'd had some questions for her accountant.

She tugged again on her braid, blew out a short hard breath.

Sim could run the operation of the pub just fine, but the financial stuff was still tricky, and she needed to concentrate to avoid making mistakes. She'd even put Tara into a rare day at childcare so she could focus on the numbers.

And four-year-old Tara had not been happy about it. Her angel had turned into a demon as soon as Sim went to leave. She'd clung to Sim's legs and yelled, screamed for Sim not to go. It had taken two of the childcare staff members to unwrap her baby's arms. And then the tears had started—great boulders of devastation that had rolled over the round cheeks, past the completely turned-down mouth.

No way Sim could leave Tara like that.

So she'd cuddled her close, and eventually, Tara had let one of the older staff take over the cuddle duty. Even as she'd walked away, Tara's hiccups had sent shards of pain through Sim's heart.

And now she'd missed her appointment.

Damn it. Sim sighed, dropped her head into her hands. What the hell had she been thinking? She was a server—sure, she'd even managed a café back in the city, but now she'd gone and purchased an old hotel, was actually an owner and manager. Biting her lip, she shook her head. She must've been loco.

But that's what you get when miracles happen, and you win the lottery.

With just over a million dollars in hand, Sim had suddenly been able to look after her family. From the moment Tara had come into the world, Sim had wanted to live somewhere her baby could grow up, could grow *into*.

And now she had the Warragul Grand Hotel. Not that the building was all that grand anymore—but it had been, once upon a time.

She was going to make the old girl a beauty again, eventually. And become part of a community in a way she'd never been before. She *could* do this. *Could* be a successful businesswoman—and not just because she'd won some money. She'd make this business work because she was smart enough, capable enough, to do it.

Sim took another breath, lifted her head. Repeated her mantra. *You've got this. You're going to be fine.*

She just had a lot to learn.

The enticing scent of coffee drifted through the air, followed by the hum and whirr of the steamer out front. Her mouth watered.

A knock sounded at the door to the office, and Frank walked in holding a steaming mug. "Figured if you were still here, you'd want one."

Sim almost groaned. "You're an angel, Frank Williams."

The older man smiled, the wrinkles around his eyes scrunching up.

"What happened? I thought you had your meeting?"

Sim sighed over her coffee. "I did. Only Tara wouldn't let me go, so I was late. And of course, Ellison had another meeting booked after mine, so I've had to reschedule. Damn it."

Frank gave her a crooked smile.

"Why don't you take some time for yourself? Stu and I have the place covered, and the brekkie crowd's gone. There are only a couple of rooms to do—we can look after them. Go enjoy your coffee. Take a moment to stop."

Sim smiled up at Frank. He'd been a godsend since she'd taken on the pub, always willing to help, and the locals loved him, given he'd known most of them from birth. She leaned over and gave him a peck on the cheek.

"You're amazing, Frank. But no, I'll do the rooms. Like you say—there's only two, and you do enough around here without carting linen up and down those stairs too."

"But—"

"Nope." She held up a hand. "But once I do the rooms, then I'll take that break. If you're looking for me, I'll be out back picking up some winter sun for a few minutes. Any more and I'll turn into one giant freckle."

After she finished with the rooms, she ducked up to the second-floor residence where she lived with Tara and her mother, June. She grabbed the book she'd been dreaming of having the time to read and a coffee.

Within minutes, she was downstairs and out the back door, inhaling the sweet air of the winter morning as she looked around her back lot.

Her heart swelled. This was something she was proud of, even though she'd had a lot of help.

This area had been unused when she'd moved in—half concrete, half dirt. The only saving grace had been an old lillypilly, its branches covered in a tough cracked bark that weathered the Victorian climate well. Now, broad leafy grass spread all the way to the back fence. Timber picnic tables sat beneath the lillypilly, and solar lights hung from the big branches. At night, it was beautiful out here. Almost magical.

Uh-uh, not that word.

Images from two months earlier—of the bonfire up at Nate's family farm flittered through her mind, of Nate, his tall frame silhouetted against golden tongues of fire as the wind raced to howl around them, of his brilliant blue gaze holding hers.

Shivers raced over her skin as if she were back there, and the heat and energy pouring off him was a cord reeling her into him. Enticing her into his hard, wide chest. Closer to the tang of his scent.

Sim moistened suddenly dry lips. Uh-uh, no more Nate thoughts, and definitely no thoughts about the ... the *things* she'd seen that night.

Nope, she was here for some peace. Not the niggling, eerie sensation that something existed outside of her already hectic world.

She forced her focus back to her garden. Right now, those picnic tables invited *her* to take a seat. She slid onto one, looked up at her old building. Her heart filled.

Damn, but she loved this place. The worn timber handholds, the wrought iron balustrades. She'd even planted a climbing rose on the building's corners out here. Couldn't wait to see leaves and blossoms cover the building in time.

The redbrick building was built at the start of the last century. After she'd purchased the hotel, she'd only had enough money left to replace the most damaged carpet and fix the safety issues.

As hard as the work was, as steep as the learning curve was, it was hers. Theirs—Sim, Tara, and Sim's mother.

Inhaling deeply, she closed her eyes. Lifted her face to the sun. Welcome warmth settled on her skin, seeped into her pores. Contentment eased through her.

Then her phone played a tune. She took one more moment to enjoy the sun, then with a sigh, opened her eyes.

But before she could pick her phone up, a cloud passed over the sun. Goosebumps pricked over her arms.

Suddenly something icy and razor-edged speared into her chest, shoved away the warmth of the sun. Her breath whooshed out.

She gasped, tried to inhale, but then a huge punch of pressure smashed into her. Her body flew back off the bench.

Cool grass cushioned her fall. Clear sky filled her view until a dark silhouette moved into her vision and blocked the sun.

Sim tried again to draw a breath, but her chest was too tight, too compressed ...

And the world went dark.

2

Sim opened her eyes, blinked against the sun, against the fuzziness in her mind. Why was everything upside down?

The cobwebby sensation gradually drifted away, a plume of smoke on the wind. A sensation of *difference* remained.

She lifted her head, and the world righted itself. With a groan, she eased her head back to the grass and looked up again—straight into the winter sun. She cursed and shielded her eyes. Awkwardly rolling over, she drew her knees up and under her belly and pushed herself onto all fours.

Tentatively, she turned her neck from side to side.

No sharp pains. Thank the stars, an injury was the last thing she needed. She shuffled to the bench, snagging her phone from the grass on the way. Right, now, all she had to do was stand up. But what the hell had happened?

With another curse, she braced her palms on the bench seat and unsteadily rose to her feet. Tiny darts of silver crowded her vision from all directions. She fought back the dizzy sensation, held herself upright.

Eventually, her head cleared, and she stood up. Damn it, this wasn't how her rare moment of quiet was meant to go. What *had* happened?

That's right—her phone had been ringing. And something had hit her in the chest. And then what? Something else niggled at the back of her mind, but the thought faded beneath the sudden need to check herself.

She lifted the neck of her sweater, looked for an injury. Nothing.

Scrubbing a fist over her chest, she sat with a thud, took a shuddering breath. But then something deep inside her, right in the middle of her chest, shivered.

What the hell?

She let out another shaking breath, waited a moment, then inhaled slowly, cautiously again. That thing within her tingled right at the end.

Sim reached out a trembling hand for the coffee. The cup was barely warm. What the hell was the time? She scrambled to check her phone screen.

No way. It was after ten o'clock. Had she been on the ground for forty-five minutes?

Bloody hell, had she hurt herself after all? She couldn't afford to be hurt—couldn't afford to be away from her business.

Shit, shit, shit, shit, shit.

Okay, she forced herself to take a slow breath. *Calm, Sim.* She wouldn't help herself if she panicked. *Try again.*

She cautiously inhaled, not as deep ... Her chest tingled. Hell. Maybe she'd busted a rib when she fell?

Sim swallowed the lump that rose in her throat. So maybe she *had* hurt herself. But that didn't have to mean it was a severe injury. People busted ribs all the time. She'd just go see the doctor. She was certainly no stranger to them after what had happened to Tara two months earlier ...

Her intuition rang low and long, a chime ringing deep inside her chest.

She could either ignore it, which she'd occasionally done throughout her life—always to her dismay—or she could listen to it. Well, hell. Time to listen to her gut.

Breathing as shallowly as she could to avoid that odd sensation, Sim headed into the hotel and up to her apartment, vaguely registering the walk up the two flights of stairs.

Inside, she used the weight of her body to close the door behind her, resting her head on the timber and taking a cautious breath.

Maybe she'd imagined that weird sensation? Only damn, there it was again, deep within her chest. Her skin went clammy.

Sim forced a shallow breath and pushed off the door.

June, her mother, sat in her usual seat at the dining table, staring out through the back window. She wore her usual soft blue cardigan, white long-sleeved T-shirt, and beige pants, looking closer to eighty than her true age of fifty-five.

Sim tugged on her braid, forced on her everything-is-okay face.

Then her mother slowly swiveled, luminous gray eyes filled with tears. Sim's heart lurched; she dropped her calm façade, and she darted over.

"June, what's wrong? Are you okay?"

June's hand, a close-to-lifeless pale limb, came up to rest on Sim's cheek—a move unexpected, rare.

Sim held June's hand there, willed warmth into it. She moistened her suddenly dry lips. This day was turning even crazier.

"June, come on. What's wrong?" Her mother rarely spoke, rarely showed any reaction—physical or emotional —or did anything more than sit and look out the window. A state she'd been in and out of for most of Sim's life.

"Come on, June. *Mum*. You can tell me."

Her mother whispered something.

Sim leaned in, so close their cheeks touched. "Say that again."

"They're here."

A knock sounded at the apartment door. Sim yelped, jumped to her feet. The door opened and revealed a tall, slim figure—Nate's cousin.

"Bloody hell," Sim said. "India, you scared me."

"Me?" India asked. "Ah, I called earlier, left a message to say I was coming over."

"Oh no, not *you*, the door. Something June said."

"So is now an okay time for a visit? I could come back—"

"Actually, yes," Sim said in a rush. "Now is an *excellent* time for a visit."

Sim turned back to her mother. June's luminous eyes once more looked outside. Straight out over the picnic tables. Had June seen everything?

Sim's heart thudded. Biting her lip, she turned to India. "I'm so glad you're here. I could use some help, *your* help, right now." Sim briefly dipped her eyes to her mother. "How about we head out back, chat there?"

"Sure, sounds good." India eyed June too. "I could do with a chat in the sun."

Sim patted her mother's shoulder. "Right, June, I'll be downstairs. If you need me, here's your phone."

Sim moved the rarely used mobile beside the teacup on the table. June nodded but didn't turn her head from the window. Sim swallowed a sigh, gestured for India to follow her.

"Can I get you a coffee on the way?"

"That would be lovely, but only if you're having one. Also, Nan's downstairs, no doubt talking with Frank."

Sim glanced sideways at her friend as they walked down the old steps to the first level. Out of habit, she checked the short corridor—all seemed in order—before she turned back to India.

"It could be a good thing that your grandmother's here." She touched India's hand. "Seriously, I'm glad you're both here."

A surge of something powerful, electric, zapped where her fingers met India's skin, and silvery fog seeped across Sim's vision. India disappeared, replaced with an ancient tree with gnarled bark, dark and aged, with mighty limbs spearing into the sky. The silvery fog swept back in, obscuring the tree before disappearing. And India was back again.

"Bloody hell. What was that?" Sim whirled around. Where had the tree come from? And where had it gone? Was she going mad? Her heart began to pound. She wiped sweaty palms on her jeans. "Uh, India, did you just see anything ... odd?"

India's eyes were wide. "Apart from the blank way you were just staring at me, you mean?"

"Yeah, apart from that," Sim muttered. "We definitely need to talk."

When they reached the bar, Frank had already made three coffees and was talking with India's grandmother, Liz. "Nan" to the family.

Trying to act normal—like she hadn't gone loco—Sim mustered a smile for her bartender. "Thanks, Frank. Listen, I need some time with India and Liz. Would you mind not sending anyone out back for a few minutes?"

"No worries, I've got it here."

She went to pat Frank's arm—or maybe not. She dropped her hand to her side and ushered Liz and India through the back door.

The picnic tables and chairs were the same as earlier, all innocent and inviting. A shiver prickled down her spine, but she made herself step forward and sit down with Liz and India.

She'd confront this thing, whatever it was, head on. But where to start? Well, she had to start somewhere. She took a deep breath.

"Ladies, I can safely say this has been the weirdest morning of my life. Even winning the lotto made more sense than today." Sim tugged at her braid. "And you're the only ones who won't think I've lost the plot. Okay, here goes."

She recounted what had happened from when she'd fallen off the chair up to when India had disappeared, and a tree had appeared ... then disappeared. Then another thought struck.

"But you called me," Sim said. "I should've checked what brought you to town?"

Liz toyed with her coffee mug. Then her blue eyes lifted, sparkling with intelligence and something else, something powerful and unspoken.

"Simone, dear. India saw a vision, too. Of you in trouble. She ... we ... had to come to town and find you."

"You saw a *vision*? Of me?"

India had become a genuine friend since she'd come to live at her grandmother's farm a couple of months earlier. And India had been the first person to push Sim's understanding of her own intuition. And around a crackling bonfire beneath a new moon up on Nan's farm, India had done something Sim had never imagined possible.

India had made magic. There, she'd thought it.

Sim placed her coffee mug down, moistened her lips as she tried to put her contemplation into words. "India, are you a ... a ..." She shook her head. "I can't even say it."

India gently smiled, and Sim looked, really looked, into her friend's eyes. Their green depths were unusual. Cat eyes, some locals called them, but right now they also sparkled, overflowed with the same force, the same power as Liz's.

The same force that shone from Nate's eyes.

The world quieted. Or maybe Sim was so focused on this moment, this conversation, that nothing else penetrated. Either way, in that welcome silence, beneath the warm winter rays, a whisper of air moved against her skin. The currents brushed over her, played with the end of her braid, soothing, comforting.

And the tingle, the shiver, whatever it was inside her, whirred to life. Didn't stop. She took another deep breath. "Are you *witches*? Am *I* a witch?"

"Yes, Sim. We are," India said, exchanging a glance with Liz. "And so are you."

Sim's breath whooshed out. Well, there it was. She stilled. The question that had hovered at the edge of her mind ever since the night of the bonfire had an answer.

And one by one, every single atom inside her zeroed in; her heart leaped, her pulse sang as if aware of a rightness, of acceptance as if at last the world made sense.

Yet this all seemed unreal. *She* was a ... a witch?

"How?" Sim asked. "How is this possible? I mean—I figured out you were all, even Nate, well, different. But you're all family. I'm not related to you." Sim's gaze lifted to the top level of the hotel. To where her mother, June, would be sitting at the dining table against the window, no doubt looking out. "Is Tara? June? Is that how it works?"

"Yes, Sim." India nodded. "Your mum, I don't know how to say this, but we believe your mum has—"

"Sim. Sim!" Frank stood at the doorway, worry tugging at the creases on his face. "Sim, I'm sorry to interrupt you and all, but there's someone here. You need to come in. Now."

That little chime, the one she associated with her intuition, rang clear and long. She scrubbed her chest as she stood.

"Sorry, ladies." Sim gave India and Liz a tight smile. "Something must be wrong. Will you wait? I'll be back out as soon as I can."

Frank held the door open, lowered his voice. "Your next check-in's here."

"That's the problem?"

"Ah, well, yes, but not just that. He says that he's Tara's … That Tara's his—" Frank's cheeks reddened, and he ran a hand through his already mussed silver hair.

Sim strode up the short corridor to the front of the hotel. Spoke over her shoulder as she did. "Is he in the guest parlor?"

"That I am." A man's voice drifted from that direction.

That chime rang inside her again, hard. She slowed. Stilled. That voice … it had a familiar, European old-world lilt, a smooth roll of the vowels. Her heart stopped. Everything in her swayed.

"Bloody hell," Sim whispered.

Every muscle in her body tensed, and for one moment, she froze. Then she swallowed hard and with leaden feet, clumsily took another step forward. Another. Until she stood in the doorway.

His features were barely changed from her memory—the angular jaw, a cleft centered in his chin, the straight hard nose, those piercing cool gray eyes. Even from the doorway, their chilled crystalline depths were more silver than gray. The only difference was his thick blue-black hair was shorter now.

He wore buff chinos with brown leather boots and a creamy thick-knit sweater that hugged his impressive frame. He looked expensive. Like he'd backpacked his way into a well-paying job.

"Hello, Sim."

"Luc?"

3

In the cramped, shabby room of the pathetic little shop, utterly unsuitable for the glory it contained, Ri'Anit bent her will to the altar of bones—darkness shed like oil on water, out from its center. Broken bone after broken bone emerged from the dark; each one smashed into the next until the mighty structure was revealed.

The Mortalworld did not deserve such magnificence, but she'd chosen this path of assault. Chosen to tread subtly, precisely in this pitiful town until she found the perfect place for an attack.

A shudder rippled through Ri'Anit as the perfection that was her god formed atop the mass of bones.

Irrika lay supine, luminescent skin gleaming, hair so black it sucked in all light, flowing in a river over the end of the altar. One stray wisp caught on her blood-red lips. A single razor-sharp platinum chain linked around her neck, caught at ruby breast studs before slipping in a hard V to her crotch.

Ri'Anit sank to her knees, dropped her head low.

"My first. What news have you?" The purr of her god's voice crossed the room.

Ri'Anit's heart leaped at the new address. She glanced up once, knew the adoration on her face would be fully evident before she bowed her head. "My god, as you ordered, I am in place and ready to proceed."

"Beware the Keepers, my first. Your predecessor did not heed their danger, and in doing so, lost my closest opportunity yet." Irrika gave a sharp laugh. "And his life."

"My god, I vow this to you. In your honor, I will infiltrate this place. Once they trust me, I shall take their Tree's defenses one by one until none here may stand in our way. And then we shall hold the Tree until the next black moon rises."

Irrika languidly reached out, softly stroked her cheek. Ri'Anit held her breath at the exquisite touch.

"My first, this is your decision," Irrika purred. "Though know this, I have heard rumors the Angelkin are becoming interested in this fight. You will be up against a lineup of enemies, old and new."

"It matters not who they are or where they are from, my god, I will take down any and all who stand in our way."

Irrika laughed, her slim neck arching back. "That is as it should be. It appears I chose well with you, my child. But my desire is that you strike while their backs are turned, and they think us vanquished. Know this; you have until the new moon rises to prove yourself worthy. Use your every tool, your soldiers and your magic with absolute prejudice and control. Or I shall be forced to find another to anoint."

Ri'Anit inclined her head. The moon was in the first quarter now, leaving her seven nights to locate the Keepers and destroy them all. She lifted her chin. She was more than up to this task.

"Your desire is my will," she promised. "I will deliver this world for you."

"Never has one been given such honor with such little time in my ranks. Do not make me regret anointing you first follower."

Ri'Anit resisted the urge to shout her elation, instead bowing her head. After two hundred years of dealing death to those she was ordered to kill, *she* would lead their war.

"I will do this, my god, and use all means required to reach your objective. These humans, witches or not, are no match for me."

Irrika's touch hardened, clamped tighter and tighter.

"Do not fail me—my first. My love," Irrika's voice crooned even as her form shifted from solid mass to mist, then faded into nothing.

Ri'Anit slowly released her breath and then called out her spell to conceal once again the altar. The magic rolled from her hands in a wave of heat.

Then she fluidly rose to her feet. Time to enact her plan.

Using the dark of night to cover their arrival, Ri'Anit brought two of her seasoned soldiers in through the shop's rear entry.

Slaying local witches to steal their meager power for her soldiers would risk alerting the Keepers to her presence; therefore, her soldiers had to be accomplished killers already.

And these two were pure muscle, their minds and bodies completely bent to her will—for both her pleasure and her orders—with multiple kills to their names, so they had been her first picks for this mission.

Bespelled through physical release, these soldiers would obey her orders when and how she wanted.

They both murmured her name before dropping to one knee at her feet. Their hands slid up her calf muscles beneath the hem of her long skirt. She let them each take one leg, let them warm their cold hands on her heated skin, sent a beat of heat for her own enjoyment as they reached higher to her thighs.

Ri'Anit dragged one back to the wall, let him come close and lift her skirt, plant his face between her thighs and lick her. The other moved in, slid his hands to stroke high inside her. Between the rasp of that thick tongue hitting her clitoris over and over and the rubbing of those fingers hard and deep inside her, they pushed her over the edge.

Still on their knees, one went to open his pants, but she kicked out with her black heeled boot, and the hands dropped away. Play time was over. They had work to do. Then she recalled her god's words. Control.

Ri'Anit inhaled the scent of her release, resolved herself to take the time for this step. Necessity meant she needed these two muscled males biddable and pliant. Sex served both purposes after all.

"Stay." She pressed her boot back into the first soldier's chest until he was prone.

Breathing rapidly, gaze locked on her, he unzipped his pants, and his cock sprang free, thick and ready for her.

The other soldier, she pulled to his feet.

"Undress," Ri'Anit ordered.

He obeyed without pause, and she took his length into

her palm. He groaned, and his hips surged toward her. She regarded her soldiers for a moment—their willingness to follow her commands had to be absolute. But she was going to enjoy herself while she was at it.

She murmured her spell, chanted it over and over as she lowered herself onto the length of her first soldier, all the while gripping her second, bringing him closer.

Finishing the spell, she took her second into her mouth and sucked him hard. Beneath her, her first soldier groaned and jerked. She slammed down, again and again, ground into him until the pressure exploded, her internal muscles clenched, and her body convulsed. He came too, shouting his release. She cupped her second soldier beneath his heavy balls, pressed deeply between them, and then he roared, coming down her throat.

The spell consummated in an electric surge that sent a residual tingle through her core.

Licking her lips, drenched from her release and theirs, Ri'Anit stood.

"Our mission is this ..."

4

Nate stalked through the station and into his small office. He left the door open, shrugged his jacket off and dropped into the chair at his desk.

Kat, short for Kathryn, appeared a moment later. She was Warragul's senior sergeant. She had smooth, deeply tanned skin and stylish hair cut short enough that she didn't have to effing bother with tying it back—her words. She was muscular and as strong as she was direct. She cocked a hip against his door.

"The probie's grabbing coffee. You want one? And I'm not talking about instant. My shout since I owe you for last time." She raised a brow. "Your usual?"

"Always remembering the details, Kat. Which is why you're the best senior ever."

"I bet you say that to all the seniors. Plus, we've only known each other since preschool." She folded her arms. "How'd it go with the magistrate? And how's the noggin?"

"Turns out the guy's wanted in the big smoke for a serious assault too, so he's on remand here, transferring up there later today. My bet is he'll be spending a fair amount of time behind bars. And as for my head ... sore as you know what." Nate scowled, touched the still tender skin at the back of his head.

"Well, at least you got some good news. We won't have to worry about him hanging around town," Kat said.

"Any other news I need to know?"

"Did you know that Matt, the florist over on Queen Street, moved up to Melbourne? There's a new florist already moved in, apparently."

"Wow, no, hadn't heard. That was fast."

"Yep, and that's pretty much the news."

Kat smiled and headed back to her desk. Nate sighed and dug into his jacket, pulled out his mobile phone. He'd had it on silent during court, but the screen showed several text messages. He thumbed through them as he loosened his tie with the other hand. He was out of court now, so the neck-choker could go. Hallelujah.

A message about Sim caught his attention. What the fuck? He grabbed his jacket and raced out of the office.

"Nate, where are you ... your coffee!" Kat called out from her workstation.

"Heading out. I'll call in later."

He broke into a run and rounded the corner to the car park. Barreled into a young woman. She rebounded off him, and he snagged her arm and stopped her from completely smacking into the ground.

"Shit, sorry." He helped her back to her feet. "Are you okay? Did I hurt you?"

A pale face surrounded by masses of golden blond hair turned to him. Early twenties, aqua-hued eyes. She shook her head, and her baby blues widened. "No, not hurt. Just surprised."

Nate cursed under his breath. "If you really are okay, would you mind if I keep going? I've got something urgent to attend to."

"Of course, no harm done." The woman waved one hand. "Please don't let me stop you."

"Thanks. Appreciate your understanding."

"That's okay." The words cheerfully rang out behind him.

It took a whole three minutes to drive to the hotel. *What the fuck* spun over and over in his mind, matching every spin of his wheels.

The foyer of the hotel, with its old timber and wide corridor, was quiet. Nate ducked his head into the public bar. He eyed the locals spread through the room. Nothing looked untoward.

Frank was pouring a beer from the taps, and Nate caught his eye. The older man gave a short jerk of his chin, darted his eyes up. Nate took the stairs at a run all the way to the dim landing on the second floor.

The door to the residence was closed, so he knocked once, pushed it open—walked into a wall of tension, found Sim, June, India and Nan seated around Sim's dining table. Three of them looked up; only June kept her gaze locked on the window.

It was amazing how the craft flowed from a witch without any conscious will. He knew Sim had some low form of power. Tara was definitely a witch. Even Sim's mother, June, had the remnants of the craft.

Now, the air vibrated with the varying levels of power in the room.

Sim's braid was undone, and a firestorm of hair framed her face. Her normally creamy skin had a pallor he'd only seen once before.

"What's going on?" Nate asked.

No one answered.

Then something different registered—from the magic that roiled around the room. There were three full-strength witchcrafts. He opened up his own. The magics in the room were tactile, identifiable by the rub against his own. Brail for witches.

Nan's magic had been within him his entire life; its force and depth as recognizable as her face, as was his cousin India's.

But there was a new presence. Strong. It teased at his magic, but he couldn't place it, not at first.

He frowned. This witchcraft was velvety, warm. Inviting. His magic rose to meet it—magic always met magic. Then his gut tightened. His gaze flew to Sim.

"What the fuck—"

"Nate," Nan said.

"Sorry, Nan." But Nate didn't take his eyes off Sim, even as he stumbled back, hitting the couch behind him. He leaned for a moment against the sturdy furniture.

"Someone needs to explain what's going on. Now." He blew out a low breath, met Sim's gaze. "Why is your witchcraft hitting me?"

"I don't know, Nate." Sim scowled. Color flooded her cheeks. "But how about why didn't anyone tell me I was a witch before now?"

"Ah ..." Nate looked at Nan and India.

They looked helplessly back at him.

"Hell, Sim," he said through gritted teeth, stabbing a hand through his hair. "You've always had some level of it, but it never appeared to be significant. And it's not something that you just go and blurt out. Like, hey, you're a witch."

Sim's eyes fired up—their whiskey-brown color tinted with a coppery fire not unlike her hair. Heat poured off her as if her magic lashed out along with her ire.

She was magnificent.

He forced down the surge of desire that spiraled through him.

Bloody hell. Now was not the time. But she'd always turned him on—and now, all afire, it was impossible not to react to her physically. He bit back an oath. *Not the time. Not the time.* He told himself that over and over until he was almost certain his body wouldn't give him away.

"But, Nate, I *am* a witch." Sim's hollow laugh echoed through the little apartment. "And damn it, that's not even the bad part."

Her eyes closed as if the comment had taken everything out of her. Even the heat in her cheeks drained away.

"Okay ..." Nate slowly exhaled. "Tell me what's bad."

Sim opened her mouth, but nothing came out. Finally, she closed her eyes, and her fists clenched.

"Hey, come on, Sim. I ... we ... can help, but you need to let us in." He rubbed her back in slow, soothing circles.

Shit, looked like words weren't going to work. He was about to try again when finally, Sim opened her eyes. Her gaze was filled with raw, hard pain.

"Luc's here," she whispered. "Staying here, in one of the hotel rooms."

He froze, stared hard at her. "Hold on. You're not talking magic. You said Luc? As in *the* Luc?"

"You know who Luc is?" India asked.

Nate gave a short nod. "Ah hell, Sim." He racked his brain to recall everything Sim had let on about Luc—it hadn't exactly been a talking point. He swiftly pieced together what he knew. "You haven't seen him in, what, over five years?"

Sim nodded, mouth still tightly shut.

"And Luc is ...?" India said.

Nate glanced back at Sim. She opened her mouth, but nothing came out. Which made fucking sense given everything. He kept his gaze on Sim's and raised one eyebrow.

She swallowed and then dipped her head once.

"Luc is Tara's father," Nate said.

Sim cursed even as he said it. Reflexively, he stepped forward and ran his hands up and down Sim's arms. She looked up at him, skin waxy.

"That's one hell of a shock," Nate said. "I take it you didn't know he was coming?"

Sim shook her head, apparently all she could do to respond. Her eyes were locked on his as if he was her tether in the storm. A dim part of him registered he liked being that for her.

But she looked like she was in shock. At least he knew what to do with that.

"India, Sim doesn't keep anything hard to drink up here. Could you duck downstairs and get something stronger than coffee?"

"Absolutely," she said. "Here, have my seat."

"Thanks, but I'm fine here." He wasn't leaving Sim's side. Not when she was so upset.

Somehow, Nate managed to keep a calm outer appearance. But inside ... inside, he was ready to destroy every fucking obstacle in Sim's path.

And what the fuck was Luc doing here, really?

5

A whirlwind of sensations and emotions caught Sim up. Tossed her around and left her stranded—like flotsam after a storm. *Luc was here. She was ... a witch. Luc was here.*

The life that she'd worked so damned hard to build for Tara and her, for June too, suddenly it was all on the precipice of coming apart.

Every single sense, every layer of emotion, screamed *no!* Things were just getting on track.

And then there was Nate. Steadfast. A lifeline through the squall.

He'd reached out and touched her. His warm, capable hands were a tether when she was going to shatter into a million pieces.

Sim dragged in a breath, and finally, finally, the seething storm receded—it didn't disappear—but it gave her enough room that she could drag in another breath, another, then another.

She kept her eyes steady on Nate through it all.

And then a little shift, so tiny, barely noticeable, moved inside her. In a day of so many changes, she wasn't sure why —how—she could even notice such a small thing. But that didn't make it any less real.

She had welcomed his touch.

For the first time in her adult life, she didn't disengage from contact with another human being. She wanted Nate's hands on her, even to let herself lean into his heat, his strength. To inhale that warm, spicy scent that was all Nate.

And it was okay.

Which was another first. Because she had never leaned on a man. Ever.

She almost swayed when Nate's hands left her. A chill claimed the places where they'd been, and she hugged her arms tight.

"Sim? Simone? Did Luc say what he's after?" Nate asked.

She mentally shook her head, forced herself to focus.

"Ah, no. He said he'd been looking for me ... us ... after he heard about Tara. And that he wants to get to know his, our, daughter." She swallowed the hard knot lodged in her throat. "Bloody hell. I'd gotten to the point that I never thought I'd say that."

Nate's jaw clenched, and Sim had the absurd desire to reach out and cup that hard plane, soothe it like he'd soothed her.

She didn't do it, though. That wasn't the nature of their relationship. Nate had asked her out when she'd first come to town, but Sim was a pro at keeping men in the friend zone. And they'd become so close she'd even mentioned Luc once or twice. As sharp as Nate was, he'd probably pieced the rest together.

"What?" Sim eyed Nate's face. "You look worried."

"I'm trying to figure him out."

"Great. Let me know what you come up with."

Nate laughed, but it was strained, and Sim couldn't even bring herself to smile.

"Where's India?" she asked, looking around the apartment.

"She's grabbing something strong to drink."

"Why?"

"You were looking shocky. And considering you didn't even notice India leave, I'm guessing you need something strong."

"Huh. Thanks."

Liz made a sound, kind of like a smothered laugh.

"Sorry, Liz. I've pretty much ignored you since, well, since Luc arrived."

Sim had to hold back a grimace at even saying his name, which on a logical level, she knew wasn't fair to the man. But it wasn't something she had control over—just saying his name made her stomach clench, sent a roil of nausea through her. She blew out a shaky breath.

"Liz, can I get you a tea, a coffee? June, I'll get you a tea, too." Sim turned to her mother, but June's gray eyes were still as distant as the hills on the horizon.

"Why don't I make the tea?" Liz covered Sim's hands with hers.

"Thanks, Liz, but I need to be busy."

"Well." Liz stood up too. "At least let me help. And please, Simone, call me Nan."

Sim darted a look at Nate. He leaned back against the couch again, but his eyes had softened.

"Looks like you're part of the town now, Sim. Only the chosen few get to call Nan, Nan."

"I'm back," India said, pushing open the apartment door. "Man, Sim, those steps are a killer. No wonder you're in such good shape."

She placed a full bottle of amber liquid on the table.

"India," Nate said, "I meant a nip, not the whole bottle."

India sniffed. "That's fine for Sim, but what about us? And anyway, Frank dug this out, said to bring it up."

Sim looked around at Nate, India, Nan, and June. Somehow, her move to a quiet country town had turned into a bizarre witch landscape. And even more loco, it was … right.

"Well, I was going to make everyone a hot cuppa. But this looks way better. Thanks, India. Let's crack it open." Sim turned the bottle around. "Wow, Frank went all out."

"What is it?" Nate turned the bottle so he could see the label too. He blew out a low whistle. "This is a good drop. Are you sure you want to open it?"

Sim raised one eyebrow.

"Right. I'll get some glasses."

Nate brought over four glasses, and Sim cracked the seal on the decade-old scotch. Nose tingling at the scent of the aged, liquid gold, she poured a finger's level into each glass.

She downed hers in one gulp.

Flames ignited in her throat, and once she could get past the fire consuming her, she wheezed in a breath. Tears stung her eyes.

Nate clapped her on the back, and as he downed his in a much smoother, less oh-my-God-what-is-this-wretched-fiery-thing-in-my-throat way, she couldn't help but admire the long column of his neck. The firm line of his jaw.

She wrenched her gaze away before he caught her staring.

The burn of the liquor dwindled, a warm mellowness remaining in its place.

"So." Sim looked at India and Nan, who were being much more sensible and sipping their scotches. "Now that I've burned my throat and can think clearly, it looks like I've got two issues at hand. Tara's father has turned up, and only the stars know what that means. But I ... I won't lie. I'm shit-scared."

June looked up briefly. A whisper of recognition stirring in her eyes before she turned to look back outside again. That was odd, but Sim had more pressing things to think about.

"And secondly," Sim continued, "I'm a witch, which is a whole different kind of scary because I have no idea what that actually means for Tara *and* me. And both things are new." Nate went to speak, and Sim held up her hand. "No, no, I realize that the witch thing isn't new. I mean, new to *me*. *Me* being a witch. I knew my intuition was good. How and why this has all happened is beyond me."

She bit back the whole truth that wanted to tumble out. *Scared?* Scared didn't even begin to explain the strength of what rattled inside her. Because at the same time as her fear, deep inside, that little thing that always chimed and guided her—when she listened—said that she'd discovered something vitally important about herself. How had she not known this before? And what were the implications for Tara? She had no bloody clue.

"Hmm." Nate rolled his now empty whiskey glass in his hand. "Coincidences, genuine coincidences, are very rare."

With greater care than a simple water tumbler would normally receive, Nate placed his empty glass back on the little kitchen table and flexed his fingers around it. The morning's events flew through his mind, and as was his way, he compartmentalized them. Looked at each critically as both a stand-alone and a connected event.

Finally, he blew out a low, controlled breath.

"Sim," Nate said, "maybe you should ask Luc to clearly state his intentions. The fact is, he's Tara's father, and he has rights he might want to assert. You also have rights, like financial support."

Horror, swiftly replaced by anger, lit Sim's face.

"Don't get all mad at me. I'm just saying that there are some laws here you can't ignore but also some options you should at least be aware of, even if you don't take them up."

Nate looked at Nan and India for support, but they both frowned back at him.

"Hey, not you, too," he said. "I'm just stating it like it is."

Wrinkling her nose, India muttered, "Well, I don't like the fact that he can just show up here and suddenly have 'rights' to Tara. I mean, who is he? What does he do?"

"It's okay." Sim gave India an encouraging smile. "But thanks for caring."

Nate stared at Sim. To be going through this—all in one day—yet she was still thinking about others. Of course, he was head over heels for her.

But he'd known that for some time.

And this was why he wasn't going to answer the call of the World Tree and join the Keepers in their war. Sim and his family mattered to him. Needed him. And he needed them. Being called into an eons-long war and leaving all of this behind was unthinkable.

"Luc does have some rights," Sim said, and Nate snapped back to the conversation. "He's Tara's father." Sim's cheeks reddened as she spoke. "This is a little embarrassing, but you might as well know the truth. Luc was a backpacker traveling around Australia.

"He got a job for a week as a dishy at the restaurant where I worked. The night before he was due to move on, we all went out after closing and had a few drinks, and then, well, you can guess the rest.

"I tried to get in touch with Luc, but I barely knew him. And the phone number the restaurant had for him didn't work. I looked for him through social media, friends, anything I could think of. But I couldn't find him. And I didn't even know his full name. The restaurant paid him cash to keep it off the books, and they didn't keep records of that kind of payment. But I left word with the manager in case Luc ever came back."

Nate scrubbed his jaw. "Is that how he found you?"

"That's what he said, and then he looked me up on social media. I'd always used my full name at the restaurant, so it was easy for him to find me. He saw my page on the hotel and came here."

"Right." That was all very convenient for Luc.

"How do you feel about it?" India asked.

India was asking how Sim *felt*? They needed to focus on finding out what this Luc was after.

"Honestly, I'm conflicted," Sim said, rubbing her arms. "I'd begun to think that Luc wasn't ever going to be a factor in our—Tara's life. And in one way, that was okay because Tara is *mine*. I'm the one who gets to have a say in how she's raised. I'm the one who gets to have her with me all the time. But the facts are what they are. Without Luc, well, I wouldn't have Tara. And Tara deserves to know her father ... Every child deserves to know its father," she whispered.

Instinctively, Nate's magic gathered, then surged at Sim in a protection hex. But not to protect her; instead, it would protect *him* from losing her. Nate reined the acidic-edged spell in before he lost control of the magic. Something he hadn't done since he was a teenager.

That would have been one fucked-up spell.

Nate slowly let out his pent-up breath, made sure no one else could see his struggle. He'd purposefully chosen a service vocation. One that mattered, that could help others. He'd seen what happens in the aftermath of tragedy. Look at when his uncle had died, and India's mother had moved her away.

Using his magic in any other way than to help was the opposite of everything he believed in.

And shit, the spell had surged from his emotions. He was jealous. Because Luc had a part in Simone's life that Nate didn't. He stabbed a hand through his hair.

"Simone," Nan said, standing and picking up the whiskey tumblers, "you should come out to the farm. Tomorrow. We'll all help you learn about witchcraft."

"Ah," Sim said, "that would be lovely, but I don't want to ask for your help. I mean, I don't want to trouble you ..."

Sim looked at Nate, eyes wide, like a deer caught in headlights. He kept his face neutral. What was his wily grandmother up to now? And look at Sim—she'd been refusing help from them all for such a long time now; he wasn't surprised she was going to refuse Nan now.

"You didn't ask, dear. *I* offered. And don't try to say no."

Nate laughed, turned it into a cough, then looked innocently at the group. Hell, Sim didn't have a chance. Once Nan started on a course, there was pretty much no hope for budging her off the path.

Nan cut him a glance. She raised one eyebrow and nodded sideways at Sim, then impatiently frowned at him.

Understanding her request, dipped his head in acknowledgement.

Nan dusted her hands on her pants. "Sim, dear, Nate will bring you out. And June and Tara. But you'll need your energy and focus for the magic. Because on this, I'm right. Magic needs magic. You must learn what your power is, its strengths and weaknesses—how to control it, how to feed it. You would never want to harm someone through an accident or misuse, would you?"

Nate held in a snort. That was laying it on thick.

But Sim's eyes widened, and her cheeks paled.

"No, of course not." Sim looked at them each. "I just don't like ... to ask for help—to impose, I mean. But you're right; I need to work this out." She scrubbed a hand over her chest. "I need to work out what this thing is inside of me. And I need to know why it's happened. So I'll bring something for lunch with me, then. In exchange for your time."

He mentally rolled his eyes. Of course, Sim would offer an exchange. But he was finally going to get to the bottom of the mystery that was Sim's magic. Something he'd itched to do for the last year. And he was going to get time with her. On his turf. Something else he'd been itching to do.

"What about Luc?" he asked.

"He went to get settled in his room," she said, chewing on her lower lip. "But I need to talk to him before he meets Tara."

"Do you want company?" Nate checked his watch. "I can take some time off."

"No, though thanks, Nate. You've all been great coming over here and helping as is. But I need to do this on my own."

Jealousy pricked him. But he shoved it aside. This was Sim's decision. All he could do—would do—was support her choices, as hard as he might find them.

Sim waved goodbye to Nate, and his family, and emptiness echoed through her. She rubbed her arms to find some warmth. But there was no time to stand on her doorstep feeling crappy because she'd agreed to meet Luc—Tara's *father*—in the guest parlor.

Oh God, what if he demanded custody? Could he? What if he was a complete asshole? She swallowed the lump that suddenly clogged her throat. This wasn't the time to panic. She had to let the man talk. She wouldn't prevent Tara from having a relationship with her father. But she was going to make sure he was a decent bloke before she agreed to anything concrete.

She fixed her hair into a tight braid and strode into the hotel.

At first, she said nothing, just eyed the muscular form of Luc's back where he perused the bookcase by the window.

He was still an attractive man—but then, that's what had got her into trouble in the first place.

"You have an ... eclectic taste in reading," Luc murmured without turning.

"Oh," she jumped. "Didn't know you'd heard me come in. And yeah, it's a good mix. Though the books aren't all mine," she said, forcing calm into her voice. "It's a book swap. Guests of the hotel take some, leave others. It makes for an interesting assortment."

He slipped his hands into his pockets and turned around, taking in the space.

"Your hotel is lovely," he finally said, taking a seat on one of the two comfy couches.

"Thank you. It might be small, but this is my favorite room in the whole hotel. The homey feel of it, I guess." At least, it was *usually* her favorite room. Right now, it was the opposite of where she wanted to be.

But she had to face the fact that Luc had turned up, which meant the only choice was to stay right here and work out what that meant for Tara.

Sim forced a smile and took a seat facing him.

Nate's words about coincidences echoed in her mind. Sim set her jaw as all her protective instincts sharpened.

"So," Sim said, "I'm sure you want to meet Tara, but she's not here right now. That's probably just as well because you and I need to talk first. And I'll need to prepare her. She's a determined little thing, but this is going to be a massive change in her world."

"Truthfully, I'd like to meet her as soon as possible. But I understand you wanting to talk first." Luc smiled—which seemed genuine.

Sim kept her face calm, even though she wanted to run in the opposite direction at a million miles per hour.

"Thanks. Now, Tara can be a little reserved around strangers at first. A little while ago, she had an ... accident —" Sim swallowed at the word. It hadn't been an accident at all, but now wasn't the time to tell Luc what had really happened. "Anyway, just be aware it might take her a little while to be comfortable around you. Don't push her, and she'll come around."

"Okay." Luc shrugged, the cream knit of his sweater bunching over his wide shoulders.

"So, would you like a coffee before we start?" Sim asked, unsure whether she was procrastinating or giving in to her need to control every situation. Probably both. "The machine's on, so it won't take long. Or I can get you something else."

"Coffee would be fine, thanks."

"How do you have it?"

"Whatever you're having will do."

Who didn't have a preferred way to drink coffee? "No worries, I'll be back in a few minutes."

She quickly made the coffees, preferring to do it herself and keep her hands busy, then returned to the parlor, carrying two mugs.

"Here you go." She handed Luc one mug. Sitting down, she took a sip of her coffee, fortitude building with the hot, rich taste. "Luc, before we say anything else, you need to know that my only priority here is Tara. Her well-being is everything. Tara has to come first. She's the only thing that counts, and I won't let her be hurt. And that's why I have to ask a serious question. Though it's tough, because to be totally honest, I'm not sure what I want the answer to be."

Sim placed her coffee down and took a deep breath, surreptitiously rubbed her hands on her jeans.

"What are your intentions? Will you get to know Tara, let her get to know you? Are you planning on being a regular part of her life?"

Luc slowly placed his cup down. His watchful eyes seemed to gleam brighter for a moment before their silver depths subsided back to cool gray.

"I do want to get to know Tara. And yes, I would like to be in her life as a regular figure. When I found out about Tara, I was … well, for honesty on my part, I can say delighted. But I understand you must have a fear of what my being here means. And I can see you're a lioness, guarding your cub even while letting Tara feel her claws."

6

That night in bed, the warm spice of everything male teased Sim's nose. Where she'd been cozy under her winter quilt, now she grew hot; her legs moved restlessly, kicked blankets away. Her head turned first, following the beguiling scent she recognized. She rolled into a hot, hard body.

Nate. She knew it was him, even with her eyes closed.

She raised one leg, rubbed her thigh along his. She pressed into his side, gasped when her breasts hit his chest as his heat met hers in a blast of need.

Desire rocketed through her, pooled in her groin.

The lure of his skin beckoned her to run a hand over the smooth, heated flesh, the hard, sinewy muscles beneath. She smoothed her hand down his stomach, brushed against his hard length.

She slid her palm around him, moaned at the heat of his satiny skin, the width of him almost too big for her small palm, and she brushed her thumb over the head. A bead of moisture rose, as did her need for him.

Urgent. Hot. Now.

She needed his touch. Needed him. She rolled again until she straddled him, gasped as his heat brushed her core.

She cupped his jaw, and his eyes opened.

And hers did too.

To an empty bed. To a quilt tangled in her legs. To a sense of emptiness, of wrongness, when moments before everything had been right.

Sim groaned, looked around once more, then dropped her head back to the pillow. She pulled the blankets up high to her chin—the steamy dream was all well and good, but the icy morning air was way too cold to just lie there, even wearing her flannelette pajamas.

Damn. She hadn't had a sexy dream in ages. It had been way too long since her last erotic activity of any kind if her subconscious was coming up with this kind of action.

But best it was just a dream. The urge to sink into Nate and never come up for air was too much. Too needy. She needed to rely on herself, no one else.

But man, that had been one hot dream.

She blew out a breath. *Men.* And holy hell, she'd even forgotten about the other man right now sleeping in her hotel one floor away.

And what in the hell was going to happen there? He was still handsome. Just a slightly older, more worldly version of the man she'd known for a brief time.

She'd never kept Luc's identity a secret from Tara. Had always tried to be honest—well, as much as possible. But as the years had passed, part of her had begun to feel like Luc wasn't ever going to be a part of Tara's life. And the only thing that she was at all okay with in that scenario was that it meant *she* could do what she believed was best for her daughter.

But in all other ways, Tara deserved to know her father. She sure as hell deserved to know any medical issues, any siblings—damn, that could get messy—and she just deserved to decide for herself, one day, if the man who fathered her was someone she'd want in her life.

Sim rolled over and checked her mobile phone. Ten minutes to six. Well, there was no time to lie in bed worrying about something she couldn't change. She could either edge cautiously into the chill morning air or jump into it and embrace whatever was coming her way.

She chose to jump and landed her bare feet squarely on the cool carpet. It was weird, but no matter how cold the nights got, she couldn't wear socks to bed, so she grabbed a pair of sheepskin-lined boots from her wardrobe and pulled them on.

Sim changed her pajama top for a sweater, added a knitted cardigan, but left the warm bottoms on. She was going to make coffee; who cared if anyone saw her at this time of the morning.

She eased open Tara's bedroom door. A little unicorn-shaped night-light revealed squishy toys strewn across the floor. Sim stepped around the noise-landmines until Tara's face was visible, the gentle sweep of her dark brows, her soft cheeks, the little upturned nose. Something from Sim there. But the little monkey's coloring was either from Luc's side or maybe even Sim's father, given Sim had no idea what he looked like.

She eased back out of the bedroom and headed downstairs to the coffee machine in the public bar. Not too long later, she was taking a blissful sip of the rich, hot brew when footfalls echoed from the lobby.

Luc walked into the room. She sighed but didn't do anything as he stood in the doorway, looking way too well put together for this time of the day.

"Good morning, Simone."

It looked like she was having company with her coffee. Drat. But she was also the hotelier, and he *was* a payingcustomer.

"Morning. And please, call me Sim. Can I get you a coffee or tea?"

"Coffee, thank you."

"How do you want it? No, wait, let me guess, whatever I'm having will do?"

Luc nodded again, though this time a small smile curved his lips. She made another cup of the hot, aromatic brew, and when she turned around, Luc was standing at the bar. She jumped but luckily didn't spill the coffee.

"Shit. Sorry, didn't hear you move. Your boots must be the quietest shoes ever made."

"Hmm." Luc stood still, hands in his pockets, silver eyes watchful.

"Right. Well, here's your coffee."

She kept the bar between them. Luc's eyes gleamed brightly for just a moment before their silver depths subsided into smooth gray, and he took a seat at the bar.

Sim's heartbeat kicked up. Her intuition chimed low in her chest. Something wasn't quite right here, but what? Well, for Tara's sake, she had to find out. She placed her cup on the counter.

"So," Sim said, "yesterday you mentioned you were traveling with work when you found out about Tara. Do you have to travel a lot?"

"My work keeps me on the move, but I do have a permanent home. Not in this country, though. I'd like to stay here for a few days this trip, and then work out the best way to see Tara regularly in the future."

Her belly turned to lead. That was the worst outcome—that he still lived overseas. "And where is your permanent home?"

"When I met you, my base was located in Vienna. However, my permanent home is now in America. New York, to be exact."

"Wow, New York." Sim couldn't contain the crack in her voice. Right, time to ask the number one question. "Will you want Tara to go there?"

Luc regarded her for a moment; she had the sense he was trying to figure her out, probably doing the exact same thing as she was.

"No, that's not my intent. I can see that to bring Tara to New York is not the best course."

"Okay." Her breath whooshed out, and her shoulders relaxed. Thank the stars. "Well, you're welcome to stay at the hotel for a little longer. I'm fully booked next weekend due to a local festival but can provide you a room through till then."

"That will be perfect. I'll have to leave by the weekend for work anyway but should be able to come back within the month."

"Wow, that's quick. So, what do you do?"

"It's a family business, but I run the company now. We're pretty diverse in our interests."

Sim finished her coffee, rinsed her mug out in the small sink. "Backpacking around the country wasn't by necessity?"

"Necessary for me to see the world, really see it, yes," Luc said and smiled gently. "Necessary financially, no."

Heat prickled up Sim's cheeks. "I didn't ask that because I'm fishing for how much you make or anything like that. I just need to know what your, well, what your circumstances are."

"I understand that. And I would not mind either way."

Luc finished his coffee, placed the cup back on the counter. Sim searched his calm gaze. Believed him. It was odd because she didn't know him. Hadn't when they'd worked briefly together in the Melbourne restaurant. And their one night together—well, that had been after too much alcohol to the point her memories were pretty damn vague.

Sim touched his hand, but the moment their skin connected, a tumult of information poured through her. It came in a tsunami of colors and sounds and images, all at the same time, but too fast, too much to make any sense at all.

She gasped, pulled her hand back. She cut him a surreptitious look—had he felt that too? But his expression was calm as if nothing had happened at all.

Was it her? Had that reaction been all her own? Was her witchcraft flaring up again? Liz had said she needed to learn how to control it. Sim swallowed hard, forced herself to breathe evenly for just a few seconds, and finally caught her balance. Whatever that—that wave of information had been, it had receded and left nothing more than the impression of something massive, something bigger than she could even comprehend.

It looked like she needed control of her magic because that sudden information overload had nearly overwhelmed her, both physically and mentally. And she couldn't afford not to have full control in her world. It was her one absolute must.

"Although," Luc's voice broke into her thoughts. "When Tara's old enough to travel on her own, she will be welcome to visit me at any time. And you with her. Perhaps we could arrange a trip for you both sooner, though. I would be more than happy to pay for your fares. You could see my home, learn about my family. Me. See for yourself that we will be of no harm to Tara."

"Sorry, I was a million miles away. Did you just say Tara and *I* could visit you?"

"Yes, of course. We may not know each other well, but I recall enjoying your company." His liquid voice lowered. "I would be happy to spend more time with you, especially given we will no doubt see each other ... often."

Oh shit. Was he—did he—

A knock on the hotel's front door grabbed her attention. She checked the clock. It was still early, but she had a feeling who it was.

"Well," she said. "That's certainly a lovely offer. I just need to answer the door. It's probably Nate. Tara and I are heading out to his place for a ... visit, although he's a bit early. Be back in a minute."

She didn't wait around for any questions—had no idea

how to describe Nate and his family if Luc asked about them—and headed into the lobby.

When she unlocked the front door, Nate was on the step, one arm raised against the old timber frame, standing well over a head above her. He wore blue denim jeans with a fleecy Geelong Cats hoody. His blond hair fell over his forehead, and his too-blue eyes sparkled down at her.

"Morning. I wasn't expecting you till later," Sim said, keeping her eye contact brief. No way was she getting caught in that gaze.

"Hi, yeah, I was up, so figured might as well get a start on the day. Knew you'd be up by now." Nate cut a look toward the bar. "Is the coffee machine on?"

Sim laughed. "I swear that's the only reason you come here."

"What? No way." He waggled his eyebrows. "Your kitchen cooks a mean steak too."

"Yeah, we do." She kept laughing and swatted his chest.

The moment she made contact with that wide, hard expanse, an echo of that dream rose in her mind. She dropped her hand.

"Are you going to let me in or keep me standing in the cold?"

The deep timbre of Nate's voice cut through her distraction, and she stepped back, tried like hell not to blush. Tried not to think about that comment as figurative as well as literal. Her cheeks heated against all her efforts.

Seriously, why couldn't she curb her reactions around this man? She'd been doing fine, at least, she thought she'd been doing fine for the last twelve months. So why now? It had to be that damn dream making everything too real.

Nate looked sideways at her, smiled, and those dimples came out to play. Damn them.

"Hey, is something up?" Nate asked.

"Huh?" Sim caught herself staring. Damn it, this was not going to plan. "No, nothing's up. So, do you want that coffee?"

"Do ducks fly?"

Sim forced a laugh and led the way into the public bar. She halted when Luc swiveled to watch them enter, slipping his hands back into his pockets. Hell. She'd forgotten about him. And how in the world had she done that?

7

___

Nate knew himself well. Knew his craft, knew his strengths, his weaknesses. He'd known he was a witch like he'd known he could breathe. It simply was.

As a child, it had been steeped in reaction, in feeling, and in a burgeoning understanding of the world around him. As a teenager, it was exciting and steeped in emotion—and he'd begun to see its delicate nature, how he could carefully, skillfully intertwine the spells that he knew and those he was creating for himself, to make powerful, strong magic.

With time, he'd learned to master his magic rather than be mastered. And all along, he'd known his magic was a guide as well as a barometer of his emotions.

And right now, his senses went on high alert. The hairs on the back of his neck prickled. Adrenalin kicked through him.

Luc.

Male, six-two, dark hair, lean build. Dressed in expensive country-casual clothes that no actual country person wore.

Relaxed body language, but the tension in his shoulders made the pose seem ... forced.

Even as Nate's detective logic kicked in to assess Luc, his magic roared *threat*. Yet the man had no visible weapons.

Nate forced a calm smile even as he whispered a probe spell, waited until the silent, invisible tendril met Luc. The beauty of the spell was that the probe remained connected to him and would shiver if it met magic.

There was no tingle.

His breath released. Not that he'd known he was holding it.

Nate nodded at Luc when Sim rushed through introductions—she gave Nate's full name and explained his role with the police.

"Nice to meet you, Nathanial. Well, Simone," Luc said, voice smooth. "Do you think I could spend some time with Tara today?"

Sim's face scrunched. "Actually, I accepted an invitation to Nate's family's property for lunch, and I don't want to pull out now. But we'll be back this afternoon, and then we can work out how you and Tara ... get to know each other."

Luc's face tightened, then relaxed a moment later. Nate kept his expression passive, but inside he was cheering. While he might not have detected an overt threat, he still didn't trust Luc.

But why?

Could this be all about Sim? Nate was sure as hell jealous of Luc's part in her life. Was that what this was?

Or was it something else? He eyed the other man again and took a seat beside him. "So, what do you do for a living, Luc?"

"I'm in the import-export business."

Nate withheld a snort. That could mean anything.

Nate was driving Sim, Tara, and June to Nan's in his twin cab utility, and a sense of calm, of rightness settled over him the moment he turned the vehicle off the main road and on to the now paved street that curved its way up to the farm. It was a vivid measure of time across his life—red dirt from his childhood, gravel as a teenager, and now here it was, paved as an adult. He loved that he'd been here to see it grow and change alongside everyone and everything else in this valley.

The farming pastures of mellow jades and deep khakis, interspersed with rich red-brown—not unlike the deep amber of Sim's eyes—ushered them past with a familiar sigh.

Sim sat beside him, staring out the window. She looked pensive, as if whatever thoughts captured her mind obliterated everything else. He cut a glance in the rearview mirror. Tara's face shone back at him as she happily played with a little figurine in her car seat. She looked up once and smiled with genuine happiness as they made eye contact.

He gave her a quick wink, and when Tara scrunched up her entire face to wink back, Nate swallowed a laugh. June was sitting beside Tara, her gaze locked on the world outside, as usual.

The moment he drove over the cattle grate and closed the gates behind them, the calm morphed into relief. Of home.

Nate sensed that was more to do with who was in the ute with him than anything else. Everything in him wanted to tell Sim—*show* Sim—how he felt about her, physically and emotionally. And for the first time in twelve months, he sensed Sim's interest back.

But she had enough on her plate without him adding to the mix, for now.

Though he couldn't help giving her one more glance. The dark denim jeans she wore hugged her like a second skin. Back in the hotel, when she'd changed and come out wearing them, she'd turned around and knelt to tie up her bright joggers. The tight curve of her butt had his hands itching to cup her, stroke her, haul her into his arms. He'd had to turn away to hide his raging hard-on.

Then, as soon as Sim had hopped in the ute, warm air blasting, she'd undone the zipper of her black puffer vest and had revealed a red scooped-neck sweater. The swell of her breasts and a glimpse of smooth skin had made his mouth go dry.

He forced his gaze away. Again.

Driveway. Focus on the driveway. It curved up through the front horse pasture. The grass was green but patchy—hopefully, they'd get a good rain soon and the patches wouldn't grow any larger. If not, he knew Nan would weave some magic into the land to bring water there another way, but it was a complex spell, and since Nan appreciated the need for balance, she wasn't about to bring water into the region that would leave other valleys and farms without enough.

It was one of the earliest spells he could recall Nan, and his father with her, creating.

Nate had cornered Nan and his mother the night

before to talk about Sim and his feelings for her. Nan tried to go the innocent route, but she hadn't held out long and had told him she supported him. What a thing to hear from your grandmother. And then Mum said she'd always liked Sim and was happy to have another witch in the family.

He'd groaned and shaken his head.

That's when he'd laid down the law—or tried to—with them. Please, please do not scare Sim away. She had to be okay with this, and his strategy was to go gently, gently. He'd eyed both his mother and Nan after his plea. They'd shared a look and meekly promised they'd behave.

Nate almost snorted as he turned the steering wheel and maneuvered his ute between the huge gumtrees that towered up into the sky beside the driveway, their dappled gray bark cut with spears of brown before their upper limbs branched out to sway in the ever-present breeze.

The movement recalled him to his moment with the World Tree, and sure enough, as if even the thought was enough to bring it front of mind, his eyes cut to the north—where the Tree stood, not more than a ten-minute drive away.

"Look, Mum, Nate, out the window! Horses!"

Nate shook the image of the World Tree from his mind. Sure enough, two mares stood at the salt brick beside the water trough. They both picked their heads up as he drove by, ears flicking toward the ute.

Sim turned too, tuned in to whatever Tara said.

"See the bay horse?" Nate asked, checking for a nod from Tara through the rearview mirror before he continued. "That's Jemma, she's got one white sock on her front right leg; that's how we know it's her. And beside her is Lady E, she's one of my mum's favorites. She's the sweetest girl."

"The gray one, that's Lady E?"

Nate smiled at the excitement in Tara's voice and couldn't help but check out Sim's face. By her expression, she appreciated the wonder in Tara's voice too.

"That's right," Nate said.

"Mum?"

Nate held in a laugh. He knew that tone from Tara.

"Yes, monkey?"

Clearly, so did Sim.

"I'm not a monkey. But do you think I could ask Nate's mum if I can have a ride on Lady E?"

Nate glanced at Sim, right as she rolled her eyes at him. He bit back a laugh. Sim might not be a fan of the horses— but *he* loved them. How could he not respond when Tara loved them so much, too? He made an innocent face back.

Sim narrowed her eyes at him as if to say, *don't encourage her*.

He raised one eyebrow. *Why not?*

Sim raised one back.

Right, he got the message—because that would piss off Sim. That *wasn't* the plan for today. He cleared his throat and replied to Tara, "Not sure about going for a ride today. My mum has some work to do, and Lady E looks like she's having a nice rest out in the paddock."

"Oh." Tara turned, gazing through her window. "Okay."

The forlorn little voice was like a paper cut he couldn't ignore. He blurted out, "But maybe we can take her something to eat, and you can have a pat later on?"

Sim shook her head.

He mouthed, "What?"

But she just smiled, shook her head again, and went to looking back out her window.

Nate couldn't help the smile that spread over his face. Looked like Tara had just gotten one over him. But he was okay with that.

The smile stayed on his face as they crossed the grate into the house yard proper.

8

The summons hit Ri'Anit like a piercing cut to the heart. She gasped and tried to inhale, but breathing past the stab of red-hot pain was impossible.

She staggered to her feet from where she'd been sitting behind her too-fucking-pretty flower shop counter, and a blast of uncontrolled magic erupted in a flash of laser-sharp heat from within her.

Her soldiers leaped to their feet, one not fast enough—the pathetic lump—because her magic rammed straight into him, through him. The acrid stench of burning flesh filled the room, and the man dropped to his knees, toppled to his side.

The other dodged the blast, looked back at her in shock.

Ri'Anit ignored them both.

She had no choice but to heed the pull of her summons. And for the summons to be this hard, fast, it meant something was wrong. Her god had never called her so, not in two hundred years.

Heart pounding, Ri'Anit ran into the back room faster

than even the pull of the summons. She threw a holding spell against the door. Her men—man—could not see what was about to happen.

And she released the glamour on the altar.

Irrika materialized, her forked tongue hissing.

Ri'Anit dropped to her knees but looked straight up immediately. "My god?"

"Your instructions have changed."

"But—"

A perfect white hand sliced through the air. Ri'Anit's cheek split open, blood welled, ran down her face to drip on the floor.

Ri'Anit balled her fists and took the flash of pain. That had been her due for daring to question her god. She bowed her head lower.

"Apologies, my god. I am yours to command."

"One has come to my attention who must be dispatched with full prejudice and haste. She is a child living in your location. The daughter of a witch. Her name eludes us yet."

Ri'Anit kept her eyes on the floor. "Do you have an image of the child you can share with me?"

Irrika hissed, but no further pain came with the sound.

"May I approach to gather the image?" Ri'Anit asked, keeping her head bowed.

Irrika stretched out her hand once more, and Ri'Anit shuffled over, pressed her forehead into her god's hand, and received the image instantly.

"Well?" Irrika said. "Go. Now. You are not welcome to my attentions until the child is dead. She grows further in power and further in protection every day. You must act now."

Ri'Anit waited only until the air pressure in the room had evened out, mere moments before she looked up to ensure Irrika had left.

She'd find and kill this child. No mere witch could withstand her.

9

Sitting beside Nate was torture. Even if his monster truck hadn't been heated, Sim would've been on fire—his body poured off warmth like a furnace. And every time she looked at him, all she could think of was that hot, hot dream.

Was his body really that delicious? His arms, his chest ... his di—oh no. No way was she going there. She jerked her gaze back to the scenery as hot prickles washed over her cheeks.

Please, *please* don't let him have noticed her checking him out. She forced herself to pay attention to their surroundings because somehow, they were at the farm already. She'd been lost in her thoughts the entire drive.

As always, the Jones property took her breath away. For a city girl, it was both a mystery and slightly unsettling to see so much space. So many living things. And who knew animals would be so big? Sure, Sim had known horses could be tall, but when you got up close, they were huge.

And Tara was drawn to them like a lodestone, which had

sent a shudder through Sim more than once. Because while Sim was short, Tara was tiny. Any of those animals could step on her baby, and even if it was by accident, they could do a lot of harm, no matter that everyone out here tried to convince her otherwise.

But it was also magical.

Hah, that word again. But there was no other way to describe it.

A simple fence bordered Nan's house yard made from pine rails and wire electrified on the side of the animal paddocks. Nate had pointed that out to Sim and Tara on their first trip here—he'd even touched the wire to show that though it gave an uncomfortable shock, it wasn't more harmful than that.

But past that fence, the magic came to life.

The driveway wended around a mini botanical garden. Lush green lawn spread in a carpet around mature trees and beds of flowers of all kinds and colors that were both soothing and stunning. There were the obvious blooms, the roses and jonquils and daffodils. But so many more she had no clue about. And without question, a lot of love must have gone into creating and tending the garden, because only a lot of care and attention could create such beautiful serenity.

Nate pulled his monster truck—she swore everything was giant in the country—around the gravel driveway, past the cottages and the garden and pulled up in front of the double barn.

Sim murmured a thanks to Nate as she opened the truck's door to the chilly bite of the morning air. She zipped up her vest and had to swing herself out of the seat, since she couldn't reach the ground, and landed on the cold hard earth. She rubbed her hands together as the icy air hit them.

"Mum. Mum. Let me out." Tara glared at her from the back seat.

Sim couldn't help but laugh at the scrunched-up face. June sat quietly beside Tara, her expression placid, although she smiled when Nate opened her door and helped her out.

"Okay, okay." Sim laughed at Tara. "Hold your horses, monkey. It's cold out here." She opened the truck door, hit the release on the buckle, and reached in to help Tara down.

"No, I want Nate," Tara said.

Sim sighed. This was not a new comment. "Did I hear a please in there?"

"Pleeease."

"Would you mind?" Sim asked Nate.

Nate came over, pretending to scratch his head.

"Hmm, let me think ... Nope, I don't mind at all. Come on, pumpkin."

"I'm not a pumpkin!"

"Pineapple?"

"I'm not a pineapple!"

Sim couldn't help but chuckle as the two continued to play argue over Tara's status—apparently, Nate only hit it right when he got to puppy. Of course. Tara loved everything about puppies. The thought brought a shiver, not from the cold—again, nothing new.

Ever since Tara had been targeted, a puppy used as the lure, even the thought of one made Simone break out in a cold sweat. She'd looked carefully for any signs of distress in Tara, but apart from scrapes and bumps, thankfully, her baby hadn't been badly injured and didn't seem aware of the attack. Certainly didn't associate anything bad with the little black pup.

Sim held in a sigh and went back to the truck for the picnic basket she'd packed for lunch.

"Simone, June, you're here." Vera, Nate's mother, walked over from the stables.

"Hi, Vera."

Vera wrapped Sim in a hug. Once again, Sim's inner chime tingled in her chest. If her hands weren't busy with the picnic basket, she would've scrubbed a fist over her sternum. Vera eased back, eyes wide.

"Oh, Nan told me," Vera said, "but I didn't expect to feel that. You must have so many questions, honey. Can I take that?"

"Thanks, but I've got it." Sim hefted the basket higher.

"Well, let's get your mother and head inside and catch up with everyone. Then we can get down to business." Vera knelt and gave Tara a brief hug, then glanced at her son. "Nate, why don't you show Tara up to the stables? Tim's just had a rub down and would love a carrot. Then come on back inside yourselves."

Nate opened his mouth like he was going to argue, but he quickly caught himself and whisked Tara away. Sim couldn't help but appreciate the respect he always showed for his family.

"Mind Nate, Tara!" Sim yelled after them.

Then she found her arm linked in with Vera's and herself being moved along to the house efficiently. June walked sedately beside her, the smile replaced with her normal, empty expression.

Sim glanced over at Vera. Nate's mother was a little taller

than Sim. She had laughing gray eyes and a cap of thick blond hair cut short—she'd joked more than once that long hair in the animal world was just an additional pain in the butt.

Sim had always been comfortable around Vera, and the low hum that echoed inside her carried that same sense of ease, enough for Sim to be honest.

"Are you stealing me for something, Vera?" Sim whispered.

Vera laughed, steered them along the garden until they came to the farmhouse. "India and Nan are inside, and we thought you might appreciate some girl ... woman time before we get down to business."

"Business?"

"Don't worry, honey." Vera waved her free hand. "Business is what the Jones family calls their magic. Nan thinks you might benefit from being shown what it means for each of us, and then we can help you see what it's going to mean for you. But first, this has to be your choice. Nate told us a little about what's happened, and I can't imagine what you're going through, given everything." Vera's gray eyes were warm but direct. "Are you sure you want to do this today?"

Sim took a moment to look around the working farm with its surprisingly lovely mix of machinery and trampled dirt and sweeping gardens. Seriously considered the question.

"Truthfully, Vera, I'm a complete basket case of emotions and probably couldn't tell you which way was up right now. Except for Tara. That's one direction I know. And because this thing inside me, this magic or whatever it is, might bleed over to Tara, I have to work on it. Believe me, I'm okay to do some *business*."

Vera gently smiled. "Well then, let's get out of the cold and head inside."

Liz Jones's farmhouse was anything but a simple structure. It was a single-story building with family rooms, guest rooms, a huge open-plan kitchen, dining room and informal living room, a formal lounge, an office, and a laundry and mudroom. And every room along the front took in the view over the horse paddocks to the valley below. Vera steered Sim past the front entry—where any visitor would go—and around the back to the kitchen. Liz opened the door right as they stepped up.

"Simone, June, welcome," Liz said.

"Hi, Liz. Thank you for having us." Sim held up the picnic basket. "Can I put a few things in your fridge to keep till lunch?"

"Please, call me Nan. And of course, but you didn't have to go to any trouble, dear."

"I wanted to," she said, placing the basket on the kitchen counter. "I just grabbed a few things from the cold room in the restaurant, that's all. And I don't want to cause you any trouble."

Sim didn't mention that she'd stayed up late to make cookies and a potato bake that could be reheated easily and would be perfect with the cold roast chicken she'd brought as well.

"Oh, my dear, you're no trouble."

Then Sim found herself in another embrace, and a surge of energy pushed against her, as real as the hug. She stifled a gasp. Nan leaned back, recognition twinkling in her blue eyes before she gently patted Sim's cheek.

"Yes, it's a good thing you're here with us today." Nan gestured to the dining table and chairs. "Now, June, please take a seat, and would you like a coffee? It's nothing as fancy as Simone makes, of course. Or we have tea if you prefer. And what about you, Simone?"

June simply nodded, but Sim laughed. "I've already had two coffees this morning, and it's just gone nine. I think a tea would be lovely, please, especially since you've already got the pot out. And I know Mum will have one too."

Sim guided June over to the table, then made her way back to the kitchen.

"Perfect. Would you hand me that, dear?" Nan pointed toward a rectangular wooden tray with silver handles. "Thank you. The tea's only been steeping for a minute, so will be nice and hot. It's cold enough this morning to freeze a witch's tit—er, well, you know what I mean."

"Nan!" India strode into the room. "Were you just about to say what I think you were going to say?"

Nan raised her chin and managed to look down her nose at India, which was impressive, given India was a full head taller.

"Young lady, I can call it whatever I choose. I am ... we all are, after all ... witches. We all have tits. And it *is* cold."

India and Vera exchanged a look and burst out laughing. Sim couldn't help herself and joined in, too. Looking rather pleased with herself, Nan took the tray with the teapot and cups over to the table, rebuffing both India and Sim's attempts to help her.

Sim couldn't contain a smile as she sat down. This space

was where the family lived. Sure, there was the formal lounge and big dining table through the exposed brick arch, but this was the heart of the house—the simple timber dining table and chairs, two couches in pretty country patterns, the large kitchen with its island bench that easily sat four people.

And Sim was at home there.

Just yesterday, around her dining table, she'd learned she was a witch. What else would she find out today? She unzipped her vest, folded her hands on the table. "Okay, ladies, whatcha got for me?"

"We're all witches here," India said, and poured the tea. "As has been pointed out already. Nan thinks, and we agree, that if we can show you how we practice our magic, how we call our craft, it'll give you a kind of crash course in witchcraft."

"Why a crash course?" Sim said as she accepted a teacup. "Thanks."

"Witches," Nan said, "normally go through a rite where their magic is familiarized into their family circle, coven, whatever they belong to. Or if they are a true hedge witch, their own individual ceremony."

"Did you say hedge witch?" Sim asked.

"Yes, dear. Witches who practice their craft alone, among other things."

Sim blinked. She had a lot to learn. "And I should've been through this ceremony ...?"

"Well, it usually happens when a witch reaches their magical maturity."

"That's not physical maturity, then?" Sim said, and took a sip of her hot tea.

"No, it's not. I always think of it as closer to emotional maturity because true control of your witchcraft takes stability of emotion, plus strength of mind, and sometimes physical stamina, although that's the last real requirement."

"I recall when Nate was still maturing with his magic," Vera said. "He was about eighteen. And yes, boys reach theirs later than girls. Well, he had a crush on a girl. He'd been practicing some spell; heaven knows he always had the touch with the delicate ones. Spells, that is. But he lost control and that poor girl ... let's just say she needed all of our help."

"Nate cast a love spell?" Sim burst out laughing.

"No, my son tried to grow a flower for her. Only it went wrong. He'd had the young girl hold the plant, but he'd taken a Scotch thistle. And because he didn't have full control over the spell, the awful plant kept growing until she was covered in the thing."

"So, a Scotch thistle isn't a pretty little rose?" Sim asked.

"Well, it has a sweet little lilac-colored flower. But the whole plant is covered in fine prickles. The poor girl was plastered in the weed. That's why we had to help. The bloody thing just kept growing. It took Nate, his father, and I all together to get it under control."

"And did Nate get the girl?"

"He did, though I don't know how because heaven knows that poor girl was hurting from those prickles in places I can't even imagine."

"I always thought he was a smooth one," Sim said through her laughter.

"Who's smooth?" Nate asked as he opened the kitchen door. Sim jolted at his warm, husky voice.

She lifted her head, still laughing. Nate's shoulders filled in the doorway. And from across the room, his blue eyes sparkled, those dimples flashed in his bronzed skin.

He took her breath away again. Damn him.

She ducked back to her tea, cut a look around the table. June still stared out the window. But India, Nan and Vera all stared at her. Busted. She ignored the blush warming up her cheeks and instead waved at Tara to come over.

"Hey, monkey. Did you see the horses?" Tara pressed her cold little face into Sim's chest and nodded. The tang of hay and horse made Sim's nose wrinkle. "Why don't you wash your hands in the bathroom, honey, and then I'll get you a drink."

Tara nodded and skipped off into the family wing. Her little monkey was as comfortable here as anywhere else.

"Man, it's a chilly morning." Nate rubbed his hands together. "So, anyone making hot drinks?"

"Nate Jones, are you asking one of us to make you a coffee?" Vera asked.

"Mum. As if I'd ever do such a thing. I'm completely capable of making my coffee." Nate looked hopefully around the room before he grinned. "I just hoped someone else might."

"Sorry, dear, you're on your own." Nan's blue eyes twinkled right back at Nate. "But we're about to head outside and make a little magic, so once you've had your coffee, why not join us? We're going into the garden to start with."

"Fine, fine," Nate said and looked at Sim. "Can Tara have a warm Milo?"

"That would be great, thanks." But Tara ... what did Sim's magic mean for her baby? "Can I ask a question, though? What age do you introduce children to all of this? The magic, I mean?"

Vera and Nan exchanged a glance and looked over at Nate, who cleared his throat. Sim followed their gazes to him, too.

"What?" she said. "You were all children at one point. When were you first exposed to magic?"

Nate frowned.

"Nate? Why do you look like you're trying to work out what to say in the way to least make me mad?"

"Well, you see, magic needs magic. It's one of the laws of witchcraft. And because we recognized Tara's witchcraft from the moment we met her, we all let our magic touch hers. Not to affect her at all, just to let her magic sense—at a completely subconscious level for Tara—other magic."

Nate's eyes shone with the total belief he and his family had done the right thing for her baby girl. A lump gathered in her throat, and she had to force words through the constriction.

"Thank you." She looked around the table. "Thank you all for being there for my baby when I didn't know it was even needed." She took a breath, made damn well sure the lump subsided. "But now I know, so it's my turn to do the right thing for Tara. I think it's time we did some business."

10

Once Tara was happily set up in Nan's lounge with a coloring book and pencils, a cartoon series on the television, and with June sipping tea beside her, Sim willingly walked out into the garden.

Defined beds marked the breathtaking space with all kinds of flowers and bushes and plants—she didn't have a clue about most of their proper names, but one thing she knew, they were lovely. Nan paused at the garden edge and removed her shoes. Vera, India, and Nate followed without hesitation. What the heck, if this was the way you did magic, then this was the way she was going to do some magic.

The cool grass, damp from the overnight frost, tingled. She paused, blinked. Somehow, every single blade held her aloft, made itself known to the soles of her feet. The other three women walked into the center of the garden.

Nate stayed behind. He watched her carefully, assessing her once more. She abruptly understood why and touched his arm. Even through the fabric of his fleece-lined hoodie, his warmth called to her. His heady scent, all spice and male, beckoned her closer. But she made herself keep her touch light.

"I'm okay, Nate. More than okay. It's like I'm taking a step, literally, that I've been waiting for my whole life." Her gaze drifted toward the house. "After this, I need to ask about June too. But right now, I'm here to learn about what's inside me."

"Come on, you two," India called out from farther into the garden and ducked behind a largish bush that looked more blossom than leaf, in shades of lilac and white.

Sim smiled and followed India as the flower beds opened into a little circle, surrounded by different plants and trees and flowers. At its heart stood a tall conical tree with silvery-blue needle-like leaves.

Nan, Vera, and India stood close to the tree, and with each step Sim took forward, Nate's arm brushed against hers, warm and reassuring.

Anticipation zinged through Sim. Followed by a flush of doubt. What if she wasn't a good witch and her magic fizzed? Was that even possible? Her hand being picked up in a warm, calloused grip broke her thoughts. A shock of recognition flowed straight to her internal chime. It rang once, instantly reassuring her.

She didn't look at Nate but squeezed his hand in thanks. India picked up her other hand, and then all five of them were linked by grip. Sim had a crazy urge to make a joke about witches and circles.

"Simone, dear," Nan said, "this is how we practice our magic as a family. We'll keep it short and simple. Are you ready?"

"Yes, I think so."

"Good. I'm going to call for a rite of welcome to energy, just a small one for the garden around us."

Slowly, the power in Nan's gaze changed direction to face inward. A tendril of something *other* whispered over Sim's skin; goosebumps trailed in its wake. Her internal chime rang—continued to ring and ring and ring, louder and louder, until it flowed through every single fiber of her being.

"Mother Earth," Nan said, beginning her spell. "We thank you for your water that it may feed us, we thank you for your sun and moon that they may nourish us, we thank you for your energy that it may help us flourish."

The other tendril of sensation grew from a whisper, shouted through the skin of her palms where she touched with Nate and India.

As Nan focused on the blue spruce, her gaze filled with an energy completely different, and she called out a mix of words in a language Simone didn't recognize.

A sweep of power rolled from India to Sim, then through her to Nate.

The chime in Sim's chest rang out in a resounding roar that left her deaf to all else as the sweeping energy gathered somewhere she couldn't see. But then she took flight along with that energy until it—*she*—dissolved in a spiraling burst.

Simone drew in a shaky breath.

Four stunned faces turned to her.

"What? Did I do something wrong?"

"Sim," India said, "I'm still new to this circle business; however, I can tell you that what we just felt with you, through you, differed from how our magic feels. And that's odd. Even for me."

"Okay ... What does that mean?" Sim asked.

Nate rubbed the sensitive skin of her palm. Warmth pooled low in her belly with every sweep of his thumb.

"We don't know," he said. "But we've got a couple of options to investigate."

"Why am I not surprised you want to investigate something?"

Sim had worked hard to keep her tone dry when all she wanted was to dive back into his bewitching eyes, press up against his hot, leanly muscled frame. The heat in Nate's eyes rose to simmer until it rivaled what she knew must be in hers.

"That's me, your local investigator."

He'd kept his tone light, too. Which she was both grateful and annoyed at. Sim would've smacked herself in the head if she'd had a hand free. Ugh. She was smart enough not to get caught up in a hot body and wicked smile.

"Okay, so what's the next step?" Sim asked.

"Let's keep up the magic," Nate said. "You just saw Nan's craft; let's give Mum and India a go. And then I can show you mine. We're all a bit different. And Nan's idea is for your magic to get a sense of each of us, and then we'll help you, guide you through making your first spell. That will let us get a good look at what your magic can do. Its strengths, where its preferences lie."

"My magic has preferences?"

"Absolutely. It's a sense like any other part of you. Your taste buds prefer your coffee rich, right? Well, your magic will have its preferences too. Mine's seated in complexity, both creating and unraveling. Nan's is very much tied to the earth. The spell she just did is one she and her mother and grandmother practiced nurturing the earth and the plants. Mum's is more about animals, also makes sense since she works with them."

Vera took the lead and called out another spell, and then it was India's turn. Nate's cousin smiled, then her eyes lost their focus, and for a moment, through their hands, the universe opened up to Sim, showed her a glimpse of its heart. She gasped.

"Bloody hell," Sim said. "What was that?"

"My magic is different too," India said. "I'm tied to the three worlds, whereas Nan's, Vera's and Nate's are all mortal magic."

"Mortal?"

"We'll leave that for another time. But right now, let me show you how mine works."

India ducked her head, her dark hair dropped to cover her face, and the next moment a breeze whipped through the garden, rushed around their little circle, and dipped in, tickled Sim in the side. She yelped.

"You didn't say anything," Sim said. "Don't you need words for a spell? Like Nan and Vera?"

"Nah, that's not my way. But if something exists in the three worlds, my magic can talk to it."

What on earth had she stumbled into? Witchcraft was far more complicated than she'd been ready for. Taking a deep breath, she turned to Nate. "So, what have you got?"

Nate smiled and gazed at the garden. When he looked back, he squeezed her hand once. And murmured something low, too low for Sim to hear. But the moment he said the words, a vibrating hum emanated from him, and its warmth rolled into her, through her.

She was aware of India and Nan dropping their hand-holds and looking over their shoulders and of Vera's chuckle, but the rest of her focus centered on Nate.

Heat that had pooled all morning gathered in a storm, and she clenched her thighs as it threatened to ricochet off and make her body do something totally uncalled for. Right here. Thankfully, everyone else had turned to look at the garden. But while Nate's eyes were on the garden, too, he kept Simone's hand.

Then *his* hand tensed. *His* breathing shallowed.

Sim risked one look at him. She blew out a surreptitious breath. Nate was laughing with the others, and she let herself have that one moment to drink him in. Hair gilded by the winter sun, carved jaw granite hard, eyes like lasers focused on his task. And then a subtle change ebbed in the magic flowing from him, as if it had done its task, so began to subside.

Sim finally looked at where everyone else stared. "Holy cow, Nate. That wasn't there a moment ago, was it?"

"Nathan Jones, I do not grow Scotch thistles in my garden," Nan said, shooting Nate a scowl. "You'll dig that out, thank you very much. Afterward."

Vera just laughed and swatted his arm.

"Yes, Nan." Nate somehow combined a laugh and groan.

He let Sim's hand drop, but as he met her eyes, the smile playing about his lips made her wonder if he'd known what had been going on inside her. She narrowed her eyes. Two could play at that game. Whoa! No, she made herself step back from that thought. No playing games with Nate. He was her friend.

But he could be a friend with benefits. Sim's heart picked up.

Oh no. No way. Heading down the friends-with-benefits road was not on her agenda—that was the surest way to mess up their friendship. Except, she was more tempted than she'd ever been before.

She forced out a laugh. "Nate, that is a truly beautiful plant. A thistle, Nan called it?"

"Ha, more like a weed." India scrunched her face up at Nate.

"Hey, that's a good-looking thistle," he replied. "Trust me, I know thistles."

Sim just smiled. The comfortable banter between the family members showed their bond, and for a moment, she simply enjoyed seeing them all so at ease. But it also made her aware that she'd never had a connection like that. She shook off that thought. Today wasn't about self-pity. Today was about magic.

"Well, looks like it's my turn," Sim said. "So, what do I do? How does this magic thing work?"

"Sim, before you start, you've been using your magic all morning," Nate said. "Every time you've touched one of us, we've felt your magic against our own. The way I feel magic is like a physical barrier against my own and, believe me, yours has been up and running all day."

What did Nate mean? Sim glanced at the others, searching for answers. India placed a hand on her arm.

"We all experience magic differently," India said, "which is normal. And what I see with you is that every time you touch something, your magic is right there. And it's growing in strength. Quickly."

"But I'm not making a spell or anything ..." Except, what about that feeling she'd had all day—the moment her feet had touched the ground, the moment Vera had hugged her? And it made sense. All this time she'd thought she was reacting to other sensory impacts, but maybe they'd been reacting to her? "So, my magic is always there?"

"Our magic is as much a part of us as any other sense," Nate said. "Unless you have a cold, your sense of smell is always there, right? But until something out of the ordinary happens, you don't actually think about smelling, do you? Your magic is part of you. But what we usually do, except India, who's some kind of wonder kid,"—he glanced affectionately at his cousin—"is we move it from a subconscious state to a fully conscious state when we want to fully employ it."

"Why, Nate, that was one of the loveliest explanations I've ever heard you use," Vera said, beaming at her son.

"Thanks, Mum." He gave Vera a quick hug, and as tall as he was, she fit under his arm.

"Well, dear," Nan said, "it looks like it is indeed your turn." Nan smiled gently, but the steel was clear and present behind her regard. "To help guide your magic consciously, you can either give it a go on your own, or one of us can direct you. If you want to just try, then it might be best if we all create a circle again, and we can be there to help in case anything ... er, wayward happens."

"Wayward?"

"You see, at your age, your magic would normally have found its level, and you would know how to control your power. Given none of us know what your magic will do, it's just a precaution."

"Great, I'm an aging witch with no control. I'd prefer to do this on my own, though."

"That's fine, dear, so what do you want to try? Something like Nate's grand plant? Or maybe some of India's wind?"

As Sim looked about the garden, her childhood dream of an English cottage covered with roses came to mind. At one end, an arbor framed an opening that led to the other side of the garden. A climbing plant, devoid of any blossoms, grew up and over the graceful arch.

"What about that plant? The one wrapping around the arbor. Can I try to grow it?" she asked.

"That would be lovely," Nan said, a smile blooming on her face. "And I'll be right here, so if anything goes wrong, I can even it out. But it's winter, and that's a rose plant—roses shouldn't grow too much this season, so why don't you try a small energy spell to push a new shoot out of the stalk?"

"Okay, sounds good to me. So how do I do that?"

"I can teach you the spell, but the magic has to come from you. And that's the part that you need to control. Not too much to drain yourself, but with enough force to make the magic happen."

A ball of lead gathered in Simone's stomach even as her heart picked up speed. "I have to tell you, I'm pretty nervous about this."

"What? You, Sim Morris, fully capable mother and hotelier, afraid to give one minor spell a go?" Nate jostled her with his shoulder.

"Not afraid. Nervous. Different thing."

"Really?" he asked.

The ball of lead in her tummy simmered. She poked Nate in the chest.

"Really." She pivoted to Nan. "Let's do this."

"Right, by all means, dear. So firstly, Nate, India and Vera, it's unlikely anything will go awry; however, having your magic up and ready to call on is prudent. Now, Simone dear, hold my hand, and I'll say the spell; however, I won't use my magic. You'll do that on your own as per your wish. Once I've spoken the invocation, I want you to repeat the words until you have the spell memorized. I'll squeeze your hand when you have it."

Nan smiled, that gentle steel ever present in her gaze, and held her hand out. As Sim picked it up, the now-familiar hum of Nan's power buzzed through their touching palms. Then Nan recited the spell in English.

"That's it?" Sim asked. "What about the language you spoke before?"

"Well, yes, that's the words." Nan beamed. "But the magic happens when you combine the words with your conscious intent to craft the spell. The language doesn't matter; I simply learned mine in Latin."

Sim repeated the words, then Nan squeezed her hand.

"You have it, dear," Nan said. "Now you're on your own. Remember. Intent."

Sim began once more, only this time she stared at the rose, willed it to grow as the words fell from her lips. Vibrations resonated at her hand where she and Nan connected, then moved to her mind like a soft breeze. Her heart picked up speed, and her inner chime rang softly, rhythmically, in time with the vibration.

Well, hell, she was doing this!

Nan's magic. Her magic. Like to like.

Recognition rolled through her, and in its wake, her chime still sung a low, soft note. Waited for her direction.

And then Nan's touch, both physical and magical, departed, moved to hover near the arbor where the winter rose waited. Of course, that's how it would work. Sim saw instantly that her chime—her magic—would float on the words she said toward the bush. She said the words once more and sent her chime out to follow Nan's.

Only it stopped as soon as it reached the outer limits of her skin.

Sim focused harder, pushed with her mind to force her magic to leave her body as Nan's must have. But nothing happened. The chime still rang, still hummed its low, soft note. But no matter how hard she pushed, shoved, she couldn't force it outside of her body.

Frustration welled, jagged and discontent. Sim took a deep breath, tried again. One last shove to push it out—make her magic part of the world.

Nothing.

She opened her eyes.

Nate and the others still stood, watching her closely, encouragement on their faces. But the rose plant was still a plain brown stalk, blossomless and unchanged.

"Don't be disappointed, dear," Nan said. "We could all sense your magic, and it doesn't matter how strong you are; it takes time and training to learn how to consciously use your witchcraft. Like any other muscle. You know, I've gotten rather cold out here. Why don't we go inside for a hot cuppa? We can come back out afterward and try again."

"Thanks, Nan." Sim blew out a breath, tugged on her

braid. "That was, well, more than I expected. I could do with a little time before we try that again." Sim forced a smile. "Please, you all go in; I'll be there in a minute."

Sim wandered over to the arbor. The metal frame was, painted green, and no doubt when the rose bush was in bloom, it would blend into the arbor and be just beautiful.

Bare but for the thorns that guarded it, the strong naked stem of the rose bush looked withered almost. Yet she knew life had to beat strongly inside.

Like how she'd felt for too many years. Over time, thorns had hardened her heart from ever being hurt again—from an absent father, from an absent one-time lover, from being a mother to her mum, from always being responsible for making all their lives secure.

One rose thorn was right at her arm height. The sun caught its tip, and she reached out, touched it. Like a dam bursting open, the words of the spell rushed through her mind. And then Sim could do nothing other than *feel*.

The chime roared to life, sent a blaze of wind through her entire being along with the words. And she was part of it as it unspooled to fly through her, out of her fingertip, and into the rose.

Energy, the most elemental of natural things, coursed through her. Overtook her.

11

So, this was life? Simple, basic. Vibrant. Intricate. Uncontrollable.

Sim's eyes remained blind to everything else. Her spell roared, consumed her in an endless white-hot funnel of pure energy that swept around her body, exited through her in a rush from her fingertip to the rose stem. Her spell roared again. That funnel rushed back through her. Over and over, the cycle ran.

It was exhilarating. Amazing. And it tied her to the rose.

"Sim, are you okay? Sim? Can you hear me? Sim?"

The words registered, but she couldn't respond.

Because she was so strongly connected to the rose, her fingertip had become part-Sim, part-stem. With every pulse of her blood, every beat of her heart, the vitality of the plant pulsed and flowed with her.

She breathed, the plant breathed; she lived, the plant lived.

And through the plant, she touched the soil—a distinct energy again. It didn't beat with life, it contained life. A rich metallic tang hit her tongue. And the soil brought her to the grass. Tangled roots spread into the earth, pushed life to pulse upward and sprawl out into the tendrils of grassy leaves. Those tangled tendrils brought her to an enticing, beguiling scent, spiced with a hint of ginger and a trace of leather.

Heat arrowed through Sim, pooled between her legs. She knew that scent. It had sent her heartbeat crazy a million times. The part of her mind not consumed with the rose was in awe—this was why Nate's family went barefoot when they practiced their witchcraft. Their bare skin physically connected them to the world.

Then a touch to the back of her unused hand caught her attention. She broke free from the furious rush of life.

Nate stood in front of her, the arbor a perfect frame for his wide shoulders, winter sun bouncing off his messy blond hair.

His eyes were tight with concern, but from that connection of fingertip to hand, a new sensation arose. Her blood heated. Her breasts grew heavy. Desire took over the funnel of life.

With a gasp, she wrenched her finger from the rose, stretched up on her toes, and cupped Nate's cheek. But he stayed motionless, leaving the next move to her.

Should she? Nate wanted more than just a kiss. But she wasn't looking for happily ever after. All she'd wanted was to build a home for Tara and herself and never have to rely on anyone else ever again.

But one kiss. One taste of his firm lips. One press into his hard, muscled frame ... Hot damn, but she wanted that. Wanted him.

She rubbed her thumb across the curve of his lower lip.

His eyes narrowed, their glittering fire on her. He drew in a harsh, unsteady breath then nipped the sensitive skin of her thumb.

Her core clenched.

She curled her hand around his neck, drew him down.

Nate's heart slammed into his chest. As soon as he'd touched Sim, the power of her spell—unlike any witchcraft he knew—echoed inside him.

He'd tried to cut through the power pouring out of her. She was so new to this; no way she was ready for this level of power. Hell, even he'd have to exert maximum effort to control the witchcraft she was wielding.

Whatever Sim was doing, it was off the charts.

Then suddenly his skin was too tight. Something inside him clawed to get closer to Sim. Fucking hell, he wanted her.

And then, with a wrench, she pulled her hand back from the rose. The soft, warm pad of her thumb smoothed over his lips.

Nate's chest swelled; his dick went hard.

Her gaze, rich intoxicating fire filled with cognac flames, captured his. And she drew him down, down and into her.

He almost resisted. But hell, he couldn't battle that pull, no way on earth.

Her lips touched his.

His heart kicked into a sharp beat. Holy hell, all he wanted was to fit her body tight against his. Her sweet taste made his mouth water. He let her kiss him again, let her pull him in harder. Nowhere near hard enough.

Somehow, when all he wanted—fuck, *needed*—was to get closer, he let her keep the lead, reigned in the furious need. Focused on Sim. She'd always held back from him. How close was she going to let him?

His gut tightened. What if it was the spell, not her intent, driving her? Nate didn't want her to regret it after. And damn it, he didn't want her because of some goddamn magic. He wanted her to want him. One lover to another.

Abruptly, Sim pulled back, asked in a low, husky voice, "Is this okay?"

Missing her already, he growled, the sound rumbling through his chest.

"Yes. Damn, yes. Why?" he muttered, gaze locked on her lips. Lips he wanted back under his.

"Well, you aren't kissing me back."

"Not because I don't want to." He blew out a hard breath, lifting his eyes to hers. "I don't want to take more than you're ready to give." He peeled her hand from around his neck and pressed it to his chest. "Feel that? My heart's going to explode. From your kiss. I want this."

Her lips slowly curved. "One more?"

"One more?" he growled.

Even as he saw her mouth move to answer, he couldn't wait. He cupped her cheeks, and the silken perfection of her skin elicited a groan from deep inside him. He ducked his head, ran his tongue along her full flesh.

"More," Nate said.

He tightened her hand against his chest then pressed his lips hard to hers. Explored her mouth, her full, sweet lips he'd been entranced by for over a year. Slowly, luxuriating in her silky softness, he ran his tongue lightly over the fuller bottom curve before her lips parted and she let him in.

He swept inside, Sim's heady taste sending him into a spin. Masculine approval rumbled through him at the sheer fucking perfection of her. And then she stroked him back, her tongue sliding along his. The chill of the morning air disappeared beneath a surge of heat. Shivers raced up his dick. God, he needed to haul her away. Hell, lay her down in the grass right here. Drive into her.

Somehow, he held back the ravenous need. Forced himself to just enjoy the kiss. Enjoy Sim like he'd wanted to from the first. Tongue to tongue, taste to taste. Moan to moan.

Until a cough sounded behind them, and Thrane's rough masculine voice asked, "Should we interrupt? Or is it an acceptable thing to stand and watch mortals make out?"

Nate groaned and eased back. But kept his gaze on Sim. "I refuse to be interrupted. Can we pretend they're not there?"

Sim's pulse hammered in the vein at her neck. A ghost of something flickered in her eyes before they returned to warm amber. "Sorry, tiger. Think that's our call."

"Sh, Thrane," India said, her voice ringing out through the garden. "I told you he'd ... they'd ... be fine."

"Right. And that's why you practically dragged me out here the moment I arrived?" Thrane replied.

"Well, you said you were planning on catching up with Nate, and Nan's going to make lunch. Plus, I *did* just want to check for myself. Sorry guys, but since you've come up for air and all ..."

Nate groaned. "You two have the worst timing. Ever."

Happiness lit India's eyes for a moment as she beamed at him and sent him a thumbs-up that Sim—luckily—didn't see. Because Sim was looking at the rose. A plant now covered in vibrant leaves and rich yellow buds.

Her mouth dropped open, and she whirled back to him.

"Bloody hell. I did it! Hey, at least the spell worked. That's good, right?"

12

Nate opened the door to his apartment above the stables and held it open for Thrane to follow him in.

"Thanks for coming up," Nate said as he walked through the studio-style loft into the kitchenette space. "I wanted to talk to you about something, away from everyone else." He opened the fridge door, ran one hand through his hair while he surveyed his options. "Mate, would you like a drink? I've got beer, juice, or"—he ducked his head and checked the back of the shelves—"water."

"I'll have a beer if you're having one." Thrane sat at the round four-seat table.

"Do ducks swim? Hell yes, I'm having a beer. It's been a ..." Nate grabbed two frosty beers, popped the tops, and sat down too. "Let's just say it's been a long couple of days."

"Thanks," Thrane murmured. "So, what's up?"

Nate took a sip of his beer, and as the cold, sharp liquid hit the back of his throat, he tried to sort out his thoughts. Sim. The World Tree. Luc. The spell. At least he could tackle one of those issues now. He firmly set his beer on the table.

Thrane was taking a sip of his drink, but raised one eyebrow and slowly settled his beer back on the table.

"Thrane, I've been around you my entire life. You've never hidden the truth from us, even when it's been bloody hard. You're also the only Keeper—until recently—that I've known. And that's what I need to ask you a question about."

"Okay."

"Why does the Tree want me?" Nate asked.

Thrane frowned for a moment. "I can tell you why I *think* it wants you. But first, why are you asking now?"

Nate let out a hard, short laugh. "All right, old man, I'll tell if you tell."

"Old man?"

"Hey, don't blame me; I call it like it is. Blame the Tree."

"That would be the truth of it." Thrane chuckled, took a sip of his beer as he considered Nate. "The Tree. Well, since that's what you've asked about, let's start there. Do you know what the Tree actually does?"

"Yeah," Nate replied, "it's the connection between the three worlds."

"That's right. The Underworld, Mortalworld and Higherworld are all connected through the World Tree."

"And you use the Tree to travel between the worlds, right?"

"Yes. Plus, I have my Connection." Thrane reached under his shirt and withdrew a small flat disk attached to a cord around his neck.

"What's that?" Nate leaned closer.

"This is how Keepers cross between two points and the

World Tree. The other end of this Connection is beside my sword in the Underworld. The lord there, you've heard of Serephena, lets me keep my sword in a locked cell under her mountain. I travel to and from the cell by touching this Connection."

"Does the Connection work for anyone else?"

"No, this was made for Keepers only. Everyone else has to touch the World Tree to cross between worlds."

"So who else travels via the World Tree?"

"Everyone. From the Angelkin to the demigods. Do you know the old gods created the Tree to construct and then constrain their domains?"

"Yeah, and the old gods each shared some of their mojo with the Tree; that's how it has the power that it does, right?"

"That's one way of putting it," Thrane said. "But it was more like they each ceded a portion of their power because that was the only way the Tree could influence the gods. Before the Tree, the old gods had their way whenever, however, they wanted it. No one, and certainly no mortal, was safe from the whims of the gods."

"So they created the World Tree. Then what?"

"The worlds separated, constraining the gods within the domain they chose. Outside of their domains, the gods could derive power from those who worshiped them, but they all agreed that the only way to physically travel between worlds would be the World Tree."

"And what happens if the Tree's destroyed?" Nate asked.

"Without the Tree here in the Mortalworld, no one from the Higherworld or Underworld will ever set foot here again, and mortals will be at the mercy of any being who's here when that happens."

"That sounds pretty fucking bad."

"It's been my purpose for over five hundred years to stop that from happening. That's what the Keepers do." Thrane clenched his jaw, then said, "And before India, I was the last Keeper. Now, why are you asking about the Tree?"

Something heavy coiled in Nate's stomach, a weight that he couldn't dislodge.

He stood up, placed his empty beer bottle beside the sink, but even moving around didn't shift the uneasy sensation. He finally turned and leaned back against the kitchen counter.

"The Tree talked to me," he said in a rush. "Communicated, fuck, I don't know what you call it." Nate ran a hand through his hair. Hell, he couldn't even find sense in his words.

Thrane turned to face Nate from his seat. "The World Tree does communicate, but it's in a language of images and feelings when I'm in physical contact with it." His eyes sharpened. "I know you haven't been there recently. What happened?"

"Two nights ago, I had an altercation at work. Got hit in the head. Afterward, out of nowhere, the Tree was knocking at my mind. It knocked." Nate rapped his knuckles on the counter. "Just like that. And I knew it was the Tree. Suddenly the Tree was right there, in my mind, like you say. It showed me a ton of images."

Nate battled back the urge to shiver, and after a deep breath, shared the impressions he'd taken from the Tree. He finished with the last impression he'd received: millions of souls crushed, destroyed.

"Have you dreamed about it?" Thrane asked.

"About the Tree? Yeah, plenty of times. Why?"

"Nate, the World Tree calls a Keeper through our dreams. It's how it called to me, and it's how it called to India. If you're dreaming of it … if it came to you while you were fucking awake, then it wants you. *Really* wants you. And there must be a reason—something about you that's uniquely able to protect it."

"Hell, Thrane, I know we haven't always agreed with each other, but you've respected my role in town with the police and as a witch, and I've tried to give you the respect due for your task."

Thrane snorted. "Mostly."

"Fine. Most of the time. But seriously, I'm torn. Being a cop and being here for my family is all I want. Becoming a Keeper … that would mean leaving everything and everyone I worked so hard for behind me."

Thrane stared at his drink for a long moment. Finally, he sighed and looked up.

"What?" Nate asked.

"Do you know when I became a Keeper?"

"Not exactly. I know it was a long time ago."

"It was in the Middle Ages. I was a mercenary, and fighting was my whole life. Fighting for a purpose that I suddenly believed in with my heart, not my head, made perfect sense. But everyone comes to this calling differently. Look at your cousin. I still can't believe how lucky I—we—are to have her. And India's witchcraft has been invaluable."

"Because she can influence the elements?"

"That too. But India communicates with the Tree without touching it. That's a first in my knowledge." Thrane tilted his head, a look of calculation rapidly entering his eyes. "Nate, I'm seeing why the Tree would want you specially."

"And that is?"

"If your witchcraft means it can communicate even when you're not in physical contact, that's damn important. I thought that was just an India thing."

"But there are other witches," Nate said. "Maybe it's something we can all do? It wouldn't make me worth singling out."

"But how many whose craft is as strong as yours? And of them, how many would be comfortable in a fight? Have the ingrained protective instinct that drove you to become a cop? It makes perfect sense to me."

"Bloody hell. Do you know the Tree's been there for as long as I can remember? But now I can sense it ... feel it waiting." Nate swiveled to look out the back window. "It's there. I can tell you its direction because the SOB is always right here at the outer barrier of my mind. It's a fucking compass."

"Well, _I_ can tell you this," Thrane said. "The Tree is patient. And very, very stubborn."

"This family fits right in, then." Nate straightened up against the counter. "What would happen to the old gods' powers if someone destroys the Tree?"

"Theoretically? They'd be released."

"Why would the gods give their power to the Tree only to take it back again?"

"What makes you think the old gods are the ones trying to destroy it?" Thrane asked.

"What makes you think they're not?"

"The fact that they've helped us plenty of times

throughout the centuries to start with. But there are other gods not among the elders."

"You don't mean that God ..."

"No," Thrane said. "He's aided as much as he can. One of the oldest angels, Moyarn, has been helping us on and off for centuries. And if we really needed help, they'd probably even send their youngest, Amadis. Not that I've ever met her."

"Then what happened in Europe?"

Thrane's lips thinned, but after a moment he sighed, low and long. "The World Tree that I first came to know existed deep in a European forest. The Order had been trying to find the Tree for centuries, and as you know, they use mortals in their ranks. Well, they'd amassed an army. To give their soldiers strength, they rounded up all the witches in the surrounding area—children, men, and women—and, in one mass killing, murdered them and stole their magic. The Order gave the death magic to their mortal soldiers, and that was enough. By weight of numbers and stolen magic, they destroyed the World Tree. And my brethren Keepers."

"What the hell happened?"

"You've heard of Freya?"

"The goddess of love and war? Yeah, India's mentioned her."

"I'm only here today because I was the last Keeper to arrive at the Tree, and that's why Freya summoned me. She said the Tree would die that night. The only way for the mortal world to survive would be for me to take a seedling of the Tree, and I had to leave the fight, secret my seedling away." Thrane looked down at his hands. "I brought my seedling here. And have protected it against the Order ever since."

"Holy shit, Thrane. Who *are* the Order?"

"They're an organization that spans the globe. Their upper leadership has always been supernatural. But we've never known who's directing them. My theory is it has to be one of the deities."

"Who are they?" Nate asked.

"Offspring of the old gods who have been granted power, maybe even gathered worshipers of their own."

"And you think one of them could be after the destruction of the Tree?"

"All I can tell you, unequivocally, that in my centuries as a Keeper, I've fought off countless attacks against the Tree. All from one direction. The Order."

"It's odd; Sim and India are both witches who didn't know their power until now. And both handle magic in ways unlike any other witch."

"Don't you have a saying about coincidence?"

"Yeah, they're pretty fucking rare," Nate said. He stared at Thrane, the mirror of his curiosity reflected in the other man's gaze. "We need to talk to Sim. Something's bugging me about her magic. It's unlike anything I've ever seen before."

13

Sim finished putting away the last of the lunch dishes with Nan and hung the dish towel over the oven door handle to dry.

"Right, well, that's the dishes done," Sim said with a smile at Nan.

"Thanks for the help, dear. Now, I think I need a cup of tea. What about you? Or a coffee?"

"You know what, Nan, let me make this one. You've been making me coffee all day."

Nan went off into the formal lounge. The sounds of the television were just audible through the wall, and shortly after, Tara's voice, also muted. Sim's mouth curved. For all the craziness over the last twenty-four hours, right now, she was happy.

She picked up the kettle and, turning to fill it, smacked into a wall of hard, hot muscle. Her breath whooshed out of her. She rebounded backward, but Nate grabbed her around the hips and steadied her before she toppled.

"Crap," Sim gasped.

"Hell, sorry. Are you all right?"

"I was until I walked into a man-wall." Sim looked up into Nate's wicked blue eyes. Their glittering depths held a level of heat mixed with mischief that struck her hard. Her stomach tightened. Heat pooled in her groin. Damn it. Just like always. Then his heat entwined around her, drew her closer. She swallowed the lump that grew in her throat.

Nate's gaze dropped to her neck as if he could see her pulse pounding.

His lips curved, as wicked as his eyes. Those lips that she'd kissed not long ago. And damn, but she wanted to go there again. Wanted to reach up on her toes, nip that lower lip, mash up against his chest, and relish in his hard, sensuous mouth on hers.

Was she doing this? Was she really going to go down the friends-with-benefits road?

Nate moved closer; his hands slid up from her hips, up along her rib cage, up higher, till his knuckles just brushed the outer curve of her breasts. Sim sharply inhaled, the swell of her chest brushing against his hand again. And even under the jacket through her sweater, fire arced to her breast, spread like lava to her core.

Her eyes slowly traveled back up to his, and dear God, the heat, the want, the need blazed like the sun just for her to see. Something Nate had never shown her before.

"Sim," he murmured.

She licked her suddenly dry lips, and Nate's gaze followed her movement. All the reasons she'd been keeping him in the friend zone dissolved.

Yep, she was doing this.

Sim swayed toward him; he leaned down, and she pressed her lips to his.

His chest pressed into hers, his torso, his groin, his thighs. And those hands, oh man, those hot, capable hands with their long, dexterous fingers. They ran up and down her side, each graze covering more of her breasts.

Holy crap, Sim wanted more. She moaned into his mouth.

Their second kiss.

Hot, darkly sweet. A rich, decadent dark chocolate.

"Mum, can I have a hot Milo?" Tara's voice cut through the fog of heat and want and need.

With a gasp, Sim brought her hands up. Huh. Somehow, she was still holding the kettle. With a snort, she used the kettle to push some space between Nate and her. He didn't resist, but heat and desire still simmered in his gaze. And behind that, need echoed in the tight jaw, the hard curve of his lip. For her.

A thrill coursed through Sim. This craving, this dangerous need that roiled through her—he felt it too. She cleared her throat, forced herself to turn away from Nate.

Tara was sitting on a stool on the other side of the counter. Oh God, how long had her daughter been watching them? Heat flooded Sim's cheeks, and she threw Nate a look. Nate was grinning at her. Sim's lips threatened to curve up in response, but she battled the urge, kept her face straight. Nate got away with way too much as it was.

She narrowed her eyes at him. "Get out of here, you. I'm making, or was making, coffee. And now a hot Milo, apparently." She turned to Tara, softening her voice. "Honey, how long have you been there?"

Nate slowed before he left the kitchen, and she could tell he was waiting for Tara's answer too.

"I saw you kiss Nate, Mum." A smug little grin hovered over her face.

Nate coughed, and Sim whirled to glare at him, but he moved quick smart out of the room.

"Mum, why did you kiss Nate?" Tara asked.

Sim mentally bit her lip. How to answer this one? Finally, she tugged on her braid, tackled the question the only way she knew how.

"Honey, sometimes people kiss because they like each other, and kissing is a nice way to show that. Kind of like when you give someone a hug."

"Oh, okay, but when you kiss me, you just kiss me on the cheek."

Sim laughed, mussed Tara's shiny black hair. "That's right, baby, and that's the only place you need to worry about kissing."

"Mum, I'm not a baby. I'm a big girl."

Sim rested her arms on the bench, lowered her face to Tara's level. "You'll always be my baby, sweetheart. But you're right; you're not a baby anymore. And you know what?"

"What?"

"Because you're a big girl, why don't you ask what everyone else wants to drink. Then you can come back and give me their orders."

Tara let out a theatrical groan, but Sim sent her a stern look, and Tara grinned again, hopped off the stool, and raced into the lounge. Because apparently, walking anywhere was the absolute last thing a four-year-old did.

14

Taking the warm drinks into the formal lounge, Sim found June at the large dining table, staring out the far window. As far as Sim could tell, the quieter it was, the better her mum seemed to be.

She paused midstep. She was a witch; Tara was a witch. Surely that meant June was too? She'd have to find out how to tell if her mother was or not. She placed June's cup in front of her and, for a moment, rested a hand on her mother's shoulder. June lifted her eyes briefly to Sim's, then turned to gaze back out the windows.

Sim settled into one of the couches with Nate and his extended family—Thrane, India, Nan, Vera. Tara sat on the floor, using the coffee table between them to do some drawing. Sim was used to being the alpha of her little family of three, not that you'd know it sometimes with Tara, the little monkey being so strong-willed. But around the oversize couches here, the power construct varied, even seemed to shift with the conversation topic.

Of them all, Thrane was the most unknown to her

because he'd always been quiet about himself—a kind of man-mountain, all broody and dark. But on the rare times Thrane was in town, only Nate and Nan, and now India, ever disagreed with him.

So Thrane was seemingly the alpha, but then you had Nan—the matriarch of the family. Although more and more, the family were responding to Nate on a similar level to the way they did Nan. Even his parents, when it came to the family business—she mentally shook her head; what a name for witchcraft—seemed to give way to both Nate and Nan. Maybe Nate's parents' magic wasn't as strong? She'd have to find out later.

As India sat forward and placed her mug on the table beside Tara, Sim tuned back into the conversation.

"What are you drawing, Tara?" India asked.

Tara gave India a quick glance, then turned back to her work. She had a bright blue crayon in her hand. "Where Grandpa was from."

She'd drawn a blue river with a bright yellow sun at the top of the page. Green covered either side of the river, and a lighter blue colored in the sky around the sun. The hairs on the back of Sim's neck pricked. She rubbed a hand over them. Bloody hell, what was going on now?

Sim cleared her throat, forced her voice to remain steady. "Wow, that's really pretty, honey. Did you say your grandfather lives there?"

"He used to. But he doesn't anymore," Tara replied, head still bent over her task.

Sim pursed her lips. Nate and everyone else were watching her. Nate's frown was the most telling, though, because he knew Tara had never met her grandfather.

"So, how do you know this is where Grandpa is from? Did Nannie June tell you that?"

Sim held her breath. *Come on, baby, please, please say yes.* Finally, Tara put down her crayon and looked up, her dark eyes bright.

"No, silly. Not Nannie June. Grandpa showed me in my dreams. This is where he lived." Tara picked up the paper and held it directly in front of Sim.

Her heart sank. *Oh hell.* Sim somehow swallowed the lump that lodged in her throat and exchanged a glance with Nate—his expression was as tight as hers must have been—and then looked back to Tara.

"So, do you know any of Grandpa's family?"

"Only from my dreams. But I think they've been here before because they know where Nate lives," Tara said and peeked up at Nate and gave him a cheeky smile.

Nate's eyes cut to the kitchen door, once. Sim nodded with a single small dip of her head.

"Well, of course, everyone knows where I live," Nate said, ruffling Tara's hair. "Hey, Miss Tara, now that you've had lunch and done some drawing, would you like to visit the horses? Maybe, my mum"—he tipped his head sideways at Vera—"could take you out to say hi to Gemma." He looked back to Sim. "If that's okay?"

Sim swallowed. Right then, she wanted nothing more than to pick Tara up and hold her close. Never let her go. But Nate was right, she also needed to have a conversation that was best had away from Tara's too-sensitive hearing.

She forced a wooden smile to her frozen face. "Sounds great. If it's okay with Vera?"

"Of course," Vera said. "In fact, Tara, I don't think

anyone's brushed Gemma today. Would you like to help me do that?"

Her little munchkin in a stall with an enormous horse? Sim bit back the urge to yell, "hell no."

Tara picked up on her unease, though, of course. She turned around and wrapped her little arms around Sim's shoulders. "It's okay, Mum; I won't go *into* the stall. I'll just stand with Vera."

Sim hugged her daughter, took comfort in the steady beat of her heart. Finally, she leaned back, pressed a fast, firm kiss to Tara's little head. Forced her helicopter-mum instincts down.

"No, baby, that's okay. You just do what Vera tells you. She knows the horses," Sim said.

Once Tara and Vera were outside, Sim tugged on the end of her braid. "I didn't see that coming."

"Neither did I," Nate said.

Sim went to laugh—maybe cry—but it came out as a snort instead. She'd have been embarrassed if she had the energy left, but it was all she could do to look at the others.

"I suppose you should know a little more about my fami-ly," Sim said.

"Only if you want," India said, shifting on the couch closer to Thrane. "But given what we're learning about your ... odd magic, it might be helpful."

Sim turned back to the drawing still in her hand and placed it on the coffee table where they could all see it.

"That *picture* was odd," Sim said, rubbing suddenly sweaty palms on her jeans. "The thing that made Tara's comments ... well, odd is the right word ... is that she's never met my father. Neither have I. And with Luc, I can safely say she's never met his father either. I don't know of any other family that we have."

"Sim, do you really not know anything about your father?" Nate asked as he picked up the drawing.

"No, nothing. June's barely spoken for as long as I can recall. I've never even heard his name. And there's no name listed on my birth certificate, just father unknown." Sim looked back down at the paper. "Why?"

Nate shared a look with Nan.

"Nate? Why are you asking that?" Her hackles rose at being excluded.

"Simone," Nan said, "I see now why Nate asked about your father. I should've guessed; after all, India went through something similar."

"What did I go through?" India glanced around quickly.

Her friend was as clueless as she was, which was a kind of comfort.

"Sim," Nate said, "you don't know India's story. But I think, if it's okay with you, India and Thrane, that Sim needs to know everything. Now. Starting with why you came home, India."

After a long moment, India and Thrane both nodded.

"Okay, Sim," India said. "As you know, I came back to town a couple of months ago. Well, I left when I was just a kid after my father died. My mother moved the two of us to Queensland, and we lived there for fifteen years until Mum passed away.

"After her death, I learned Mum had cast a powerful protection spell to keep my magic hidden. A side effect of the spell was that it hid my magic from even me. But the reason she chose that spell was so that no one from the supernatural world could track me.

"Because through my mother, my magic is connected to two of the three worlds, the Mortalworld and Underworld. And through my father, my magic connects me to the Higherworld. It turns out that my combined heritage makes my magic unique. And dangerous."

"How dangerous?" Sim asked.

Thrane squeezed India's hand, and Sim's heart blipped in her chest—their support for each other was beautiful.

"My magic can destroy the World Tree."

A chill slid through the room. India's comment carried some importance, but Sim had no clue.

"The *what* tree?" she asked.

"The World Tree. You know how I spoke about the three worlds just then? The Mortalworld, Underworld and Higherworld?"

Sim nodded.

"Well, the World Tree connects them. The Tree acts as a point of connection and travel between the worlds, as well as a containment, so the gods and beings who live in the other worlds can't come here and physically force their will on us—you mortals."

"Huh," Sim said. "So, your magic can destroy this World Tree. But you're not a bad person; you're not going to do that, right?"

"While India would never harm the Tree," Thrane said, "there are others who would. In fact, they want to destroy it, we think, so that they can take dominion over the Mortalworld. They can steal the magic from witches through a sacrifice, and if they do … then they would have the ability to finally destroy the Tree."

"Are—are you in danger?" Sim asked India.

"Not anymore. I've discovered the depth of my ability now and think it would be very hard for anyone to kill me." She looked up at Thrane, her green eyes mellow. "But if anyone tries, I've got my own Keeper here to help."

"Keeper?"

"That's right." India nodded at Thrane, and a look passed between them before she sat forward. "It goes like this…"

"Holy shit," Sim whispered, rocking back in her seat after India finished describing the World Tree and the fight to keep it safe.

"That's about what I thought when I found out India was a Keeper, too," Thrane said, his eyes locked on India's.

The clear connection shining between Thrane and India was beautiful, and Sim automatically looked away. Would she ever have that? Did she even want that? She turned, without thinking, looked at Nate. He was staring at his clenched fists. His jaw tightened.

What was that about?

And then his gaze cut to hers. His blue eyes deepened to a glittering indigo.

"Nate, are you okay?"

He stared at her for one long moment, then his jaw unclenched. He smiled and nodded, but his fists remained clenched. Whatever was going on, he wasn't going to tell her.

Fine, he didn't need to tell her everything. It wasn't as if that was the nature of their relationship.

"Right, well, that's a lot to take in, you know?" Sim said.

"I know," India said. "Believe me, I know. But I think the reason everyone wants you to know my story is because that's where you and I are similar. I didn't know my father's family—and their influence on my magic—until it was almost too late. And I'm still learning the intricacies of my power."

"Okay, so you've got an ... interesting heritage." Sim looked at Nan and Nate. "What does that have to do with me?"

"Sim, dear, this is all about genetics. We think you need to learn about yours. When you cast that spell in the garden, that was unlike any magic we've ever known."

"What? Why? How was it different?"

"When you grew that rose," Nate said, "you channeled something through yourself that I've—we've—never felt before. When my family casts a spell, except India because she's different, we ask the world to work with us, and then because we carry the gene of hereditary witchcraft, the world responds to our requests, and the magic is made. You did something today that we haven't done. You became a funnel for the magic through your touch. So, yes, you have the genetic spark that will let you make the spell, but there's something else in your magic."

"Holy cow. Seriously? I can't just have plain old everyday magic?"

"Looks like it."

"You know, I need to try and talk to Mum. When this all started—" Her memory of the actual moment her witchcraft had surfaced hit her fully for the first time.

"What were you going to say?" Nate asked, leaning in.

Sim turned to India. "Do you remember when you called me yesterday morning? You had a vision of something coming and called me?"

"Yeah, of course."

"Well, that's when this all started," Sim said. "And I just remembered what happened. Fully remembered. I was sitting out the back when this ... this thing, right here in my chest, started to spin. And then the sky clouded over, and something cold speared through me, shoved me off the bench seat. And I think—no, I know, before I blacked out, someone else was there, right before I blacked out."

"What the hell?" Nate jumped up. "You were attacked? You didn't mention that—"

"No, no one attacked me." Sim grabbed his hand, tugged him down. "Whatever happened, it happened *inside* me, not to me. But someone was there. And when I came to and went upstairs, June spoke. That was unusual enough, but she was crying. June never cries. She said, 'They're here.' That was right before you got up to the apartment." Sim shot India a look. "I thought she must've meant you."

"Right," India said, "I remember. I thought I'd surprised you."

"Yeah, but what if June didn't mean you?" Sim said. "When I spoke to her, I saw her view out of the yard. She had a perfectly clear—what do you call it?—line of sight. She would've seen what happened to me."

"You think June saw all of it, and said nothing?" Nate asked.

"June doesn't speak." Sim shrugged.

"Ever?" Nan said.

"Pretty much. She's kind of—the best way I can put it—

is absent. She was in and out of institutions when I was growing up. And after I turned eighteen and got out of the foster homes, I took her to see some specialists. But no one could find anything medically wrong."

"Have you always looked after her?" Nate asked, voice low.

"Of course. As much as I could before I was eighteen, although when she went into facilities, I'd get put into care because I was a minor. But she'd come back eventually, and we'd be together again for a little while. And then, like I said, after I turned eighteen, I could look after her myself." Sim's gaze drifted to June where she sat at the dining table. "But she just sits there. Looking outside. She goes through the motions physically, but inside, it's like she's not there."

"June spoke to me, once," India murmured.

"When? What did she say?"

India rubbed her arms as if a chill had run over her. "It was when Tara ... when we found her at your hotel. I ran inside to call Nate and saw June then. Your mother grabbed my arm and told me to be careful not to send myself so far."

Sim rubbed her arms as if the chill had moved from India to her. She had the same reaction every time she thought about what might've happened to Tara when she'd been attacked.

"India, dear."

"Yes, Nan?"

"Why do you think June said that to you?"

"I think that was the second time I used magic. Consciously, that is." India looked at Thrane for a moment. "Thrane asked me to check if anyone was around, who we couldn't see. I sent my energy currents—that's the only way I can describe it—to see if I could sense anyone else so that I didn't have to leave Tara and Thrane physically."

Sim swallowed the lump that formed in her throat. "I'm so grateful for what you and Thrane did. Who knows what might've happened if you hadn't found Tara when you did?"

Another spear of cold echoed through her. And this time when Nate held out a hand, she picked it up without thought. Clasped it tight.

"I might know what happened to your mother," Nan said and slowly placed her teacup down. "My dear, there's a spell that witches can use, a very difficult one, where they can send their self, their inner-self, to see or receive or send a message to another place or person. Only a very strong witch could master the spell, though. And if it goes wrong, if you lose control of the spell, you can lose your inner-self. Your physical form would be present, but only the shadow of you would be inside."

15

S im bundled Tara into the car seat behind Nate and secured the clasp on her harness buckle.

"Do we have to go now, Mum?"

Sim gave Tara a soft tap on her button nose, belying the urge to run, or scream, or throw something hard like she really wanted to do.

"We do, honey-bug. There's someone you need to meet, and Mumma's got to work tonight. That means we need to head home."

"But can't we have a sleepover here?"

"Not tonight. But maybe if you're extra good, we can ask Nan if we can come back another time."

Sim closed the truck door firmly, steeled herself against Tara's forlorn expression, then made sure June was in her seatbelt too. With a sigh, she said her goodbyes to everyone else except for Nate. He was already in the driver's seat, talking to Thrane in a low voice.

"Bloody monster truck," she muttered as she hauled herself up.

"What's that?" Nate asked.

"Nothing."

"Did you just call my beautiful ute a"—Nate cut his gaze to the rearview mirror where Tara was happily watching them—"a something monster truck?"

"Well, if you heard me, why did you ask?"

He groaned, turned the key to start the engine. "I'll just sit here and mind my business, shall I?"

Sim rewarded him with a tight smile because the rhetorical question didn't need any response.

Gravel crunched beneath the truck wheels as Nate slowly reversed and then drove down the driveway. Sim waved a last goodbye to Nate's family, and then it was just Nate and her little family of three.

June sat as quiet as ever in the back seat, and Sim couldn't help but eye her carefully, looking for any traces of what Nan had said.

Tara was watching a movie on her tablet. The quiet chatter of the character voices was a soothing counter to the feelings roaring inside Sim.

"You okay?" Nate asked, voice low.

Sim forced a smile, automatically hiding how close she was to losing her shit, and almost answered yes by rote. But damn it, she didn't want to lie.

She surreptitiously checked that the movie had Tara engrossed. Only then did she let her smile drop.

"Okay is the polar opposite of how I feel right now," she said, turning in the seat to face Nate. "I'm scared—no, I'm absolutely, completely consumed with fear. And it's coming from all directions. For Tara ... what if Luc's not a good father? I mean, I don't know anything about him, other than he can clean dishes, comes from Europe somewhere, and has a family business."

She swallowed the lump that rose in her throat, checked again on Tara.

"She's fine," Nate murmured. "I'll keep an eye on her through the mirror and let you know if she tunes in to what you're saying. What else?"

Sim took a deep breath, slowly exhaled. The need to get her feelings out and into words was too strong to smother.

"I'm scared because ..."

"Because ..."

"Because what if he's actually a *great* father? What if he does a better job of parenting than me? I don't want to lose control over what happens to Tara, hell, for at least another fourteen years. And then there's June. What if Nan's right? That June's the way she is because she lost herself. What does that mean? Is her soul flying somewhere through the universe, trying to find a way back?" She pitched her voice as low as she could. "That is just horrible."

"And? What else?" Nate murmured, the rumble of his voice soothing, comforting.

Trust Nate to pick up that there was more. She looked away from him, out over the hills. Did she even want to acknowledge this to herself?

Nate's monster truck was cozy, secure somehow in the late afternoon sun. But it wasn't the heater that made it cozy. It was Nate. Oh shit, it was *Nate* who made her feel safe. His strength, his solidness, and his warmth—physical and emotional—all spun together and made the cabin of the truck, somehow, right.

And she didn't want to lie to him.

"I'm ... I'm frustrated. And this will sound awful, but this amazing thing has happened. I'm a witch. A *witch*. I need to know what that means. But I feel, well, selfish for even thinking about focusing on myself. Except that the witch thing also bleeds over to Tara and June. So, I have to know." She slumped back on the seat. "My head is going to explode."

She only kept one thing back, one last teeny-tiny thing she wasn't ready to face yet. Nate. That would be going down a dangerous road she didn't have a single hope of controlling. Dangerous to her heart and his. Because she didn't do relationships.

Sim blew out a breath, slow and long. Tried to at least calm the clamor of emotions inside her. She wasn't kidding about the whole imminent brain explosion thing.

"You're entitled to lose it, you know," Nate said. "You're always so controlled ... and I know you have to be most of the time, but maybe you should think about letting yourself lose it, just once in a while."

"No, thanks. No way do I want Tara seeing that." Lose control? A shiver trickled through her. Sim tugged on her braid. "You know you're talking to a complete control freak here, right? I don't want to lose control at all."

She turned to the window. Outside the car, the countryside sped by, her thoughts racing just as fast.

They were almost at her hotel when Nate's mobile phone rang, jarring Sim from her thoughts.

Nate glanced at the truck display synced to his phone. "It's the station. Do you mind if I take this?" he asked. "I'll just pull over here for a moment."

Nate finished his call and minutes later pulled into the car park behind Sim's. He turned off the engine and as Tara had fallen asleep on the drive, said quietly, "There's been a break-in at the new florist's place, and Kat's asked me to head over. I can help you get Tara upstairs, and then I'll have to go."

Sim smiled, but it lacked her usual life and energy. "Not needed, but thanks for the offer. It's already close to four, and if Tara sleeps much longer, she'll never go down tonight."

Nate hopped out of the ute and opened the passenger door to Tara's side as Simone came around. She gently woke Tara up, and the little girl sleepily rubbed her eyes and looked around, met his gaze. A smile blossomed on her face.

That smile hit him like a sucker punch. Tara was genuinely happy to see him. Sim looked at him too, and another smile came over her face. Still tired, but genuine. She was the two in the one-two punch.

Man, he was a goner for these girls.

He took a steadying breath and helped June out. Then he had to muffle a laugh as Sim wrangled Tara out of the high back seat of his ute.

Sim must've sensed his mirth because she grinned. "Don't say it, Nate."

"What? You don't like my monster truck?"

Sim shook her head, but her expression had lightened, and this time there was a little more life to her face. Good.

He grabbed Tara's backpack from the rear tray and knelt

to help put the straps over Tara's shoulders. "Here you go, munchkin. You're all set."

Nate turned to Sim. Her hair had come loose from her braid, and the afternoon sun caught the red strands, gave her a red halo of fire. She was magnificent. And she took his breath away.

He had to clear his throat before he could speak. "Would it be okay if I stopped by later this evening if it's not too late once I'm finished with the florist?"

Sim regarded him carefully, and after a moment of silence, he didn't think she was going to say yes. His gut dropped. And then she moistened her lips, and after cutting her eyes to the back of the hotel, she finally nodded.

"Luc's spending some time with Tara this afternoon, so I'll be with them, of course. Then I'm working the dinner service through till we close," Sim said, "but feel free to stop in. And if you haven't eaten, I can make you something."

Nate gave Tara a hug and said bye to June. He wanted to lean in and give Sim a quick kiss—okay, not so quick. But it didn't take a cop's sense to see now wasn't the right time. So, he just smiled, made sure his eyes did the talking for him.

Sim got his message because her creamy cheeks reddened, and she shook her head even as she walked past him and ushered her little family inside the back door of her hotel. She looked over her shoulder before she disappeared out of sight, a genuine smile curving those lush lips.

His lips tipped up in response. Nate probably looked completely foolish, standing there smiling like that. But man, he'd kissed her. She'd kissed him. Twice. It made his reasons for not accepting the call of the World Tree even more important.

As soon as he had the thought, the Tree registered in his consciousness. That same sense of waiting. Watching.

Blowing out a low breath, Nate forced that door in his mind to close tightly and shut the World Tree out. Right now, he had a job to do, and he started his ute up and headed toward the florist shop.

It was just after four o'clock when he turned onto Queen Street. He slowed down as he drove past the old street-front shops lining both sides of the road, noted who was coming and going.

These businesses represented everything he loved about country towns. Large windows displaying wares. People watching out for each other, helping when times got tough.

The street was quiet, normal for this time on a Saturday, with most of the businesses closing up for the day around two hours earlier. Queen Street would continue to die down until the only people around would be those using it as a go-between for the night spots in town and the exceptional Asian fusion restaurant at the end of the street.

He pulled his ute into the diagonal curbside parking in front of the florist and cut the engine.

Only four other cars were parked on the street, two of them beside him, and one of those was a marked police car.

He quickly changed his hoodie for the jacket he always kept ready for these unexpected moments when he needed to appear professional and took his police ID from his wallet.

He noted the registration of the other car as he walked up to the front door.

The shop was classic '50s-style—brick, a window running most of its length, and a glass door that should have had four rectangular panes. Old advertising remnants of paint and writing were still visible on the glass window. So, the new owner hadn't made any changes there yet.

The door was open, a rectangular Shop Closed sign hung facing outward. The lower left panel was smashed in with a large fragment of glass still caught in the rim, and more shards and splinters were covering the floor inside.

Nate raised an eyebrow at the obvious damage. It was unusual for a shop, especially on this street, to be broken into in broad daylight. Another car drove past, slowed down, of course. Word had spread quickly. Not surprising.

Kat was already in the shop. She acknowledged him with a nod but continued talking to a blond female.

The blond glanced up, and the view was pretty amazing. Pale golden hair fell straight to her lower back, and she wore a plain white T-shirt, which fitted very well indeed around impressive curves. From her position behind the counter, he presumed her to be the new florist.

Stunning blue eyes, awash with a sheen of tears that somehow managed not to fall, widened as he walked in, and she visibly tensed.

Man, she was familiar. Where had he seen her before?

A perfectly pink rosebud of a mouth quivered, and the woman swallowed once before she responded to whatever Kat had said. Then a light bulb triggered in Nate's brain. She was the woman he'd run into when he'd left the police station in a hurry to get to Sim's. Nate held out his police badge, and she visibly relaxed.

Nate nodded and murmured a greeting. Kat had things under control, so he looked around the shop instead. It was hard to tell what damage there was—if there was any—and what were the remnants of the remodeling.

The counter ran almost the length of the space. A door, currently closed, led to the back area. The shop itself was pretty small, but he knew it had to be to allow room out back for cold storage.

There were no flowers anywhere, and all shelves in front of the counter were on the floor in pieces—not smashed though, more like disassembled. He turned around on the spot, took a last thorough look over everything there was to see.

"Senior Sergeant," Nate said to Kat, acknowledging her as the first responder who had ownership of things for now. He'd learned early on that if he didn't acknowledge a uniformed officer, sometimes *others* didn't give them their due respect.

"Hi, Nate." Kat looked down at a small spiral notebook she had on the bench. "This is Anna Johnson. Anna is short for Annalise. Anna, this is Detective Nate. You said you wanted a detective, and Nate is ours."

He looked closer at the woman, and her eyes filled with more tears.

"I'm sorry to get you out on the weekend, Detective." She sent Kat a grateful look, then turned her stunning gaze on him. "Kathryn did mention you were on your day off, but you see, while this might just look like another break and enter, I've got some history with certain people in the city, and I'd hate for trouble to follow me. I thought it best to bring it to your attention right away."

Kat hadn't given the new florist her preferred name,

which told him straight up how she felt about the newcomer. And he trusted Kat's impressions.

Nate kept his expression completely welcoming, his standard poker face when dealing with an unknown situation.

"Ms. Johnson, is it?" he asked.

"That's right. Anna Johnson. But please call me Anna." Her lower lip quivered again but bravely stayed up. Just. "You see, I had a shop in the city and had some trouble with my neighbors there. That's why I came here, and then—"

Nate held up his hand. "Okay, okay, before we get to that, why don't you tell me what happened here." He looked at Kat. "I take it this happened this afternoon?"

Kat nodded, struggling to contain a smile. The bugger.

"Oh, well, I was out the back, you see, working on my plans for the shop. And then I heard glass break, and I ran out here and saw the door ... the damage to the door , that is."

"And did you see who did it?"

Anna shook her head, blue eyes wide.

"Okay, so what did you do next?"

"I ran to the front of the shop." She moved out from around the counter, brushed past Kat without a word, and took a couple of steps as if to act out what she'd seen. "I didn't want to step in the broken glass, but through the window, I saw some figures— at least two—running down the street. And I was so scared, I didn't want to run out after them. What if they came back?"

Her gaze lit on his and didn't let up. She moved closer. Her breasts grazed his sleeve.

Nate shifted his weight to the back of his heels, created a

little breathing room. He cut a look at Kat. She was enjoying his discomfort way too much to be any help.

He surveyed the shop, nodded to a piece of brick paver on the floor beside the door. "Was that what they used?"

"Yes, and I—I think it's from the planter in front of the next shop over. It's similar."

"And what time was this?"

"Oh, maybe an hour ago."

"An hour?" Nate traded looks with Kat.

"Oh yes, you see, the telephone here in the shop isn't working. And I got such a scare that I ran back out to get my mobile phone but couldn't find my bag. It was beneath one of the boxes, and then I finally found it and had to find the number of the local station. I didn't want to call it in as an emergency, and luckily Officer Kathryn was able to come here as soon as I made the call."

"Of course. I was at the station, so it was easy to pop over."

"Well, there's not much chance the offenders are still close by," Nate said.

"I checked the premises inside and out," Kat said. "Couldn't see anything else amiss. Unfortunately, Anna hasn't set up any kind of surveillance yet, either internal or external, so there's no camera footage to check here."

"We can ask around the local shops. Maybe some of them have camera vision that might show something." Nate took another look around. "Have you been able to tell if they stole any goods?"

"They didn't take anything."

"Are you sure? You're still remodeling, right? It's kinda

hard to tell. We can dust for prints and check if they got inside."

"Honestly, I came out as soon as I heard the glass smash—there was no way they could've come inside and me not have seen them."

"Okay, well, that's good to know."

"Right, well, I'll bag this up." Kat nodded at the brick. "Who knows? We might get prints."

"If you're good on that, I'll head out and see who else is around," Nate said, moving to the door. "Sounds like the damage was opportunistic, so there could be other premises they hit, and if they're already closed up for the day, the owners may not even know it."

"Oh no, please, Detective, I think you'll find this was targeted at me. Perhaps Kathryn could ask around, and I can tell you about the other incident?"

"Actually, Ms. Johnson, this is technically Kat's investigation. She's our senior sergeant, and I'm only here because you asked for a detective specifically, and Kathryn agreed. She's more than qualified to manage your case, and I can help her if needed." Nate turned to Kat. "What would you like me to do?"

Kat's eyes twinkled as she clearly considered whether or not to feed Nate to the wolves. He held his breath. She was normally a decent person, so hopefully ...

"Ms. Johnson—Anna," she said, "it's standard procedure for me to prepare a report for the CIB."

"The who?"

"The criminal investigations branch. That's where Nate works. They'll decide if they need to assist with the case. Though it's Nate's day off, maybe he can check around for us before he heads home. But he'll be back in the station on Monday, and I will certainly make sure to include all of your information about your prior issues in my final report."

"Oh, well, okay." Anna began to wring her hands. "I really only want to make sure it's not the city problem happening again. I'll definitely go with what you think is best, Officer." Anna returned her baby blues back to him. "I'm sorry to interrupt your day, Detective, and thank you for coming so fast."

"No worries, I'm sure everything will be fine. Do you have friends or family in town?"

"No, not yet, although I have hired some workers through an online agency, they should be here tomorrow. But for now, it's just me."

The full force of Anna's hope-filled gaze hit Nate hard. And while he seriously wanted to get away from the too-close attention of the florist, it'd be a prick move not to help her out. And Anna Johnson had become one of the towns-folk. They looked after their own.

He'd get the info from Kat and look into what had driven their newest shopkeeper to their little country town.

Nate held back a sigh. "Then how about I help you clean up the glass once Kathryn takes the evidence? And then I'll ask around your neighbors, just in case they heard or saw anything."

16

———————

As night fell, Ri'Anit finally dropped the spell that had hidden the bodies of the previous florist and his partner. Then she opened the shop's back door to the rear laneway and used the dark to cover her soldier's return.

He dropped to his knees and placed his hands on her legs.

"Fool, there is no time for this." She kicked him away. "Did you find any witches?"

Her soldier shook his head.

She spat out a curse. Damn these witches. "At least I found one. He was here in the shop today. He's the local police detective—you are to find him now and let me know his movements—where there's one witch, there's always more. And I will find this child."

At least her plan had worked. Bring the witch folk of the town to her so that eventually she'd be in place to find the Keepers and bring them down. It was rewarding to find a powerful witch so soon. She was just temporarily switching her focus.

That the male witch had taken none of the lures she'd laid out was only a minor inconvenience. Perhaps this visage wasn't the right one for him. But no matter, with time, her skills would bring him around.

17

The hotel's public bar was humming by six-thirty that evening. Weaving between tables, Sim carried a tray of freshly poured beers to a group of regulars.

"Hey, guys, got your ales," Sim called out as she stepped around another table.

A customer at the table stood up and stepped into her path.

"Yikes!" she yelped, stumbling to a stop. But the large, frosty glasses of beer kept going.

She yanked the tray up. The glasses tumbled back at her and icy liquid splashed down her shirt. The metallic scent of hops and malt bloomed in the air; then the glasses smashed onto the floorboards.

Shit. She didn't need this on a busy Saturday night.

"Sorry," she called out, dropping to her knees to scoop up the broken glass. "No one move till I've picked this up."

"No, I am sorry, Simone."

Sim stiffened at the lilt of Luc's voice. Of course it was him. He'd been with Tara for an hour, and he'd been ...

great. Not too full-on, but engaging enough that Tara had opened right up. Sim had wanted to both cry and laugh.

"Here, let me help," Luc murmured. His cool gray gaze caught hers as he knelt in front of her.

"Thanks, but you don't have to—"

"Nonsense. It's my fault, after all. I was the one in your way." Luc deftly deposited more broken glass on her tray.

A tangy scent tingled in her nose, the freshness welcome against the malty beer stink. It was Luc's aftershave—on his clean-shaven, perfectly shaped jaw.

She looked away, hurriedly picked up the last large piece of glass—and sliced her finger. She hissed and awkwardly grabbed the wound with her other hand, balancing the tray between her arms.

"Double shit," she muttered.

"Is it bad?" Luc asked. He went to take the tray, but she turned so he couldn't.

"No, just a nick. And thanks, but I've got this. Though would you mind letting Tammy—she's behind the bar— know I need a hand with some cleaning here?"

"Hm, well, at least let me help you up first." Luc put a hand beneath her arm, helped her rise to her feet. He pulled a little square of fabric from his pocket. "Here, wrap your finger in this."

"Thanks."

Luc regarded her like he wanted to take the tray—what, did he expect her to faint from a teensy cut?—then pivoted and strolled to the bar. Sim kept the pressure around her fingertip while making sure no one walked over the broken glass until Tammy came over with a long-handled dustpan and broom.

Sim dumped her tray of broken glass into the kitchen glass bin and gave her dinner team the heads-up she was getting a plaster and a clean shirt.

Nose wrinkling, she headed into her office. Luc leaned against her desk, holding the white metal tin that contained her medical kit.

"What are you doing?" She couldn't contain a sigh.

"Your bartender told me where to find this." Luc opened the kit. "And I am here to assist you. I imagine it will be easier than trying to bandage your wound yourself."

"It's a minor cut; I'm sure I could've done it myself." She didn't want to be indebted to him. At all. She was still figuring out how Luc was going to fit into their lives. This ... this domestic side of him made the hairs on the back of her neck prick. But why?

"You seem a very capable, independent person, so undoubtedly you could. But since I am here, there is no need."

She didn't bother to hide a snort but unwrapped his hanky or whatever the fabric was that he'd given her and stuck out her hand. "Fine. But I'm in a hurry."

"So gracious."

Nate walked into the foyer of the Grand Hotel just before seven with Kat and one of the probation officers, Marlee.

"I'll see you inside. Just need to grab a word with Sim and see how her afternoon went," he called out over his shoulder as he headed into the parlor.

He didn't need to turn around to know Kat had rolled

her eyes. Still bemused by the afternoon's events, he ducked his head into Sim's office.

Sim and Luc were standing at her desk. Their heads were bent over something—what, he couldn't see—then Sim laughed. That genuine chuckle she made when something amused her. Luc laughed too.

Nate's stomach dropped.

He backed out of the doorway and slumped against the wall. Fuck, what if Luc wanted to start something with Sim? And what if Sim was interested? Luc had a role in Tara's life —and Sim's—Nate could never have.

Footsteps echoed from the office, and then Sim darted through the doorway, holding her work shirt away from her body, smelling of ... beer?

"Hey, Nate, when did you get here?" A smile lit her face.

"Just now." His heart flipped. Man, she was gorgeous. "Looks like you've been in a beer fight."

"You could say that. I have to change, and quickly. We've got a bit of a rush on. The beer and ribs specials are going out the door like nothing else. The dining room's full, but if you're hungry, grab a table in the bar, and I'll be out when we've got some breathing room."

"Do you need a hand? I can pick up plates and stuff like that."

"Nah, we're good for now, thanks. Though if we get a second rush, that might change. Gina, Frank's granddaughter, is helping tonight with the restaurant and Tammy's behind the bar, so we should be okay. Gotta run. See you soon."

Sim took off at a race up the stairs, her jeans cupping her perfectly shaped butt, braid swinging with every step.

"What's the serious face for?" Kat asked, walking out from the public bar carrying two drinks.

"Me? Nothing. But I'll smile if one of those is for me."

"Then get your grin on. Here you go. I came to tell you we've got a table."

"Thanks. I'll be there soon, just going to walk around, say hi to the locals." And check what the mysterious Luc was up to.

In the small dining area, all tables were in use, and after saying hi to the people he knew, he went through the connecting door into the rear of the public bar. There wasn't a spare high table, and a stack of people gathered at the main bar, still more around the pool table.

And there was Luc. Alone at a high table in the back corner, a beer in front of him.

Nate purposefully stopped by. "Evening, Luc. How are you finding Warragul?"

"Detective Nathaniel." Luc took a slow sip of his drink. "It's a great little town. Everyone's been ... welcoming."

"Glad to hear," Nate murmured, containing a grin.

The locals had welcomed Sim as one of their own, so they wouldn't be friendly to someone they thought could make Sim's life difficult. And Luc was going to make things difficult. Everything in Nate's gut screamed it.

"So how do you know Simone?" Luc asked.

"We became friends when she moved to town."

"Just friends?"

Wow, so much for subtlety. Nate took a sip of his beer, bought a moment to consider Luc. Was he curious about Nate and Sim's relationship because of Tara, or was he interested because of something or *someone* else ... like Sim?

Nate bared his teeth. "I'll leave Sim to answer that. But I can tell you she does an amazing job running this place. And she's a wonderful mum. I—my entire family—love Tara." He paused. "Would do anything for them. And to keep them safe."

"Are you trying to say something, Detective?" Luc asked.

"Just that country folk look after their own." Nate took a sip of his beer and tipped his glass toward Luc. "See you around."

Across the room, Kat caught his eye and held up her drink, waving him over. He weaved his way through more people and tables and chairs till he got to Kat and Marlee. How they'd snaffled a high table, he didn't ask.

"So, who's Luc?" Kat asked and took a sip of her drink.

"We've only been here for what ... five minutes?" Nate said. "How did you hear about him already?"

Kat shrugged. But then Louise, Kat's partner, came up to the table with a glass of wine in one hand, a basket of hot fries in the other.

"Hiya, Nate," Louise said. "I snagged these from the kitchen. Fresh out of the fat."

Nate sent Kat a look, but she missed it since she was busy kissing Lou. Marlee just dug into the fries. Hell, he was hungry, and the fries were hot and salty. Perfect on a bloody cold winter's night. He dug in too.

Once Kat and Lou had come up for air, and Marlee had gone off to talk to some young guy at the bar, Nate nudged Kat with his elbow.

"Okay, spill. What did you hear?"

"Oh, you know. Just the usual gossip that the town's newest, hottest single publican had a visitor who may or not be her baby's daddy." The mirth dropped away from Kat's eyes. "Seriously though, Lou heard it from Gina, who heard it from Frank. And Gina only told Lou because her sister works with Lou at the hospital."

"Wow. Impressive. But okay, got it."

"How's Sim?"

"She's managing. Just. She's got a lot going on, though, and Luc is only part of it."

"How are you doing?" Kat put her arm around his shoulders.

"Thanks for the support." Nate smiled, genuinely touched. "I'm okay. Hoping to hell Luc's only staying around for Tara—although my gut's saying otherwise. And I can say Sim and I are ..." Their kisses earlier in the day replayed through his mind. "Barring Luc, we might be in an okay spot, too."

"About time, Detective." Kat's eyebrows shot up; a grin covered her face.

"Sh, not so loud. I'm still in my strategic-positioning phase here. No putting any pressure on her."

"Sure, sure. But she's lucky to have you. Remember that."

Nate rolled his eyes, then gave Kat an affectionate shoulder nudge. "Thanks for the loyalty." Lou came back, settled beside Kat. Nate nodded at Lou and said, "You've got a good one."

"Who's got a good one?" Sim asked, wiping her hands on a dish towel as she came over to their table.

Nate choked on his beer. "Lou. I was talking about Lou and Kat."

"Well, of course they do—are. Either way." Sim used her

forearm to brush some wisps of red hair back from her fore-head. But she missed one.

Nate reached over, and without a thought, tucked the errant strand, silky soft, behind her ear.

Three sets of eyes turned to him.

"You kinda missed one," Nate said in a gruff voice, nodding at her hair.

"Right." Sim shot him a look. Oh-oh, guess she wasn't ready for public displays of affection yet.

But man, all he wanted right then was to lean in, flick open the buttons on her black long-sleeved shirt. And since when did work shirts look so sexy? But hers did, tight over the curves of her chest, offsetting her pale skin. And he wouldn't have to lean far. He'd nudge open the buttons, then duck down, touch his lips to her smooth, lush—

"Good evening, Simone." A too-smooth voice inter-rupted the fantasy.

Nate straightened as Luc appeared at Sim's side.

Sim's eyes narrowed, though, whatever her thoughts, she kept them hidden behind a pleasant smile. She took care of the introductions, which was just as well because Nate was caught between wanting Sim more than ever and wanting to get her far away from Luc.

It was fucking frustrating that he couldn't make either a reality.

Nate tuned into the conversation right as Luc said he was heading out to look around the town. Marlee came back to their table and somehow ended up offering to show Luc around. Nate caught Kat's eye, nodded at the doorway, then excused himself to the bathroom. But he ducked inside the guest parlor. Kat met him a few moments later.

"What's up?" She asked.

"Kat, I'm not sure I ... trust Luc."

"Jealous much?" She gave him a mock jab to the shoulder.

"What? No way. Okay, even if there's a little—totally natural—jealousy, it changes nothing. We still don't know him, who he is, what he does."

Kat regarded him for a beat, then nodded, a guarded look entering her eyes.

"Can you give Marlee the heads up—be aware, if not wary," he said.

"Okay. I'll go talk with her now." She turned to leave right as Sim walked in. She gave Sim a fast smile. "Hey, Sim, Lou and I were thinking of staying for dinner. How long until there's a table free?"

Sim laughed. "Kat, honey, those tables out back won't be free for at least an hour." She looked around the parlor and shrugged. "Can I set you up in here? Do you know what you're after?"

"That would be awesome. I'll be right back with Lou. And we definitely know what we want. Ribs all the way."

"Can do." Sim smiled up at Nate after Kat left the room. "You know, this Saturday night special is going gangbusters. Who'd have thought beef ribs and beers would be such a hit?"

Nate raised an eyebrow. "Everyone?"

"Let me guess, you want some, too?"

Kat reappeared with Lou and gave Nate a quick nod that told him she'd at least had a word with Marlee. He dipped his head once in acknowledgment.

"Do ducks fly?" he said to Sim. "And hey, can I head up

and say hi to Tara while they're cooking? These two can have some alone time."

"Of course."

Kat sat down on one couch and patted it for Lou to sit beside her.

"So, Nate,"—Kat shot him a discreet wink as he was about to walk out the door—"how'd it go with the florist?"

Nate held in a frown. What was Kat up to now?

"It went fine," he warily replied. "I helped to clean up the broken glass, took a walk around. You'd already left by the time I got back."

Sim perched on the arm of the couch.

"Wow, it's good to get off my feet." She cocked her head to one side, looked from Kat to him. "Was this what you had to leave about earlier today?"

Nate went to answer, but Kat cut in. "Yeah, and if I had to guess, I'd say our newest town member certainly enjoyed having the attention of Detective Hottie here to help the poor little damsel."

Nate almost choked. Detective Hottie? "Excuse me—?"

Sim cut in this time. "Oh, really? And what's our newest florist like?"

A note entered Sim's voice he hadn't heard before.

"Oh," Kat said, "about five foot eight, with long blond hair, striking blue eyes. Kind of like a Norse goddess, you know." Kat cast Lou a loving smile. "And I do like my blue eyes. And she had the biggest pair of—"

"Right. Okay, well, thanks for that review, Officer Indiscreet." Nate turned to Sim. "She was just another woman."

"Just your average everyday stunning, goddess-like shopkeeper?" Sim straightened.

Nate put his hands in his pockets. What on earth was Kat thinking? He shot her a sideways look. Kat ignored him.

"Yeah," Nate said. "Sure, she was attractive. I mean, I guess you could say that based purely on the physical. Not that I even thought about that."

"Right," Sim said, rolling her eyes. "So anyway, I've got to cook another three meals. Head to the bar and order yourselves a drink when you're ready."

Sim pivoted on her heels and marched out of the snug. Kat pulled Lou to her side and gave Nate a satisfied smile.

"You can thank me later," Kat said.

"Thank you?" Nate asked. "For what?"

Lou laughed, but Kat just sighed, shook her head. "Oh, Nate, didn't you see the look in Sim's eyes?"

"Yeah. She looked like she was ready to do murder. I'd be worried about our dinners if I were you."

"No, no, no. That wasn't murder. That was *bloody* murder. I just gifted you the best weapon you can have in a strategic push for a romance. Jealousy."

"Great, but I'm still worried about my dinner." He snorted, then headed upstairs to have his visit with Tara.

18

Feet heavy, shoulders drooping, Sim locked the main door to the pub. It was well after midnight, and she was beat.

She did one last walk-through of the bar. All she had left to do was count the till, and then she could head up for the night.

Nate was asleep on one of the parlor couches, feet propped up on the coffee table, head resting on the back of the couch at what had to be an uncomfortable angle. She smiled at him for a moment, listened to his deep breathing.

He'd helped pack up earlier, even though she'd said it wasn't necessary. Sim had to admit she was happy he'd stayed. Not just for the physical help, but he was good company. And right now, given the last two days, she was more rattled than she'd ever been. Having him around was a comfort.

Sim grabbed her till, poured herself a chamomile tea, then eased down beside Nate. It was too late for coffee, but it was cold, especially now the kitchen was closed and the mass of bodies had gone home. The hot, soothing tea was what she needed. That and sleep. The till didn't take long, and she counted out her float for the next day, bagging it all up to store in the upstairs safe overnight.

Finally, she sank into the cushions. Bloody hell, what a day. In fact, that made two days running that had been plain crazy. Thank the gods of hospitality that she didn't work the Sunday breakfast shift. She could have a sleep in ... that magical moment where she didn't have to get up before the sun. Where she and Tara could snuggle in bed. Make a lazy breakfast together. Watch Tara's cartoons.

Bliss. Sim almost sighed.

But she needed to get Nate moving first. His lean, tall body was going to be in all sorts of pain and discomfort tomorrow if she left him to sleep here.

"Nate, time to wake up." She shifted closer and placed a hand on his arm.

His eyelashes, shades darker than his hair, gradually lifted, let her glimpse the glittering blue of his eyes. His lips were soft, his face at rest. And as he blinked the sleep away, his eyes darkened, his pupils dilated. One capable hand snaked out to cradle the back of her neck.

When Nate drew her in, Sim didn't resist. When he brushed his mouth over hers, she didn't stop him.

And when their tongues touched, she moaned. Nate groaned, and his other hand moved to her waist, pulled her in until her body lay flush to his. He kissed his way to her ear, down her neck.

A shiver racked Sim's body where the hot, wet touches landed.

"Sim," Nate said, sending another shiver through her.

She brought her palm up, worked her way beneath his layers of clothes. The moment she met his hard, heated skin, that frisson returned, spreading over her body. She pressed harder with her fingers. Oh God, he was all hot, hard, burning muscles. A dusting of hair. Smooth, delicious skin.

And then Nate hauled her tight, rolled and pinned her beneath him. He knelt, powerful thighs on either side of her hips, and she dragged her eyes over the breadth of shoulders, the strong V of his torso, down to his lean hips, to his crotch—his desire was clear.

Her body clenched.

"Nate, I think ..." She licked her lips. "That is, you and I—"

"Yes, Ms. Morris?" He leaned in, nipped her lip.

Sim took a deep breath. Closed her eyes to shut out the magnificent view, tried to collect herself. "Nate, we need to talk."

"Mm," he murmured against her throat, then his hot, wicked tongue traced her pulse, sent a shiver of fire through every nerve ending.

She groaned as he scraped his teeth over the base of her neck. Fire speared into her core; her hips rose off the couch, pressed into that part of him she wanted—needed—right there and then.

Sim ran her hands over his hot, smooth skin. Ropes of sleek, curved muscles clenched, shivered beneath her touch. Dear God, she loved that she'd made him do that. Loved the way he didn't resist when she pulled him in close, pulled that massive body tight and hard into hers.

He kissed his way down to her collar, talented fingers

flicking her buttons open, and then those sinful lips touched her chest. Then moved lower and lower, as far as the gap in her shirt allowed.

She swallowed, skin ready to burst.

Nate glanced up, wicked blue eyes alight with fire and desire. His lips curved before he bent again and undid the third button. His hot breath washed over her exposed skin, sending a wave of heat rolling through her. And then his mouth closed in on her nipple through her bra.

Heat welled, pooled. A moan escaped her, but she couldn't help the sound, couldn't do anything other than try to get closer, get skin to skin somehow.

Sim was desperate for him.

An icy shiver trickled through her. Damn, she was *desperate*. For Nate. She never relied on another person, yet here she was, desperate for someone. What had happened to that hard-won control she'd prided herself on?

"Nate. Nate, we still need to talk."

His body tensed, and his lips hovered above her skin for one moment before he rose.

"Talk?" His gaze darkened to the fathomless blue of the deepest ocean.

"Yes."

Sim steeled herself. She'd started down a path today that she wasn't sure about. Not the kissing part because she was into Nate. Damn but was she into him. Temptation gnawed low in gut to throw caution to the wind and tear off his clothes, her clothes, and get them both naked right here. Get him inside of her, right now.

But she was ... scared. If she and Nate had a relationship

and then broke up, it would devastate her. And Tara would be heartbroken.

"I need to lay down a ground rule," she blurted.

Nate's eyes narrowed. Finally, he pushed himself up, moved to sit back on the coffee table.

"Ground rule ... okay." He ran a hand through his hair, mussed the blond strands further.

She resisted the urge to crawl over to him and get things back on track. Resisted the urge to moan at the loss of contact with his hot, hard, leanly muscled body. She closed her eyes. Somehow controlled her rioting hormones.

"No kissing in front of Tara. I don't want her to read anything into this—you and I, I mean."

"What *should* she read into ...?" Nate gestured between the two of them, wariness creeping into his gaze.

Sim bit her lip. Of course this moment had come. It was inevitable. Though how did she explain something that she could hardly understand herself? But she owed it to Nate to at least try and explain.

"Nate, I'm saying that I want to do this—what we're doing right now. I'm saying yes. But with some rules, that's all. Although honestly, I'm the last person you should ever be interested in being with. In a relationship, I mean. I've got this thing ... and I understand it, I really do. But I've got this little issue about control. And trust. Classic story of a woman whose father left her, and then she gets pregnant, and sure enough, the child's father leaves too."

"But—" Nate shook his head.

"I know, I know. Luc didn't even know I was pregnant. But the thing is, I feel it, all of it." She pressed a fist into her chest. "Right here. And then, a couple of years ago, I tried again, another relationship. But that turned into a bloody train wreck. And that's the real issue here. Control. I've had to be the one, every time, to make the hard decisions and make the calls that are right for my family. And I can't relinquish that now."

A lump grew in her throat, and she had to swallow hard to move past it.

"So what are you saying?" Nate blew out a slow breath, his gaze never straying from hers. "Is this about me? Or ... is Luc a factor now, too?"

"What, Luc?" Sim recoiled. "As in a *relationship*? Oh God, you're loco, Nate. No way. I'm saying that I'm no good in relationships—even a friends-with-benefits type of deal. They always end up going bad. And as Tara gets older, well, I can't imagine ever bringing someone into my life who Tara might bond with, and when things don't work out, that person would leave, too."

"First, I have to tell you I would never leave you or Tara."

"I know you say that, even believe that, but—"

"But you don't believe me. Okay, I'm going to be honest. You're saying you're holding back on having a meaningful romantic relationship because of Tara? Of course you have to think about her first. But that doesn't mean you don't get a chance to have something for yourself too. Come on. You're a perfectly healthy, very attractive"—his voice lowered—"very much alive person. You get to enjoy your life to the fullest. Hell, even if it's not with me, you shouldn't be scared off from ever having a relationship."

"Nate, hell yes, I'm scared. I could fall for you way too easily. But what if it goes wrong? And look at us right now." Sim set her jaw. "We're already arguing."

"Sim." Nate took in a deep, obvious breath then let it out just as slowly. "I'm. Not. Going. Anywhere. Look at me. I'm not telling you what to do; I'm saying you're crazy to imagine never having a genuine connection with someone."

He was angry. Of course. But he didn't get what she was trying to say. Maybe couldn't. After all, he didn't live in her head. She sighed, and a chill shivered through her.

Rubbing her arms, she stood up. "I'm tired. And out of sorts after everything. Maybe tonight wasn't the right night for this. Maybe we should just shelve this till another day."

"Fine. Not *tonight*."

"Anyway, before we ... kissed, I was going to say since it's so late and all, I can grab a key to one of the empty rooms, and you can stay the night?"

Nate sat back on the table. Luckily, it had wide, sturdy legs and didn't buckle beneath him. Every inch of his regard raked over her raw, exposed fears. She hugged her arms to her chest. Finally, he glanced down at his watch.

"Hell, it's after 1:00 a.m." He scrubbed a hand over his jaw, up into his hair. He eyed her again. "I can still stay?"

Sim almost winced at his tone but figured he was due his anger.

"Sure," she said, amazed she'd kept her voice even. Well, hadn't this night turned as crappy as a night could get?

Sim sighed as she walked up to the apartment. Her legs dragged, and her heart was against taking even one more step. She wanted to turn around and head straight to Nate's hotel room door. But she had to think longer term than just one night of sex—even if it promised to be the most spectacular, stars-and-fireworks, rock-your-world sex in the world.

Nate thought it was simply a matter of choice, but it

wasn't. Not for her. She'd been living this way for years. She'd been the child who cried in her bed at night when she couldn't help her mother, had cried when she'd been in new foster home after new foster home, had cried when she didn't have the answers to help her baby. Always on her own. Those years had made her who she was.

So if she wanted some ground rules between her and Nate, that's the way it had to be. Sim took a deep breath. She was doing the right thing. She *was*.

After checking on Tara and June, both deeply asleep, Sim did the bare minimum to get ready for bed and was in her pajamas and under the thick quilt in minutes. She dropped her head to the pillow. Thank the stars this day was over.

Sim's eyes popped open as she woke up. She was on her side, facing the window. Going by the dark of the sky, it wasn't morning yet. She didn't move—still tired from the day before, but her gaze roamed around the room. She rolled onto her back. No visible sign of anything amiss. Except her gut churned, and the little chime in her chest clanged.

Something wasn't right.

Had she left something on the stove? Had she forgotten to lock the front door?

She had to get out of bed and check. Now. She kicked the quilt back, heedless of the icy air. Didn't wince as her bare feet hit the floor.

Something was wrong.

Heart beating faster in her chest, she walked, then jogged the few steps to Tara's room. The door was ajar, and she pushed it open.

Weak light spilled into the small bedroom, but not enough to fully see Tara's bed.

Her heart beat harder.

Sim stumbled to the bed, ran her hands over the blanket. Nothing. Just sheets, cooling with no body to keep them warm.

She flew out of the room. Ran into June's room, threw the light switch. June sat up, eyes blinking owlishly in the sudden flare of light.

No Tara.

Sim ran back out, opened the doors to the bathroom, to the laundry. Nothing.

Downstairs. Maybe she was downstairs? Sim ran to the apartment door, wrenched the handle. But it didn't budge. It was locked. The deadbolt thrown.

She whirled around. Her mouth went dry. Tara wasn't in the apartment. She couldn't have left *and* dead bolted the door behind her.

Adrenaline shot through Sim. What the hell was going on? Where was Tara?

Luc.

Hands shaking, she fumbled with the lock and hurtled down the stairs to the first-floor corridor and Luc's room. She bashed her fist against his door. Nothing. She tried to open it, but the door was locked. The key. She needed her keys.

She ran past Nate's room. Skidded to a halt. She tried to open his door, but it was locked too.

"Nate! Nate!" she called out, rapping against the wood, heedless of waking up any other guests, and was about to bang on it again when Nate opened the door.

"What's wrong?" he asked.

"Tara's not upstairs. I need to find her. I'm looking for Luc."

"Fuck. Have you checked his room?"

"It's locked, and he didn't answer." She took off, yelled over her shoulder, "I'm getting the keys now. Can you check downstairs—just in case?"

The bottom floor was lit only by the night-light for late returning guests. Sim darted through the snug and into her office. The room was dark, silent.

Turning the light on revealed it was as empty as everywhere else. An icy wave coursed through her, but she pushed it aside, grabbed the master keys as Nate appeared in the doorway.

"No sign down here, and everything's locked," he said.

"I've got the room keys." Sim took off back up the stairs, three at a time.

Tara.

Three more steps.

Tara.

Three more steps.

Tara.

Three more steps.

Pressure grew in her chest with every footfall, but she couldn't think of anything else. Only getting to Tara. She reached Luc's door and unlocked it, threw it open, turned on the light.

Nothing.

She checked the tiny bathroom, the wardrobe. No sign of Tara. No sign of anyone at all. Her hands shook.

Where was her baby?

Someone grabbed her arm, and she whirled. It was Nate, face grim.

"Sim—you need to stop for one moment. I need to ask a question. Was the door locked?"

"What?" She frowned, keys clattering in her hand. "Yes, Luc's door—"

"No. Not Luc's door. *Yours.* To the apartment. When you started looking for Tara, was *your* door locked?"

She swallowed, tried to think past the crashing of her heart against her ribs, the pounding of blood in her ears.

"Yeah ... yes, it was. I remember; it didn't make sense. How could she leave and throw the dead bolt?"

"Fuck," Nate growled. "She couldn't." He grabbed his mobile phone and dialed someone. "Thrane, I need you over at Sim's. Tara's missing. So is Luc."

Nate's hawkish gaze locked on her even as he bit out the words as if he guessed how close she was to flight—if only she knew where to fly and find her baby.

Oh God, please, please, please let her be okay.

"Yeah, no sign in the hotel at all. But it might be super-natural. Your friend, Serephena, can she help us find Tara no matter where she is? Yep. Got it." Nate's jaw tightened as he hung up the call.

"Tara. I have to find Tara." Sim squeezed words past the solid knot in her throat.

Nate held her arms. She grasped him back.

"Sim," he said, "we will find her."

She took a breath, and another. And another. The room

spun. Nate shook her shoulders, and she opened her eyes. When had they closed? She shook her head. Tried to focus. "I'm here. I'm here."

"Breathe slowly, Sim. Slow it down. You're hyperventilating."

She swallowed hard, tried to inhale. A giant weight clamped around her chest.

"Can't."

Nate whispered something, and a zap of energy sprang through her. The weight dislodged. The world stopped spinning.

But her heart kept hammering. So hard, so fast, it was going to break out of her chest and tear after whoever had her baby.

"Sim, we need to work out where Tara is, what's happened. Sim. Can you hear me?"

Control. Control. Get some bloody control! She battened the storm of emotions deep, deep down, finally gasped in a breath past the razor-edged burning knot constricting her throat.

Blood welled beneath her hands where she gripped Nate's forearms. She gasped, let him go.

His skin was covered with tiny, red slices. What the— had she—? She turned her palms over. Blood, Nate's blood, stained her skin. She began to shake.

"Nate, I didn't mean to hurt ... what the hell is going on?"

"They're nothing. Wait here, I'll grab a towel—for your hands." Nate didn't even look at the cuts as he disappeared into the bathroom, then returned with a hand towel.

She was still staring at her palms when he wiped the blood off them. Then he blotted the cuts on his arms.

"Are—are you hur ..." She swallowed, unable to finish the sentence.

He wrapped the towel around his forearms, then whispered something too quietly for her to understand. His face tightened, and he grimaced, then removed the towel and tossed it into the bathroom.

The slices were closed over, blood no longer welling along the raised red lines.

"Sim. Hey, Sim. They're gone now. Come on—look at my face, not the cuts. Now, I'm going to call Kat and get a search going. Here, I'll put it on speaker."

He dialed another number. The phone rang and rang and rang.

And finally, picked up.

"Nate?" Kat's scratchy voice echoed into the room. "What on earth, man? It's barely even ... hell, it's not even five."

"Kat, I need you to wake up. Tara's gone, and so is Luc. Have you heard from Marlee?"

"Shit," Kat said. "Give me a sec." Sim kept her eyes glued to Nate as sounds of rustling, another muttered curse, and what must've been Lou's mumbling carried over the phone. "I just checked, and no text from Marlee. I'm going to call her. What do you want from me?"

"I need you here at the hotel," Nate replied. "I might need to try another way to find Tara, and we need someone I trust here to look for her using conventional methods too —just in case."

"Right. I'll be fifteen minutes."

As Nate disconnected the phone call, another chill shook through Sim, and she wrapped her arms about herself.

"Nate?" Sim said. "I don't—I don't know what to do. Where is she? Why would she be gone?"

His jaw ticked. "You need to tell me *everything* right now. And I need to see the apartment. We'll work out the fastest way to find Tara, I promise."

Nate tugged Sim out of Luc's room and upstairs. The apartment door was ajar, and he pushed it wide with his elbow. Wrapped up in her thick dressing gown, June sat at the dining table, staring through the window into the gray almost-dawn sky. Nate stopped in the middle of the room.

"Sim," he asked, "who has keys to get inside your apartment and the building?"

"Just me. I've got the front and back door, plus all the hotel rooms right here." She jangled the keys in her hand. "And Stu has a set for downstairs for when he opens up."

"Can I check Tara's room?"

Sim nodded then trailed him to Tara's bedroom door.

"Wait here. And don't touch the door. Did you turn on the light?"

Sim nodded again, close to numb as Nate stood in the center of her little girl's room and turned around, looking at everything. He used his phone to take some pictures before he stooped and laid the back of one hand on Tara's sheet and her pillow.

"Sit." Nate strode back to Sim, grasped her wrist, and led her over to the kitchen table.

She sat. But she couldn't stay still. She jumped up straight away.

"I can't, Nate." She closed her eyes for a moment. That ball of emotion within her unraveled, one strand at a time. She gulped in a breath. Forced the thread to weave back, tight into the ball. "Nate, I *need* to find her. How can I find her?"

Nate's jaw clenched, and his eyes cut to the window, looked out to the north.

"What is it?"

"Sim, I know this is fucking hard. But we need to look at this like a missing person. And the faster, the better. With the lock set internally, Tara couldn't have left the apartment on her own. But there are people—beings—who can get around locks or even up through second-floor windows. Tara could've left *with* someone."

"Who? Luc?"

"Luc's just come to town, and you don't know him or who he is. So he's a suspect and we need to find him. But we also need to leave every option open. Tara could be gone because of something else entirely."

Her gut roiled violently. Was this about her magic? Sim bit her lip till she tasted blood, and a low keen escaped her. Nate picked up her hand. She was so cold his warmth barely registered.

"I'm going to cast a spell in Tara's room," Nate said. "It'll let me trace the energy of anyone who's been in there recently, but I'll have to focus, so you'll need to stay out here. I'll do it as quickly as possible." He squeezed her hand. "Kat and Thrane are coming here now. Between them, they'll help us cover both mortal and supernatural angles."

Roiling nausea rose in a hard current, and she lurched into the kitchen, just made it to the sink to be ill.

Nate moved behind her, but she waved at him even as she held her hair out of her face. "Go, do your spell."

Sim ran the faucet, washed out her mouth and the sink.

Through the window, the charcoal dawn had lightened, now a ghostly hue as a fog rolled in. The chill of the icy morning had nothing on the frost that shoved its shards deep inside Sim's heart.

Tara was out there, somewhere.

The urge to rush into the spell to find Tara *now* surged through Nate. But he'd be no good if he let panic overwhelm him. Holding his breath, he moved into the center of Tara's room. The quilt on Tara's bed was neatly folded back, the pillow in the normal position. No sign of a struggle.

He wouldn't have long to cast the spell before the others arrived, and this spell would only work if a small number of energies were present. Otherwise, he'd never tell them all apart.

With his eyes open, Nate breathed out his spell. As the last word dropped from his lips, a tingle shivered through him. Immediately, traces of power bloomed in separate physical presences that rubbed against his skin.

Tara's magic was easy to identify, the young but undeniable power familiar to him. And Sim's overlaid it. Hers was the strongest of presences, though whether it was because of the depth of her emotions or if she'd been the last person in the room, he couldn't tell. Even June's magic was there, but it was such a shallow, light trace it was barely detectable.

Nate cast the investigatory spell again, this time focused wholly on the spell. Another energy presence rubbed against his skin. Witch-like, though not exactly a witch. But without a doubt, someone else had been here.

"Nate?" Sim's breaking voice echoed from the living area. "Have you ... have you found anything?"

"Maybe. I'm coming out."

Sim still stood at the sink, one hand on the faucet, one hand braced on the counter. How in all hell was she holding it together? When the cuts had appeared on his arms beneath her grip, he thought he'd have to use more magic to calm her, but somehow, she'd gained control when everything else was uncontrollable. Her knuckles were white where she gripped the bench, and the absolute pain in her eyes tore at his heart. He was going to find the bastard who'd done this and get Tara back.

He swallowed hard, didn't want his fear and desperation to show.

And he couldn't let it interfere. Finding Tara was everything. That meant clarity, precision. No mistakes. He was a cop. This was his job, and one he knew how to do well.

And he also knew that the moment he turned this over to the department, he'd be out. They'd never let him be a part of an investigation when he was so close to the missing person.

But his bosses would never accept, could never understand that Tara's disappearance might be—hell, he was sure now—related to a whole other world and level of life.

An oily slick sidled through him because when he'd

called Thrane, the Keeper had given Nate one other option —the fastest, surest way to find Tara and bring her home.

It meant Nate going to the World Tree.

He bit back a curse. There was no question he'd do it if it was the only way, and he had a sinking feeling it may be. But he'd wait till Thrane was there for that.

"Nate," Kat's sharp voice called out from the apartment door.

He whipped around. Hell, he'd been so focused on Sim he hadn't even noticed Kat arrive.

"Thank fuck you're here," he breathed.

Kat was in civvies, jeans and a sweater. But for all that, she held herself with a controlled grace that showed her experience.

Eyes guarded, she carefully took in the apartment, then June and Sim, before she turned to him. "I haven't heard from Marlee, but we're on days off now, so she might just be sleeping last night off. I asked Lou to head over and see her. Marlee lives on the other side of town, so Lou should get there any minute."

"Thanks. Hopefully Marlee's home, and she can tell us where she last saw Luc. Let me know if Lou finds her."

Kat nodded and picked up her phone.

He turned back to Sim. She'd picked up a photo of Tara, taken on the farm several months ago when she'd sat on the back of one of the horses. Tara's heart-shaped face was pure joy. Resolution settled over him. Ice cold. Diamond hard. He was finding Tara.

He knew what needed to be done.

"Sim," Nate said, "we have to talk."

She looked up. Maybe the edge to his voice cut through

—whatever, she didn't argue, just walked over and sat in the chair. She was pale still, her eyes haunted. Nate placed one hand on her shoulder, tried to impart some strength, some comfort. But though her mouth turned up, there was no warmth.

Kat came over, placing her phone on the table, and said, "Lou's got it covered, and she's almost there. We'll hear within a few minutes."

Nate nodded and then knelt, brought his eyes to Sim's level.

"Right, Sim, we need to talk about options. I told you before, there were two possibilities. Either way, Tara didn't leave on her own. Which means she's with someone—what we don't know is if that someone is supernatural or local."

"But how?" Sim said. "No one could get in. The lock was set, everything."

"I cast a spell in Tara's room just now and sensed a presence, someone with power, that I've never known before. Have you had anyone over? Any repairmen, anyone at all?"

Sim blinked, looked around the apartment. Finally, her gaze, wide and turbulent, came back to him.

"No, we haven't had anyone else up here."

"Right." The ice settled dead hard in his gut. He bit back an oath. He needed to stay calm. Work this through. "Okay. Given the deadlock, and the new presence in her room, it's likely that something supernatural is behind Tara's disappearance.

"Now, standard procedure for a missing child is to alert everyone—police, media, the public—and raise awareness through an Amber Alert. But if this *is* to do with the supernatural world, the Amber Alert won't do jack shit. So the safest option is to look at this from both angles." He exchanged a glance with Kat. "But first, we need to know about Luc. That's what Kat's helping with right now."

"How?" Sim swallowed, her mouth tight.

"We need to rule him in or out. So this is what must happen. Kat will cover the local angle in case I'm wrong." He cut Kat a glance; her steady eyes were hard, ready on his. She nodded once. "I'll cover the other."

"But you're our detective," Sim said. "Can't you help here?"

He quickly explained how the investigation would work, then took a deep breath. Trusted his instincts. "Sim, my gut *and* my craft are telling me there's only one way to find Tara fast."

"What? How?"

"I have to go to the Underworld and have a lord there— Serephena—scry for Tara. Serephena is the absolute best there is. She can find Tara, no fucking doubt. But I have to get to the World Tree first. I've called Thrane to help me."

"What?" Sim asked. "Why are you looking *there*?"

"I know this doesn't make sense. But I promise you. I am going to find Tara. And this is the way to do it. I don't have time to explain, but those things that you're learning about, your magic, there's more that you don't know yet. And I can tell you, someone from that world has been in Tara's room recently. So that world is where I need to go."

The World Tree nudged at Nate's consciousness as if even the mention of it triggered its presence. Nate battled the urge to turn north. At the same moment, a shiver shook through him. It was freaking cold. The cuts on his arms stung. And he was running on adrenaline alone.

And the bloody Tree was right fucking there.

He knew what was coming. And it wasn't his magic guiding him. He simply knew it.

Nate was going to make contact with the Tree. That was it. Everything he knew and loved and wanted would be changed in an instant, superseded by the requirement to protect the World Tree and join a thousand-year-old war for humanity.

He could sense it. Like the bloody universe had him on a crash course with the World Tree, and he couldn't do a fucking thing about it.

But this was the fastest way to find Tara. There was no use worrying about anything else.

"Kat," Nate said, "can you question Sim again? Go over everything from the start in case I missed something."

Kat took out her notebook and covered the same questions he'd already asked and then tried to ask June for her version. But June just stared out through the window into the misty gray of the coming dawn.

"Kat," Nate murmured, "June doesn't talk."

"No," Sim growled, lunging for June across the table. "No, you don't get to ride this one out. I know you're in there, somewhere. June, Tara is gone. My baby. Your granddaughter. She's ... gone. We need to know."

June stared up at Sim.

"Sim, why don't we try something else," Nate said, reaching out to stroke her back.

"*No*. Mum!" Tears lit Sim's eyes, the first he'd seen. Sim suddenly stood up, the chair flying out from behind her as she grabbed June's arms. "Mum! You have to be in there. You have to come back. Just now, just this one bloody time. Tara needs you. I ... I need you."

Sim started to shake her, the smaller woman frail and still. Then small lines of red bloomed through June's clothing. Just like on his arms. Bloody hell. What kind of witch was she?

"Sim," Nate said. "Simone. Come on, you don't want to hurt her. Let her go."

"What the hell are those?" Kat asked, recoiling.

"Shit." Nate shook Sim's grip. "Sim, you need to let her—"

Sim blanched—fear, abhorrence in her fiery cognac eyes—as she stared at the blood on her mother's arms.

"June—Mum—"

"She took her," June whispered.

"What?" Sim gasped.

"Nate." Kat pointed at June's sleeves. "What the fuck is that?"

"That's Sim not in control of her abilities," he said.

Sim's skin mirrored the gray of the sky outside. The fire and cognac in her eyes doused beneath a blanket of desolation.

Fuck.

"Okay, Sim, no touching anyone right now," Nate said. "June? June? Who took Tara?"

June looked at him—a rare occurrence.

A gathering of something, some kind of intent, shone through her eyes. Her face tightened. She opened her mouth once. Nothing came out. She closed it, closed her eyes, then opened her mouth once more.

"She ... took her. Up."

"Who is *she*? Where is up? North?" Nate asked, but June turned back to the window, her gray eyes absent once more. Unheeding even of the blood now covering her sleeves. "Sim, do you have something we can use for your mum's arms?"

Sim was holding her hands out, staring at them. She blinked at his words, then she gulped in a breath and nodded. "Yeah, give me a minute."

He traded a grim look with Kat as Sim grabbed whatever she was getting. Then Kat's phone rang. Nate listened to Kat's side of the conversation while Sim brought over her medicine box and rummaged through it. She finally laid out plasters, wipes, and bandages on the table, then hesitated.

Nate touched Sim very lightly on the back of her hand like he had back in the garden. He didn't get any cuts, and she met his gaze. Pain, pure, obliterating pain, shone from her eyes before she looked away.

No wonder her magic was reacting like it was. And given her ability seemed to stem from touch, it was a hell of a thing to have her powers out of control, mixed with the emotional pressure she was under. It made it totally fucking understandable.

"Hey, Sim," Nate said, "your mum will be fine; they're just like paper cuts, only a little deeper. And Sim. Look at me, Sim. June will be okay. And believe me, I will find Tara." The tiniest seed of hope bloomed in Sim's gaze. His resolve hardened. "Okay, let me help your mum first. I'm going to cast a minor spell, like I did for my cuts. It's just to get the healing process started. I'll need to be in contact with her for a fast result."

Sim inhaled, chest shaking, and nodded.

"While I do this, Kat, tell us what Lou said."

Kat came over, careful not to touch Sim, and helped him roll back June's nightshirt on one side. Fine slices marred her pale skin all the way up her arms.

Kat blew out a hard breath.

This was probably the most Kat had ever been exposed to his world. Even though she couldn't help but be aware of it, having grown up in the town like she had. And Kat was tough because after that long breath, she started to talk even as she helped him clean the little slices.

"Lou confirmed she saw Marlee," Kat said, "and that Marlee told her Luc was there. That they'd been together since they left the hotel last night. Marlee was still pretty hungover, though."

Sim swore, wrapped her hands around the back of one of the dining table chairs and gripped so hard her knuckles turned white.

"Fucking hell," Nate said. "Luc was the best hope we had of this thing being a Mortalworld matter. Okay, so I think we need to put the emphasis on my search. Stand back for a moment, Kat; I need to cast a small spell."

He murmured the spell for healing and kept his hand in contact with June until the small cuts stopped bleeding. Then he and Kat covered them with plasters and bandages.

"Right," Nate said. "Since we know where Luc is, Kat, you open the investigation wide up, same as with any missing person. I'll call it in, then excuse myself due to"— Nate measured Sim with a quick glance—"because of an existing relationship with the missing person's family. You can let the guys at the shop know where Luc is, and they can follow SOP."

"SOP?" Sim asked, a frown pulling at her brow.

"Standard operating procedure," Kat said, finishing off with June's bandages.

"And then I'm going to talk to Thrane," Nate said. "I need to find Serephena and get her help."

"Then let's go." Sim jumped to her feet.

Shit. He shoveled a hand through his hair.

"Sim, to get to Serephena, I have to travel to the Underworld. That isn't a place for mortals."

"I just cut my mother into tiny ribbons," Sim said, raising her hands. "I'm a witch. And you're talking about my daughter. Believe me. I. Am. Going."

Nate turned to June—no help there—then Kat.

"Don't look at me," Kat said. "This is way above my paygrade."

His gut began to churn, and he had to force his jaw to unclench.

"I *can't* take you into the Underworld. It's way too high a risk. Plus, you need to be here. You're the last person who saw Tara. You need to be part of the investigation, here, in the mortal world."

"What about you?" Sim asked.

"Huh?"

"You said it would be a risk. Is that for you too?"

"To get to the Underworld, I'll have to touch the Tree. That will mean ..." Nate swallowed the lump that rose in his throat. Frankly, it would mean a whole new life for him. Without Sim or Tara. But he didn't say that. "That will mean a different set of rules."

Sim's eyes darkened into a molten whiskey, and he practically felt her weighing up his words. But she didn't say anything. Thank Christ. Because he didn't know what the fuck he'd say if she did.

"Kat," Nate said, working hard to keep the fatigue out of his voice, "let's call this in."

Sim couldn't stop herself from searching the apartment, but what she looked for just wasn't there. Nate had made the call to alert everyone that Tara was missing, and she'd taken a moment to get dressed, pulling on the first top and jeans she found.

Outside, the misty fog gave way to a gray drizzle. Was Tara cold? Wet? Scared? Alone? Hur—? Sim's mind stuttered. Incapable of finishing that last thought.

Nate came to stand beside her.

"Sh, Sim." His heat reached out on unseen hands, eased the chill inside her just enough to let her know she wasn't made of ice. "I've called Thrane," he went on. "It's crazy for him to come here when we just have to drive back to his place. Can you come with me downstairs?"

Sim took a deep breath and pulled the edges of her cardigan tight.

"Okay." Her voice was a whisper.

Nate touched her shoulder. She tensed, shrugged off his hand. "Don't. What if I cut you again?"

"Your magic has been working only through *your* touch, so I'm not scared to touch you. And even if you did somehow slice me, I'd be okay." He wrapped his arm around her shoulders and hugged her into his side. "Here, see?"

Was he loco?

She tried to stay stiff, to keep her distance, but then a giant sob escaped her. Nate turned her into him, or maybe she burrowed into his chest—at the last moment keeping her hands free. A burning pressure grew low in her throat. It grew and grew until suddenly it burst.

And she cried.

Her entire body shook as sobs racked through her, over and over.

"Sh, Sim." Nate pressed a soft kiss to her forehead and brushed her hair back from her cheeks. He kept murmuring her name over and over.

The sobs came harder and harder.

Why hadn't she woken up earlier? Maybe if she'd checked on Tara just minutes faster—

Her sobs grew into heaves. Sim tried to control them, but her stomach muscles tensed. The heaves grew stronger. She pushed out of Nate's arms and ran back to the bathroom to be ill. When she returned, she was colder than she'd ever been. She hugged her arms to her chest.

"Sim, I want ... I want to stay with you," Nate bit out. "But I can't. I have to leave now. This is the fastest—maybe the only—way to find Tara."

God, she so wanted him to stay too. Except, she wanted Tara back more. She tried to speak. But her throat was too tight to speak, so she nodded instead.

He regarded her for a moment, and his jaw clenched, but then he nodded too.

"Okay, this is what's going to happen now. Kat's gone to pick up Luc. She'll take him to the station for questioning, but I don't think we'll get anything useful there. And even though Kat's got your statement, it's technically her day off, so the crew who'll be working on this will be out to see you.

"They'll be here any minute now. So I need to head off straight away because if I wait, I'll get caught up in the questioning instead of finding Serephena." They reached the bottom floor, and Nate looked around. "What time will Stu be in?"

"Um…" She somehow swallowed the lump in her throat. "It's Sunday? Six. Stu will be here by six." Sim looked at the hall clock. Half-past five. Shaking her head to display the icy numbness spreading through her, she took a shaky breath. "So, you'll head to Thrane's. When … when will I hear from you?"

Nate put both hands on her shoulders.

"Shit, you're cold as ice." He briskly rubbed up and down her arms. "Listen, where I'm going, I can't pick up a phone and call. But I'll get word to you as soon as possible. And I promise you, I am going to find Tara."

Desolation, akin to her own, flashed through his eyes, but then he cupped her cheek briefly with a warm palm, and the emotion disappeared. She pressed into it, needing that contact. Needing the reassurance of his gaze that promised he'd bring Tara home.

And then he turned and jogged to his truck. Sim followed him to the doorstep, buffeted by the frigid morning air, and stared after the rear lights as he drove down the empty streets of their little country town.

This was meant to be the safe place. The place where Tara could grow up in a caring, happy community. And it had become the opposite. The sound of a siren echoed; the rest of the police would be there in moments.

The urge which had driven Sim to get out of bed not even an hour ago hit her again. Harder. And her inner chime, that sensation which had been the start of all of this, dinged long and hard. It pulled her around until she faced the back of her hotel.

What the hell? She swallowed, and a new unease filled her. Unease at her decision to do what Nate had said—stay here and meet the police. That damned chime rang again—kicked so hard inside her chest, she lost her breath.

That chime had never led her wrong. Clarity hit. She needed to go. Wherever Nate was going, she needed to be there too.

She flew up the stairs.

June still sat at the table, bundled up in her dressing gown and bandaged. She was still, so very bloody still. Her eyes did move, though, as her gaze shifted to Sim.

"Go," her mother whispered.

Sim grabbed her car keys and bag and ran back downstairs. Strobing blue and red lights flashed beyond the windows of the foyer. Crap, she had to hurry. She raced through to the back of the hotel and out the door, and as she shut it behind her, a loud rapping sounded at the front.

Oh God, Nate was going to be pissed off. But she *had* to go.

20

The hour-long drive was torture.

The only thing Sim took some level of certainty in was that her chime was ringing, almost soothingly, gently now, tugging her forward.

Since she'd never been to Thrane's property in Hill End, Sim drove there purely from the memory of conversations she'd had at Nan's farm. Everyone said Thrane lived behind the Jones's, and they even shared a small boundary fence.

Then a different ringing—her phone—grabbed her attention. It was coming from her bag where she'd flung it into the passenger seat footwell. At least she had her phone. But the bag was out of reach, and no way was she stopping the car to rummage around and find it.

Sim kept driving, and the phone kept ringing as she followed the winding road along the lower boundary of the farm. Minutes later, she came to a crossroad. Her only insight was to follow the boundary of the farm, so she turned left and eventually approached another property driveway. It had a formal entry with a large black gate between an aged stone fence. Was this it?

She pulled the car to a stop in the driveway.

Sim took a breath, tried to calm her heartbeat, but it was near impossible, so instead, she closed her eyes. Focused. She couldn't get this wrong.

The chime rang again, low and steady. Sure.

And then Tara's face, her sweet round cheeks and bright dark eyes appeared in her mind. Oh God, her baby.

A ball of lead rose in Sim's throat. Tears stung her eyes. A sob escaped, and then another, doubling her over the steering wheel. But she couldn't stop. Couldn't give in to the terror. Not now. *Not now.* Her baby needed her.

The icy morning air, tangy from the surrounding forest, hit her hard as she left the car. Shivering inside and out, she approached the gate's intercom system and pressed the button, but nothing happened. She tried again, and still nothing.

Damn.

Sim ran back to the car and this time rummaged through her bag until she found her mobile phone. She ignored the missed calls that showed up and instead hit redial. Nate had been her last call. She reached his voicemail.

Damn it. Sim looked around, but there was no one else there. And at barely seven on a Sunday morning, it was unlikely she'd find anyone. Sim tried Thrane next. Still nothing.

She flicked to another recent call. India.

"Come on, come on, come on," Sim chanted as the phone rang. She was about to end her call when the line picked up. "India, thank the stars. Listen, I need to find Nate."

"What? Sim, where are you? Nate said he'd told you the plan."

"Never mind the plan; I need to find Nate. Now. Can you tell me how?"

"Sim, this isn't something you just do."

"Did he tell you Tara's gone?"

"Oh, hon, he did."

"This thing inside me—this chime that's always been my guide, or intuition, or whatever the hell you want to call it, well that chime *is* magic. My magic. And it's never steered me wrong. And right now, it's saying I need to go with Nate. So please. Tell me how to get to him."

For a moment, silence echoed down on the line. "Bloody hell, Sim. I'm driving on my way to you. Right now. And I've got Nan with me. We're almost at your place."

"I'm not there. I'm at Thrane's. At least I think I am. But no one's here."

"Of course not. Thrane's taken Nate to the Tree."

"The tree?" Sim hauled in a deep breath. "Okay, that's what Nate said. The World Tree. Do you mean they've gone to an actual tree? How do I get to it?"

"Sim ..." India paused. "Sim, the World Tree is *the* most important being in all the worlds. If you're a risk to it, knowingly or not, that can be very bad. For you. For all of us."

"I'm not going to hurt it. I need it to find Tara."

"It's not your intent, but what might follow you. Sim, I'm sorry, but I can't let you go to the Tree on your own. I at least need to make sure you get there safely, for everyone's sake."

"How on earth do I do that?"

"Holy crap. Let me think. Okay, let's try this. I'm going to send a message to the Tree and try to ask it to tell Thrane that you're there. Thrane can come and meet you at his house and make sure you get there okay."

Sim didn't even bother trying to understand what India was saying. "Whatever you need."

"Right," India said. "I'll have to hang up. I'll call you right back. And, Sim?"

"Yeah?"

"The Tree doesn't communicate in words, so this might take some time to get right. And that's if Thrane and Nate haven't already made it to the World Tree."

As Nate neared the World Tree, twin internal forces tore at him. He hated that either was occurring. But liking either situation had zero effect on reality. The need, the drive to find Tara still pushed him, and his resolve hadn't wavered from that task.

But competing for his focus was the World Tree.

He'd been here before—the day India had been attacked. And even then, the draw of the Tree, the call of it, had echoed in his mind, as it had in his dreams. *Come. Join this Keeper life.*

But he'd held back—had resisted the call.

Now, following Thrane around the ghostly hued gums through the mist-filled forest, pungent with fresh dew and the tang of the forest loam, that call was stronger than ever.

Nate couldn't escape the eerie sensation that the entire forest held its breath. Waited alongside the Tree.

Which was plain crazy. He scowled, looked around harder. Thrane stepped unerringly through the thick scrub, taking a path that seemingly would lead to a dead end of brush and plants, only to open into another hidden path at the last moment.

Eventually, the trail opened out, and the trees grew tall and wide with their evergreen canopies blocking out all but the misty light. His skin prickled as he entered the largest clearing yet. Thrane kept walking toward the Tree, but Nate stopped. Stared.

There it was. Smooth, dark-brown bark wrapped around a massive trunk so wide it would easily have hidden ten men. The trunk—boiler, Thrane called it—rose straight, high into the sky, its upper limbs spreading out wide with huge elbows that lifted the smaller branches high.

Nate's breath left him in a whoosh.

His heart pounded so fast he had to call on his magic to steady his pulse. And the moment he did, the Tree was there. This time fully present in his mind.

No knock, no persuasion, just there. With him. And in his mind, he saw Tara's sweet little face. She was smiling, happy, carefree like he'd seen her when they'd been working with the horses on the farm.

Contentment swept through him only to be replaced at lightning speed by foreboding, and in the vision, the light that shone on Tara's face gave way to a deep red, and her eyes changed to obsidian.

The next moment, the Tree was gone from his consciousness. He sensed its withdrawal, and then suddenly, all his other senses returned.

"Thrane," Nate called out, "the Tree just made contact,

showed me Tara. It started out all nice but then got scary fast."

"There must be something in your magic because I never get such clarity of communication unless I'm in direct contact with it." Thrane sent an exasperated look to the Tree as if it were a child or something.

"Well, I'd just opened my magic up to give myself an energy boost."

Thrane's eyebrows shot up. "I've seen India do that energy boost thing. It means she'll conk out pretty soon."

"Hopefully, I can put off the conk out part. I only used a little energy boost, plus I'm used to my spells. While India might not conjure hers like we do, she's still using magic, and she's still learning. So what do you think the Tree meant?"

"The Tree communicates to us all a little differently, and it doesn't think in linear timelines. It shows you images. Makes you feel emotions and uses your senses to convey its message."

"Well, that kind of makes sense—as much as talking to a tree ever will. Why do you look at the Tree like it's a child sometimes?"

Thrane shrugged, but the look that came over his face was one of fondness, pride even. "I guess because, in many ways, this Tree was my child. For a long time, I was its only protector. My feelings don't just stem from duty, but from a connection. And it's something I don't think you can understand, not really, unless you take the step and become a Keeper."

"It showed me Tara, happy at first, then all covered in red, and her eyes went freaky."

"We need to discover her lineage," Thrane said, frowning. "That's a very precise image about one particular person."

"And I got a clear sense of danger, like foreboding that something bad was coming."

"But it hadn't happened yet?"

"Yep, it felt that way."

"Then let's get you to the Underworld and ask for some help."

"So what do I do?" Nate followed Thrane to the foot of the Tree.

"You touch the World Tree. Are you sure?"

"Yeah. I'm going to find Tara, and that means going to the Underworld. So you're going to get me there, but then that's it, right?"

"That's right. I can't be away from here for too long."

"How long will it take?"

"How long is a piece of string? Do you know how scrying works?"

"No fucking clue."

"Right, well, Serephena will fill you in if she agrees to help. But searching through the three worlds can take a long time. Can you narrow the search?"

"Shit, I don't know. June said the word up. That could mean north or up. True up. The Higherworld."

"And you believe June? She isn't much of a communicator."

Nate paused. June had been ... trying to talk, he was sure. "Yeah, I do. She pulled herself together for a few seconds and said *she* took her. And then she said up. That was it. And it's all I've got to go on, which is better than nothing."

"Okay, so I'll get you there and introduce you to Serephena. But, Nate, Sere doesn't have to scry for you. And as the lord of her domain, you can't compel her to do anything. This isn't even Keeper business, so I can't make her either."

Nate shoveled a hand through his hair. "Damn it. Is there anyone else I can ask to help?"

"No one near as good."

Nate stared at Thrane. As an immortal, the man had been in Nate's life from the start. Thrane was family and a friend.

He grasped Thrane's shoulder. "I'm doing this, mate. If becoming a Keeper will get Tara back, then this is it. Hell, I'd give up my life if it came to it."

"Okay, the Tree will take us to the other end of my Connection in the dungeons beneath Serephena's mountain. And remember, you need to be careful; while you'll be a Keeper and immortal, true immortality is stretching the truth. And Serephena is used to having total say in her dominion. But at least as a Keeper, Serephena can't kill you on sight."

"Good to know."

"But Serephena can definitely still make things difficult for you. Remember what she did to me."

"She sounds charming."

"Funnily enough, she can be. Just don't take her lightly."

"Got it. Okay, so let's get this done."

"One more thing. I know I've been pushing you to do this for a long time now, but that's because I believe that when the Tree calls us, it means you can be of real use and make a difference to our world. Once we get Tara back, you're going to be just fine. The life of a Keeper is different to what it is as a mortal, but time, and the world you're joining, have a way of subduing the loss."

Nate let out a low, short laugh. He'd just got Sim to see him—really see him—as more than a friend, and now he was going to take on a life that meant letting her go.

Nate steeled himself against the pain that thought created. No use wasting time on what couldn't be changed. He reached toward the Tree. A blast of heat washed over him as his fingers neared the massive trunk.

"What—" His fingers grazed the bark, and everything around him, beneath him, above him, disappeared into darkness.

21

Nate's world changed. While everything around him was the deepest black of night, he wasn't alone. The World Tree was there with him.

It was warmth. It was steady. It pulsed with life as his veins pulsed with blood. Its mental weight was enormous.

He'd always known the World Tree was important. But with one touch, his understanding of that importance for everyone—for the world that he knew, and the ones that he didn't, became absolute.

The people he loved, his community, the billions in the mortal world who had no idea they all had the chance to live out their lives in ease because of one being—the World Tree.

And the fight to protect the Tree became his fight. *Because* of the people he loved. *Because* of his belief in protecting those unable to protect themselves.

The World Tree was their only hope.

And it made perfect sense he would be a Keeper. Nate was a fighter, like those who'd come before him. His witchcraft meant the Tree could communicate with him when not in contact.

What had begun about saving Tara had become about saving everyone he cared about.

He gave his vow to the Tree with determination. He'd give everything he was to protect the Tree.

Only then did Nate look around, try to discern anything in the absolute dark. Moments, minutes—who knew how long—passed as the World Tree took him on the physical journey through a space he could never have imagined.

His body soared faster than light on an invisible current of energy. Weightless. Then a bolt of color ripped through the black, only to disappear just as fast. Another jagged spear of light raced past—or maybe he raced past it—lighting the universe for a moment. He turned his head to follow the strobe-like effect, but his body tumbled forward and he fell into a spin. Instinctively, he arched his back, pushed through his body with every muscle he had, gathered himself, and managed to flatten out and end the roll.

Just as well because then the cosmic landscape disappeared.

Solid ground met his feet, and the sudden pressure of the air had him inhale.

The dark remained. Only this time, he was standing still. Luckily, he'd regained his balance midway, otherwise, he'd have ended up on his back or his head.

He wiped his hands over his jeans. Shit, the denim was icy. Though at least he was dressed. He hadn't even thought to check if you could transfer with your clothing. But man, it was cold. And dark.

"Are you okay?" Thrane's voice echoed out of the dark, and moments later, a light flared.

A candle, held within a glass and iron lamp, cast enough light for Thrane to become visible.

"Yeah, think so. That was …" He stopped. There were no words for what that was.

Thrane held the lamp up closer to Nate's face, eyed him carefully. Then he gave a shout, clapped him on the shoulder. "Welcome, Nate, Keeper of the World Tree."

Nate rubbed his shoulder. Thrane had more muscle than God had clearly known what to do with when he'd made the man.

"So that's it, we're here. Where's Serephena?" Nate asked.

"First, rule number one. Don't get dead. Immortality means you won't get sick, and you can heal from most wounds. But a bad enough strike can still take you out. Rule two, you might be immortal, but your body still needs to burn fuel for energy. There's more—"

"Can the rest wait till we find Tara?"

"Yeah, it can. For what it's worth, crossing over space can take time to get used to. You did well not landing on your backside."

Crossing over. That was a good way to describe what they'd done. Nate turned around, took in the cell. A ledge was cut into the rock, and Thrane's sword rested against it. The dark walls suggested they were underground. The cold, stale air told him it was deep.

Thick blackened bars and a padlocked gate were barely visible in the dim light.

"I keep the key to the cell here," Thrane said and picked up an old, large key. Then he grabbed his sword.

"Do I need to learn to swing one too?" Nate asked.

"If you want, but you should use the weapon you're strongest with."

"That would be my magic."

Sim stamped her feet, cupped her hands around her mouth and breathed into them. Anything to keep warm while she waited and worried.

She swallowed hard. Worrying about Tara wasn't going to help find her baby, but if she could focus on her magic, that might help. *Come on, concentrate.*

Sim's chime was her magic. Magic was tied to her touch. She opened her palms. What else could she do?

A light bulb triggered. She'd felt Nate through her magic before. Maybe *she* could find Tara?

Sim darted to the side of the driveway where the gravel gave way to grass and spread her hands on the ground. The chill and dampness registered at the same time as she found her inner chime. It was the same spinning knot of energy she'd visualized before in the center of her chest.

The chime picked up pace, spinning faster and faster, then moved through her body, just like last time. But she had no spell, and the chime moved through her till it reached her fingertips, then left her body and connected with the grass.

Sim pulled back—couldn't lose herself like with the rose —and on its next spin, somehow stopped it right at her fingertips. But all her awareness halted too. Centered right at the point as if the very last outer layer of skin held every ounce of the chime.

It was potent. Scary. Everything that made her Sim was right there. She forced herself to blow out a breath, take another.

The chime grew unsteady, and with a fast breath, she exerted more will to keep it still. So tiny, yet so bloody massive in power.

She got it under control, and with a deep exhale, she fused every part of her attention on that tiny, powerful knot of energy that was her chime. Pushed it into the ground.

Impressions flooded her. The soil was rich, with a heady metallic tang that hit her tongue. Moisture struck her next, wet the back of her throat, and for a dizzying moment, her chime—she—dropped through the earth, way, way down, and hit an underground bed of water.

Icy cold, sweet, rushing. She gasped at the shock, jumping high, then had to relax because her chime almost jumped right out of the ground. She wrangled it to a stop, and once again, a familiar rich metallic tang filled her.

Holding her breath, she focused on Tara. Her cheeky smile. Her sweet scent. The warmth of her hugs. The steady beat of her heat. *Come on, come on, come on.*

Nothing.

She sobbed, rocked back on her knees. What good was her magic if she couldn't find her baby? Eyes burning, she stared at her palms. Come on, find her. Find Tara. God damn it, find Tara!

She shoved her hands back into the soil. Please, please, *please* find Tara.

Her chime rang, pulsed in one direction.

She let her magic go. Sensations of live things digging and passing through earth came and went. Roots, small and large, came into touch with different flavors and feels, but eventually, Sim came to one different from all the others.

Strength, warmth, a taste of life, like what she'd had with the rose, hit her all at the same time.

And then her chime stopped, wouldn't move, no matter how much she willed it forward.

Was Tara close?

A breeze whispered by, chilling her skin, carrying a hint of rain. Leaves gently rustled high above her. But she was nowhere near any trees. Oh wow, that was her chime—her magic was so strong now, it picked up sensations from things it wasn't even touching.

She forced the sensations away. All she had to do was find Tara. She cast around to find her energy, any trace of her at all. But there was nothing.

What if Sim couldn't find her? She steadily took another breath. No, no thinking like that. She'd come this far—she *would* find her.

Sim swept her senses in a massive arc around her location, passing farther and farther afield, and then—finally, something. Ginger and leather.

Her stomach dropped—that wasn't Tara. But it was familiar ... Nate!

And then the scent disappeared.

Sim swept again, and again and again. Nothing. But that had been him only a moment ago.

Shit. What had happened?

She blew out a slow breath—she'd found Nate. He'd

been right where her chime had taken her when she'd been looking for Tara.

That was all she needed to know.

Sim went to bring her chime back, but suddenly couldn't sense it.

Opening her eyes, she raised her head. The world around her seemed grayed-out, a color photo changed to gray scale. She shook her head, blinked. Nothing changed.

She tried to stand, but she couldn't feel her limbs. Her heart began to pound. Bloody hell, why couldn't she control her body?

Sim forced herself to take deep, even breaths. She'd be fine; she just had to think her way out of this. Get control of whatever was going on.

She let her eyes close again, felt through the earth for her chime.

Something brushed against her senses ... she almost cried out ... but it was the root she'd come across before.

And she found the chime, right there.

Thank the stars. That moment where she'd lost touch with her magic had been ... goosebumps ran up her arms. Imagine living without yourself?

Sim carefully brought her magic back. She couldn't risk losing herself again.

Calm, Sim, you've got this.

Once she had her chime back within her body, she changed her focus to the plant with the roots. Because while she'd lost trace of Nate, that plant hadn't moved.

And she easily sensed it—without having to let her chime travel. Instead, she kept it at her fingertips, using those roots as her reference. Yep, she had her compass.

But Sim didn't think she could follow it without touching the soil. And if she took her hands out of the grass, she'd lose the reference point altogether.

Another light bulb triggered—how Nate and his family practiced magic. Shoes off. While making sure she always had one hand in the grass, Sim awkwardly pulled one knee forward, then the other, squirming her way out of her shoes and socks.

The direction Sim needed to travel veered away from Thrane's house, and she'd have to get over his fence, but the stone was too high for her to climb and maintain touch with the grass. Luckily it only ran for several meters. After that, it was timber railings, and she climbed between them, always keeping either a hand or foot on the ground.

She took a deep breath. Walking through the scrub without shoes was loco. Spiders, snakes and who knows what else. Her skin crawled, but she refused to stop.

This was about Tara.

22

Sim emerged into a clearing maybe thirty minutes later, which was a total guess because she'd left her phone in the car, and she didn't even have a watch. A massive tree filled the clearing.

Giant branches grew perpendicular to the ground before elbows broke the branches into angles that rose sharply up and out.

Her stomach tightened. She'd found it.

But there was no sign of Nate. Or Thrane. Or anyone else.

She tentatively called out, "Nate?"

No reply.

"Nate?" she called louder this time.

Still no response. In fact, there was no sound at all. No bird calls. No rustles. Even the leaves of the evergreen canopy above her seemed to have stilled.

The hairs on the back of Sim's neck prickled. Shaking off the eerie sensation, she followed the pull of the chime several more steps. The tree ahead loomed higher, larger, until it filled her view. Giant undulating roots grew out of the ground even where she stood, and she carefully stepped between their thick sinewy lengths.

And still her chime unerringly drew her toward it.

Wind whistled through the trees at her back, gathered behind her legs, gently propelled her forward. She was being guided here, no question.

Please, please let this be the way to find Tara. Sim closed her eyes, pictured Tara's face. Her resolution grew. Raising a shaking hand, she laid her palm flat on the trunk of the tree.

Suddenly, instead of standing on solid ground, her feet, her whole body, had no purchase at all and she toppled forward into a dark void. She screamed, but no sound came out. She would've tried to breathe, but her throat was too tight.

Until a gentle presence touched her mind. Warmth. Ease. Then a movie played in her mind of Tara, Nate, June. Herself ... baby to adulthood. The hotel. The climbing rose. Her little ball of energy.

And as the movie played, she stopped screaming, stopped fighting the sensations.

Her body still tumbled, but she finally opened her eyes. A landscape of the blackest black, with a starburst of color over one shoulder, careened past. She went to take a breath when suddenly the tumbling stopped.

And her backside collided with something solid, and she sprawled, knees up, arms akimbo. She braced herself at the last second to avoid splatting on her back.

A hard, even surface was beneath her.

She yelped and righted herself. Peripherally, she was aware that she was somewhere different—alien even—but all that mattered was that in the center of her vision, standing above her, was Nate shoulder to shoulder beside Thrane. She had to crane her neck to see their faces.

Nate was staring hard, straight ahead.

Thrane reacted to her yelp first, and when his eyes met hers, he flinched. In one hand he held a massive—like almost as big as her—sword. He shook Nate's shoulder.

Nate frowned, but when Thrane jerked his gaze to the floor, Nate followed his line of sight.

He stared—blinked. Stared again.

"Sim? How ... what ... how in the fucking hell did you get here?"

"Nice to see you too." She shook her head, ignored his reaction. "Is Tara here? Have you found her?"

"Here, let me help you up," Nate said, reaching out a hand. Before she grasped it, a whooshing sound echoed behind her. Thrane grabbed Nate's shoulder. Nate straightened, dropped his arm.

"Well, well, who do we have here?" A feminine voice silkily spoke behind her. "My steward didn't inform me of *three* visitors."

Sim turned toward the voice. Her mouth dropped open.

"Hello, there," said a stunning woman, who also happened to have wings, great feathered arcs in the same midnight as the landscapes Sim had just tumbled through.

She wore fluid gray pants with a tight black leather vest that showed off impressive curves. Her cap of blue-black hair set off her amazing blue eyes.

Was she an Angel? She was so perfect; surely, she had to be.

Behind the woman stood three more people. The closest

was a man, no wings obvious, standing behind the woman's shoulder. He wore similar clothes to the woman, although in a different color. He stood calmly, with his hands clasped in front of him. But the leather-clad winged women behind him *were* menacing. Each held long spears tipped toward Sim, and their expressions screamed skewer first, question later.

Sim swallowed a lump that suddenly filled her throat.

"Welcome to my home." The woman reached down with one slim, pale hand to help Sim up.

"Thank you," Sim said.

Her home. Wait—this was Serephena? Hope crashed into Sim's chest, and she let herself be pulled to her feet.

An oddly familiar tingle shivered through her palm. The sensation was odd enough that she frowned at her hand. Serephena's eyes narrowed too, before she cut a glance at Nate; then her electric-blue gaze swung back to Sim.

"Weapons down," Serephena murmured over her shoulder. "You may return to your post." Sure enough, the winged women stood their spears up and left the area.

Sim dragged her attention back to the woman before her.

"As I said, welcome to my home, little witch. I am Serephena, lord of this domain. Why were you on the floor, and how do you come to be here now, yet you were not with the Keepers when they arrived?"

Sim's chime quietly, continuously rang—caution needed. But her hope, her need, was too great to heed it.

"Well, I was using my magic to find Tara, and my chime led me to Nate and the World Tree, which I touched, and after tumbling through this kind of ... of ... Actually, I have no idea what that was. But then I landed here. My name's Simone but call me Sim."

"Serephena, if I may?" Thrane spoke quietly and withdrew a medallion from beneath his shirt. "As unusual as it is, I think the Tree brought Sim to my Connection—it's the only option possible. I'm sure your steward has told you by now that Nate and I came here to ask for your help to find Sim's daughter, Tara. As the best scryer in the three worlds, you are our best hope of finding her fast."

"Flattery will not work here," Serephena said flatly, folding her arms over her chest.

Uh-oh. That wasn't a welcoming look. Sim's gut tightened.

"Serephena," Nate said, stepping forward. "As Thrane said, we've come to ask for your help."

"*You* do not have leave to use my name. However, yes, I heard the request. But what *I* asked was what right you have to come and ask for my help in a task that has naught to do with Keeper business?" Serephena pivoted and strode away.

Nate and Thrane exchanged a look.

"I told you," Thrane muttered.

No—Serephena *had* to help. Sim's hands began to shake. Then she recalled the familiarity and connection that had flowed through her when Serephena had helped her up.

"I think you and I have something in common," Sim blurted. "And I know you felt it too."

Serephena stopped but didn't turn.

Sim licked her suddenly dry lips. *Nothing* had ever been as important as this moment right now. "I'm a witch, yes, but more than that I'm a mother, and right now, there's a four-year-old little girl somewhere, alone, who needs me. So, I will trade anything, absolutely anything, to ask for your help. But I'm hoping you'll just say yes because it's the right thing to do. Tara, my baby, she needs you. We need you." Tears rose to burn her eyes, and utter desperation consumed every other part of her. She launched forward, grasped Serephena's wrist. "Please. I am begging you. Please help us."

"You're begging me?" Serephena looked down her perfect nose.

"Of course. This isn't for me. I'm begging you for Tara. You can help save a little girl; surely that's worth doing."

"Who are you, little witch?" With a snap, Serephena's wing furled inward, their tips rising high above Serephena's head as she stepped in closer, her eyes locked on Sim's.

Serephena's gaze went from the mellow blue of an icy lake to electric and filled with an otherworldliness that far outweighed her physical differences. Looking into Serephena's eyes was like looking into the most amazing, different world of existence.

Sim gulped. "I'm not sure what you mean, but I'm a publican, and I live in Warragul."

"No, that's not what I mean. And I can see you do not understand. Who is your sire?"

"I don't know. He left when I was a baby and never returned."

"And your mother?"

"A witch. She's not ... altogether there, though. And she doesn't talk, hardly ever anyway, has never been able to tell me anything about my father."

"Is this true?" Serephena looked at Thrane, her wrist still beneath Sim's grip.

"It is," Thrane said.

"I will find your daughter."

Sim covered her mouth with both hands and tears stung. But she couldn't take her gaze from Serephena.

"Thank you," she whispered. "Thank you. *Thank you.* What do you need?"

"I'm going to enter your mind and find an image of your daughter. I will then use that image to scry for her. But I require payment."

"Yes, of course. Anything you want. Anything at all."

"I want to look farther back through your memories." Serephena stared so intently at her that the hairs on the back of her neck began to prick. "Do you agree?"

Sim cut a look at Nate. He'd never encourage her to do something dangerous. His mouth was a tight line, but he nodded. Her breath whooshed out.

"Done," Sim said to Serephena. "Just—is it going to hurt? I want to be ready."

Serephena sniffed. "A lesser practitioner may blunder through your mind and cause damage, which may cause pain, among other side effects. I, however, am no lesser practitioner. There will be discomfort, though. And the longer I am in your mind, the more discomfort you may feel. But that will be all."

Sim didn't even waste a breath and nodded once. She'd endure any pain if it meant finding Tara. Serephena put her hands to Sim's temples.

"Then let us proceed. Now stay still, lest I slip."

And then a clear, gentle presence was at the edge of her mind. Not at all what she imagined from the strong, forceful woman before her. But the presence just stayed there. Sim frowned, then remembered not to move.

What was Serephena waiting for?

Why, for you, child. I ask that you let me into your memories.

Sim barely avoided jolting. She looked at Nate and Thrane. They both watched her, and on top of their clear tension, a new level of concern entered their gazes.

Only Serephena seemed like she knew what was going on. Her perfect brow raised again.

Sim cleared her throat, finally found her voice. "No one said anything about conversations like that."

Serephena stared at her.

"Right, okay." Sim didn't even have to think about her response. It was easy with Tara sitting at the very top of her thoughts. She remembered her baby's face from the night before, all the way back through to infancy.

That will do. Take a deep breath.

Sim scrunched her face before she recalled Serephena's warning about staying still. "Is that all you needed?"

Yes. However, now I will look a little farther, as per my payment. For this exercise, I do not want you to recall a single thing. I am going to wend my way through your memories, and you must not fight me, even when you wish to. Do you understand?

Ah, yes. At least I think so. You mean in my mind, don't you?

You understand perfectly, then.

Sim carefully blew out the breath she'd been holding.

Why would she'd fight Serephena when the woman was taking what Sim had offered? But then the memories of Tara disintegrated, and millions of images, every image she'd ever seen, felt, heard, sensed, flew across her vision.

Pressure grew inside her mind, pressure to stop the flow, stop the reemergence of each feeling that went with each memory. Instinctively, she tried to steady the tumult but recalled Serephena's words and, gritting her teeth, let the slideshow continue.

But bloody hell, it was hard. And while it wasn't pain, it was more than discomfort. Sim steeled herself. Bit her lip, clenched her fists as if by keeping her whole body still she could keep her mental body still too. Because Serephena was going to help find Tara. None of this mattered.

And then, finally, the images slowed, and a much younger version of June, hair loose and long, cheeks soft and round, looked down at her. Love and wonder filled June's expression. And inside, Sim's absolute link to her mother—a total and unending bond—pulsed with love.

And then another face moved, appeared before her, a man with long red hair split into two braids at his temples and the same whiskey eyes as her own. June said something to the man, and while Simone must've heard her words, something suddenly jarred her out of the past.

No, wait. I know him. Don't go.

But her internal plea had no response. She opened her eyes.

Serephena's hand flew back, her black wings unfurled with a swift snap, and she beat them hard in a move that had her over ten feet away in the blink of an eye.

The Valkyrie's eyes glimmered, her face paled.

Sim's heart stopped. Oh God, what had Serephena seen? Was it Tara? She couldn't stand it. *No, no, no, not her baby.* The floor rushed up to meet her.

23

Nate's stomach dropped, and he leaped forward, caught Sim before her limp body hit the stone floor. What the fuck had the Valkyrie done? He gently lifted Sim's hair away from her eyes.

His heart sank at the utter desolation in her gaze. Their fire had gone, and only pain, dull and deep, shone out at him.

He drew her unresisting body into his chest, curled his shoulders around her. Dear God, he'd protect her from this if only he could. He stroked her cheek then raised his face to the Valkyrie.

"What did you do to her?" Nate demanded, but Serephena's wide eyes were glued to Sim, and she didn't respond. "I said, what did you do?"

"Let me, Nate," Thrane said, stepping forward. "Serephena, did you see something about Tara?"

The Valkyrie's electric eyes, bluer than he'd seen them yet, shot to Thrane but shifted back to Sim a moment later. It was as if she couldn't take her eyes away. Eventually, she swallowed, and then her eyes mellowed, their electric fire contained.

"Simone ..." Serephena's voice cracked, and she cleared her throat before continuing. "Simone, I saw nothing to indicate your daughter's death, if that is what you have inferred. I only saw Tara in your memories—a visual reference will make my task easier."

Sim clenched at Nate's arms, and he winced; Sim's pain was once more drawing forth cut after tiny cut. But the slicing stopped as soon as she'd understood Serephena's words.

"She's not ... Tara's not—"

"No, Sim," Nate said, "if that's what you thought. No, Serephena only found Tara in your memories. She hasn't scried for her yet." He looked at Serephena for confirmation. "Have you?"

Serephena shook her head.

Nate sighed, sent a prayer of thanks to the universe. "Is that what you thought, Sim? Is that why you collapsed? I thought you were hurt or something."

"It didn't hurt." Sim wiped away tears even as she spoke. "But I thought, by the look on Serephena's face, that she must've already seen something about Tara." Sim's gaze flew to the Valkyrie. "Your face went white, and you jumped away like you'd seen a ghost."

Serephena observed them all for a moment, and finally, her back straightened even farther.

"The act of scrying takes time," she said. "And while I have an image to search for, I must search each world, each land, until I find her. However, I will pledge to you now,

Simone of the Mortalworld, witch, daughter of Benedict, that I will find your child."

Sim suddenly scrambled to get up, and while Nate would've held her longer, hell, he'd have held her for eternity if he could, he helped her up.

"Serephena—*Lord Ursiel,*" Nate asked, steadying Sim, "what did you just say about Sim's father?"

"Fuck," Thrane said lowly. "Sere, are you serious?" His skin had paled, and he stared strangely at Sim.

"I said your sire was Benedict." Serephena nodded at Sim, her eyes somber.

"Was?" Sim's shoulders tensed.

"Yes, child. Was." Serephena abruptly turned away, spoke to them from over her shoulder. "In honor of your sire, I shall find your daughter, his granddaughter, as a matter of priority."

"Wait," Sim called out.

Serephena paused, spoke over her shoulder again, "Just because we live in a mountain doesn't mean we don't live comfortably. It is the middle of the night, so the common area is not busy yet. You're welcome to stay here and have something to eat; however, this area will grow busier come the morn. Otherwise, my steward"—she gestured to the man at her back—"can show you to our guest quarters. But I require that you don't leave these two locations. You are unfamiliar with our world, and I would hate for any harm to befall you before we find your child."

Nate risked one question. "How long?"

Serephena cocked her head, but her face stayed hidden. "That is unknown. But I find most of my targets within one full day. Though it may yet happen sooner than that."

She whispered something to her steward, whose gaze went right to Sim, and then she flared her wings, and with a sweep of the midnight arcs, propelled herself through the doorway at the far end of the cavern.

Sim was still, and Nate turned to her, risked running his hand over her arm. The cuts she'd inflicted moments ago on his forearms were already healing. And he hadn't cast a spell.

Looked like his immortality was already kicking in.

"I have to go, Nate. But can I have a word?" Thrane said, then he jerked his head to the side.

"Sure." Nate hid a frown. If Thrane wanted to talk away from Sim, he didn't want to alert her.

He followed Thrane toward the doorway.

"What is it?" Nate said, keeping an eye on Sim. She was such a petite being, but in the middle of the cavernous space, she was tiny.

"You're a Keeper, Nate; you can cross to the Mortalworld by using my Connection. But Sim ... the only way for her to get home is to touch the World Tree. I'll cross back in eight hours, check in to see if there's any update, and we can figure out how to get Sim home too."

"Fuck, Thrane. We need to get Sim to the World Tree, here in the Underworld?"

"Yes. But don't panic, there'll be a way; we just have to work how."

"I thought you were going to tell me what's going on with this Benedict. That it was something bad. Or about Keeper business."

"That is a whole other topic, and one we do have to discuss. For now, try to get Sim and Serephena to spend some more time together. And we can discuss the Keeper business once we've found Tara."

Nate nodded. Keeper business was on the back burner, but he knew that was only temporary. Because they would find Tara, he was certain of it.

"Okay, I'm going to see if Sim wants something to eat, and then if she'll sleep given what she's been through." Nate raked one hand through his hair, the almost-mended fine cuts on his arms a glaring reminder of the decision he'd made.

He'd given his life up, his dreams for that life, anyway, but now he'd done it, he found he couldn't be sorry. The World Tree needed *him*. And that meant that Sim, Tara, everyone else in his family needed him too. Just not in the way he wanted.

"I know you'll tell Nan and the family, but can you also get word to Kat that Sim's with me? Kat will be freaking out right now."

"Will do. Nate, keep your wits about you here. Sim's in more danger than she's ever been in before. These people aren't mortals. They'll react differently to how you or I would and absolutely differently to Sim."

"Got it."

Nate didn't wait for Thrane to leave before he strode back to Sim's side. As soon as he reached her, Sim's shoulders fractionally relaxed, and she gave him a tight smile.

Thrane's caution echoed in his mind. Nate quickly surveyed his surroundings. His immediate priority was making sure Sim was safe.

The top of the cavern soared high, high above him. The roof was domed, with sections cut away at the top and replaced with louvers that Thrane had told him acted as vents for air and light. Apparently, the Underworld was a mix of both ancient systems and complex advanced technology.

"Nate," Sim whispered, her gaze following his. "Are we inside a giant ... cave?"

"Basically, this cavern is the hollowed-out upper section of an enormous mountain. Thrane and I ran up countless steps to get there, so we must be damn high up."

The middle of the cavern was clearly the common area, filled with long rows of heavy trestle tables, each bordered by bench seats. Only a few people—beings or whatever—sat around the tables, which made sense given the time of night.

There were three exit options, two internal doors, one of which he'd come through. The third and largest door was at the other end of the cavern. Those winged soldiers guarded it, so that probably meant it was an entry point from the outside world.

The guards faced inward, and they eyed Nate like they'd assessed him as the threat. Hopefully, they never knew the damage Sim could do with one touch.

But they were the only overtly armed beings. Although visible weapons meant jack shit, so he also noted the faces of those at the tables. Mostly everyone else appeared to be workers, one in heavy clothing like they'd come from a raw metals workshop, another in an apron like a cook.

He couldn't dismiss them outright, but they moved lower on his threat assessment than the guards.

Regardless, Nate raised his magic in case he needed to call on it quickly. Thank fuck it responded like normal. He'd had no idea how being a Keeper would interact or interfere with that part of him that was—had been—a mortal witch.

Then Serephena's steward stepped forward and bowed his head. "Keeper, my lord has offered you the hospitality of this common area, as well as a room for rest. Please let us afford you the comfort of her home. We have food prepared if you wish to eat?"

Nate's stomach growled at the mere mention of food. He checked out Sim. She hugged her arms to her chest. Her shoulders were stiff.

"Sim? Hey, are you hungry?"

She grimaced, and he got it—she was so tense it would be near impossible to eat. But he'd get them something, see if he could coax just a little food into her. Who knew what was ahead of them? They needed sustenance, just in case.

24

S im ate but only because food was in front of her. She'd listened to everything Nate had told her about the Underworld and Serephena.

The push and pull of hope and fear overrode almost everything else. But at least she *had* hope.

She swallowed another mouthful, still unheeding of what she forked off their shared platter.

Nate's eyes flicked around the cavern every so often, but he did it without moving his head as if he were trying to keep his scrutiny unseen.

From his profile, he looked harder, more menacing, with those sharp cheekbones and square jaw covered in a shadow of stubble, than he usually did.

What would she have done without him? He'd given her a chance at finding Tara, and she couldn't thank him enough. But more than just that, he'd helped keep her sane, helped her hold it together when she would have flown apart in terror and panic.

Maybe Nate sensed her regard because, at his next

glance around the cavern, he looked at her. Their eyes locked. Heat gleamed in those blue depths, and even with everything else she was feeling, the remnant of their kiss, that need to get close to him, echoed in her memory. Like a dream she wanted to recapture.

Sim almost raised a hand to run a thumb over his firm lower lip, but then a new look stole into his eyes. Longing, layered with a pain so deep and harsh that she swayed.

"What's wrong?" Sim asked.

Nate opened his mouth as if to speak but then clenched his jaw. He blinked, and the pain and the longing disappeared.

Then Serephena strode into the cavern.

The hairs on the back of Sim's neck instantly prickled, and her stomach tightened. She hadn't expected news for hours yet.

Serephena glanced around the cavern, and as soon as her gaze landed on Sim, she unfurled her stunning wings and moments later touched down.

Sim's heart picked up pace, ran faster, harder in her chest.

"I have found your offspring," Serephena said.

Sim shot to her feet. A funnel of white-hot emotion poured through her, obliterating the rest of the Valkyrie's words. Sim grasped Serephena's hands.

Suddenly the winged guards appeared at Serephena's side, spears tilted sharply toward Sim.

Sim gasped, stumbled back.

"No," Nate yelled, lunging to stand before Sim. "Call off your guards."

"Hold," Serephena said to the women. "I am fine. The witch will not harm me."

Sim dropped the Valkyrie's hands as soon as she registered the words. But the need to reach out and have physical contact with the woman was hard to resist, and she was pretty sure Serephena knew it because she reached out and grasped Sim's hands herself.

"You will not hurt me, will you?" Serephena asked.

Sim darted a look at Nate. His eyes burned, this time with fear. Bloody hell.

"Honestly, I'll try not to hurt you." Her hands went clammy. "But I, uh, have unintentionally done some damage by touching people in the past."

Serephena raised one perfect eyebrow, but her face betrayed no other emotion. She must've been an outstanding poker player.

"I see, well, you are not hurting me now, child. However, I am ... was ... familiar with your sire, and understand why your power reached out through your hands, and the inherent need you must have for touch."

Sim held the Valkyrie's hands back, aware her emotions were very close to letting loose once again. She took a deep breath.

"Tara—is she, is she okay? Where is she?"

Serephena nodded. Then her eyes widened, and she looked down. Sim followed her gaze. The Valkyrie's skin was turning white.

"Calm yourself, child. Your power feeds your touch, and right now with no control, you are sending a blast of ice that I do not desire to endure for long."

Sim tried to break her hands away, but the Valkyrie held her steady.

"Nay, do not remove your touch. You need to learn control. But I see your fear for your offspring overrides all else, so here, let me show you your child."

Sim's eyes flew to the electric gaze before her, and the Valkyrie placed one of her hands up to Sim's temples. Sure enough, the Valkyrie's hand was icy to the touch, and once again, Sim had the sensation of a knock at the entry to her mind.

May I enter?

Sim nodded, then remembered to respond. *Ah, yes. Please.*

Tara's face clearly came into view, her rounded cheeks full of life and health, her rich dark eyes twinkling, and her beautiful shiny black hair in the braid she'd worn to bed. She smiled with her usual joyful expression.

The image showed Tara still in the same pajamas.

Is this real?

Yes, child. This is the image I found when I located your daughter. I detect no hurt or fear and can see that those with her have in her good stead.

Where? Where is she?

She is in the Higherworld, residing in a place that I cannot enter. However, I have sent my emissary to see how we might reunite you.

Sim stared at Tara's image in her mind, soaked in the face that held her heart even as Serephena's words flowed over her. Her baby. Safe. Unharmed.

Tears welled, fell over her cheeks. But she didn't care, just stared at that image, stared and stared until it burned into her soul. And the first crack of the ice about her heart wended its way through her.

"Ah, that's better. Your touch is warming."

"What do you mean?" Sim asked. She opened her eyes and flexed her hands in Serephena's grip. "Am I still hurting you? Did you know I had this ... this ice inside of me?"

"Well, your touch was not comfortable. You need to understand that when your emotions are out of control, what you are feeling will transfer into your touch. That is why you need to learn control—and until then, be cautious with your touch." Serephena folded her arms and sat back.

"Thank you," Sim said. "For finding her. And for showing me, not just telling me. Does this mean you know how I can get to her?"

Serephena pursed her lips.

"What? You've found her—in the Higherworld, you said? Do you know how I get to her? Or get her back to us?"

Nate reached out, hesitated, and then wrapped an arm around her shoulder. His warmth hit her like a blast, and if she hadn't been on a knife-edge, she would've simply turned into him, let that warmth chase the last of her ice away.

But that wasn't going to happen because Nate was eyeing her warily.

"Come on, Nate, just say it. What now? Because seriously, if you're going to tell me I can't go to the Higherworld, given I've somehow come to the Underworld, then I might have to hit you."

"Sim, we can't just go home, go anywhere, as easily as that. We need Thrane's help to return to the Mortalworld, and because we had no idea how long it would take to find Tara, we agreed he'd check back in eight hours. That's maybe six hours away. But Serephena is going to try and get a message to Thrane. He'll get here as soon as he can. And then we have to figure out how to get you home."

Sim closed her mouth, aware her breathing was coming harder, faster as frustration gathered inside her, but she battened it down. Because having her baby safe was the most important thing.

"What do you mean?"

"Sim, there are only two ways to cross between worlds. The World Tree is one way, which is why it exists in every world. Or if you're a Keeper, you can travel by Connections made from the World Tree. But you're not a Keeper, so we need to get you to the World Tree here in the Underworld and then cross back home."

"But Tara—will she be safe until I can get her?"

"Yes," Serephena said, "your daughter is safe. Of that, I am certain. While I would not say that of all locales in that world, I am sure of the Angelkin who she is with."

"The who? Could you see why she's there, why they took her?"

"Child, your daughter resides with her kin. Your sire's people. How and why she came to be there, I cannot know. But as with all Angelkin, their oath prevents them from harming an innocent."

Serephena pivoted, tremendous wings unfurling as she did. "Now, since you must wait, I suggest you rest. I have had chambers prepared in my quarters. Please follow me. Rest assured my people will deliver news about your child's return as soon as we have it."

Tara was safe. And found. Sim's knees buckled.

Strong arms swept her up against a hard, warm chest.

She closed her eyes as Nate cradled her to him.

He murmured something, and another person responded, but she kept her eyes closed. Wanted nothing else at that moment than to let the knowledge that Tara was safe sink in.

Nate's heart settled, finally. Tara was safe and not hurt. It almost brought him to his knees too. No surprise that Sim crumbled.

Sweeping her into his arms was the only option, and with her head resting on his shoulder, he wouldn't have let her go for the world.

Without stopping, Serephena beckoned for him to follow. They entered a dimly lit, wide corridor made of roughly hewn rock walls.

Serephena walked to the second-last door and took a keyring from her vest, then unlocked the door and pushed it open.

"Please bring her inside." Serephena gestured for Nate to follow her in.

Nate kept Sim securely against his chest. A lamp at the far end of the room provided just enough warm light for him to make out the space they were in.

"Your little witch may rest securely here, Keeper." Serephena regarded him for a moment. "Your room is next door; however, it may be best if you stay close. And please be mindful if you leave this chamber that you are in my domain, not the Mortalworld."

"Will you let us know as soon as word comes through

about Tara?"

"Of course." She slipped past, closing the door behind her with a heavy thud.

"Thanks," he muttered.

Had that been a warning not to get nosy in her mountain? Well, he was curious, no question. But his priority was Sim. Keeping a mortal safe and alive in the Underworld. Of course, he'd stay close.

His gut tightened, and his arms did too.

"Shit," he muttered before he could stop himself.

Sim stirred. He'd thought she'd fallen asleep, but at his oath, she'd opened her eyes.

"Ah, they've given us a room each to get some rest. Are you okay if I put you down?"

He wanted her to say no. Wanted her to tell him to keep a hold of her tight. But she sighed and nodded, her gaze leaving his to travel the room.

Nate carefully set Sim down and held on to one shoulder until she proved she was steady on her feet.

"So, as you can see, there's a bed," he said as he nodded at it, but there was no way she could miss the seriously oversized structure.

It had four tall posts carved from a deep burgundy wood. And a bed that looked big enough to sleep ten people.

Cut into the stone wall was a pool clearly meant to be a bath that would, once again, fit all ten people from the bed.

He cleared his throat. "I've got a room next to yours, but I think it's best if I stay here. Closer, you know?"

Sim wandered over to the bath—ran one hand over the stone.

"It's so smooth," she said. "I thought it would be rough like the walls because it's made of the same stone. The bath must take an hour to fill."

Nate stayed where he was, gaze locked on her, unable to look away even if he'd wanted. She followed the wall, touched one tapestry.

"These colors are magnificent," Sim said. "Look at them. I've never seen anything like it; how can yarn be so bright?"

"Ah, no clue. Maybe something about the Underworld?"

Sim kept walking, this time to the bed. She ran her palm over and around one of the gleaming bedposts.

"It's warm, like it's alive somehow." She shook her head, her red hair tumbling over her shoulders as she did. "Nate, this is amazing."

Nate swallowed. Right now, the amazing thing was the woman standing right before him. And if she kept touching things with those hands, feeling them out, experiencing their textures and surface, he'd go mad.

She gave the post one last rub, and he almost groaned.

"I don't think I could take a bath, even though that pool is amazing. But I could rest." She moistened her lips and looked up at him. "Ah, do you mind, would you—"

"No worries, you can take the bed, I'll ..." He cast a look around, his heart beating hard, fast. "I'll just stay here by the door, make sure no one comes in."

Sim blinked, then tilted her head. Her veil of hair shifted, gleamed as it swung again.

"Um, no, I didn't mean that. Would you mind coming over here, and ah, sitting with me?" She sat and patted the bed beside her.

Nate's heart jolted, then surged, pushed blood around

his body so swiftly he stumbled on his first step.

Smooth Jones, really smooth. But he got his feet walking and went slowly to the bed. He leaned back against the bedpost to give her room, tried not to read too much into her request. Kept his tone light. "What's up?"

"Nate, I need to tell you something."

"Okay ..." The hairs on the back of his arms prickled.

Sim rubbed her palms—all dainty looking if you didn't know the extent of her power. She stared at them.

"When Tara was missing, when I didn't know if she was okay, it was like this shard of ice settled deep inside me, only like a glacier it overtook me, overwhelmed every bit of me, and the only thing that held it at bay was you." Sim stopped rubbing her hands and looked up at him. Into him. "Your warmth. Your belief. You. I can't imagine how I would've gotten through today without you. And I can see that something's up, but you're not going to tell me, which actually hurts. Because you've been here for me." She scrubbed a fist over her chest in that way she did. "But you're not letting me be there for you."

Nate was undone. She'd fucking brought him to his knees without even trying. Because being there for her, that was everything to him. *She* was everything to him. But she was also right; he hadn't let her in. Hadn't been able—but also, maybe, hadn't wanted—to be that open with her and face his deepest fear. Life without Sim and Tara.

Sim seeing him, wanting him as a man, was all he'd ever wanted. And now here she was, finally seeing him, except she wasn't seeing the new him, the him who was committed to another cause, one that would take him who in the hell knew where.

But right here, lost in her cognac eyes, their fire beckoning him in, he forgot all that. Forgot they didn't inhabit the same world anymore, forgot he wasn't even sure who, or what, he was.

His next breath brought with it her scent, her sweetness, her spice, her feminine heat, and without thinking, he leaned down.

Her russet lashes closed, but he kept his eyes open as he touched his lips to hers.

Her breath, his breath, mingled as their lips connected, hers soft, smooth, sweet. Hot. Fire swept around his body, rushed to his groin. This was perfection. And he wanted, needed, more.

He touched his tongue to her lower lip, loved the shudder that racked through her. His body rippled in return.

Her lush lips parted farther, letting him in, giving him what he wanted, and he swept inside. She was heady, better than any scotch, and he drank her in, sipped her, tasted her, over and over as their tongues danced.

Sim moaned into Nate's mouth, swayed into him. He caught her around the shoulders just before her torso hit him, but her momentum pushed him onto his back, legs dangling over the side. And she was right there beside him, her lips back on his.

He breathed her in.

"Thank you." Sim pressed a soft kiss to his chin. "Thank you so much." She pressed another kiss to his cheek, then his ear. Her hot tongue ran around his lobe, eliciting a fiery shiver that ran down his spine, pooled in his groin.

Her dainty hands fumbled, grasped at the fabric of his

shirt, lifted it, and her knuckles brushed against the head of his dick, pushing hard against the fabric of his jeans.

Nate hissed. Blood pulsed heavy through his veins, and all he could think of was getting closer, getting into her, any way he could.

"Nate, thank you so much." Her kisses ran over his jaw, down his neck. And then she returned to his lips, so close her heat scorched through his chest.

If he leaned up, he'd rub against the tops of her breasts. And God, he wanted that so much. Wanted *her* like nothing else he'd ever wanted.

And then her words registered. *What the hell?*

Somehow, he restrained himself, pulled back enough to draw in a harsh breath.

"Whoa ... whoa, Sim. Give me a moment." Nate pushed Sim's soft, fiery hair at her temple away from her heart-stopping face. He searched her eyes. "I'm all for this, but let me make sure no one's going to come in."

She looked up at him through heavy lids, a wicked little smile playing with her lips. Those lush, red, gleaming lips.

Shit, she was going to undo him.

"There's a blanket; I'm pretty sure it'll cover us."

Nate scowled, jammed a hand through his hair, pushed it back from his face. "Damn it, I've wanted you for an eternity; I don't want to wait anymore."

He took a harsh breath. Fuck, he didn't want to stop this from happening. But there was one thing that he had to know. "Sim, I want you like ... Hell, like nothing else. But are you doing this to say thank you? Some kind of way to pay me back?"

"Nate, I *am* grateful to you." Sim's eyes sobered briefly.

"More than I have words to explain. But I'm also thankful to Thrane and Serephena. And I don't want to get naked with them." Her eyes lit up again, and she let out a small laugh. She swallowed, and the teasing light transformed into pure, shining desire. "Come here, Nate. I need you too."

Her simple honesty did him in. The last chink in his armor gave way. If she'd said anything else, maybe he'd have found the will, found an excuse to say no. Keep this to kissing only.

But her words—they echoed his feelings, and that she wanted him as much as he did her. Blood rushed to his dick, pushing it even harder against his fly.

Nate bit back an oath, tried to get his mind to work. But reason failed, replaced by pure, absolute lust. Dark. Needy. Urgent.

He had the presence of mind to feel around in his jacket pocket. Thank fuck he'd grabbed his jacket that morning because his wallet was in the inner pocket. And his wallet was the only place he'd find a condom right now. Hell, did the Underworld even have condoms?

"Fucking hell," he muttered as he fumbled and finally pulled the foil packet out. Thank Christ he'd popped the condom into his wallet after their first kiss.

And with that, his eyes snapped to hers. The condom had sealed it.

He strode back to the bed, his heart beating faster with every step closer to Sim.

To the most amazing, captivating, hot-as-hell woman he'd ever known. Someone who'd become a genuine friend, and someone who he needed in his world like he needed air to breathe.

Nate took Sim's breath away. He stalked toward her, all lean grace with a deadly cutting edge. Heat blazed in his eyes, answered the inferno that rose higher, higher within her, with every precise, steady step that brought him closer.

Intent shone within that glittering gaze, and she swallowed hard. She'd pulled the tail of a tiger, and he was going to claim her.

And she was going to claim him.

Finally. She was so ready for the contact, the heat. The slide of flesh, the seduction of his kisses. For the connection of lover to lover. And the one thing she knew—after everything that had happened that day, the absolute tumult of emotions, the fury and fear, the desolation—Nate had been the safe harbor in her storm.

But now, in the absence of fear, she was giddy with the need to celebrate life.

Sim had held herself back from this step for so long, but right now, the reason why was a million worlds away.

The only thing that mattered was him. Them. Together, now.

She wanted Nate. He wanted her.

The urge to be with him hummed deep inside, rose like a fever to engulf her. She was going to have him. Have the one thing she'd wanted and denied herself.

Nate cupped his large hands around her cheeks and stared into her eyes. Into her. Blue fire glittered.

"Sim, you undo me. But I'm fucking glad you don't want Thrane or Serephena because I'd have to go to war with both worlds if that was the case. I've wanted you ... wanted us together ... since I first saw you. And baby, we're going to be so good."

Sim's heart quickened. Desire swelled in her core as his deep voice flowed over her. She licked her lips.

"Heaven forbid I be the cause of you going to war, Nate." She turned her cheek in his hand, luxuriated in the heat of his palm, the rub of his callouses.

He brought her back to look at him. The need that blazed out from him radiated with more danger than she'd ever seen in him before.

This was the true him.

Beneath the façade of the easygoing, laid-back country detective was a man whose heart ran deep, whose edge was dangerous, and whose focus was laser bright, honed to a blade.

And the focus—the bladed edge—was all on her.

She swallowed hard, mouth suddenly dry. Desire and something more, something deeper, wound through her.

"I'm serious, Sim. I would fight the whole fucking world for you." The brutal force of him shone full then.

Nate was a warrior. A fighter.

And hers.

Sim's eyes widened at the truth in that statement, but then he dipped his head, and desire exploded as he took her mouth, and she tasted his need, his absolute desire to be with her.

Wonder thrilled through her. To inspire this level of want, of need, was a first and filled her heart in a way she hadn't thought possible.

She raised her hand—somehow kept her chime away from her palms—grasped his strong wrists right as his tongue swept into her mouth. She moaned into him as he stroked inside, licked her with heat and fresh spice, his taste stronger than whiskey, headier than scotch.

His hands ran down either side of her neck to her shoulders. Nate pushed Sim slowly, inexorably back onto the giant bed. She lay, heart thundering, pulse hammering.

And then Nate crawled up and over her, his knees on either side of her hips. His hair dropping forward over his brow, and a wicked glint shone in his eyes.

Blood rushed through Sim's veins, pooled at her core. She brought his head down to hers.

Her lips curved into his. "I think we've been here before."

Nate dropped a long deep kiss to her mouth, licking into her again before he pulled back, glanced down at their bodies. His eyes, hooded with desire, glittered brighter than ever.

"I promise we can try something different next time," he whispered against her lips.

She chuckled, but it turned into a moan when his hot

tongue stoked into her mouth, tangled with hers until her hips rose in supplication in rhythm with their kiss.

His breath grew faster, harder.

Something intrinsic within Sim gladdened that she'd made him this hot, this needy.

She went to grab a fistful of his top—caught herself just in time, checked her chime was still under control. It was tight, beating at the edges of her skin like a drum in an ancient mating dance, but she willed it to stay still. No way was she hurting this man.

But, thank the stars, Nate got her idea because he reared back, grabbed his shirt by the hem, and drew it up and over his head.

Sim's mouth went dry.

Rope after sinuous rope of hot golden skin drew her eyes, from his ripped abs, that wide chest, the rippling muscles of his arms and shoulders.

Like some Adonis cast in gold.

Sim couldn't wait anymore, needed to be naked with him. Together they removed her top, her bra, and then he stopped—stared. His breathing became sharp, choppy. A red tinge hit his high cheekbones, and his lips pulled tight.

She wasn't a beautiful woman. She had freckles. She was small, with curves in proportion. But now—she'd never felt more attractive.

Sim arched her back, a move she'd never consciously made before, but she wanted Nate to see every inch of her.

The ridge in his pants grew harder against her.

Her entire body clenched. She wanted that. Wanted that part of him naked, against her, in her. Sim went to touch him—needed to touch that hard, hot body—but held herself back right at the last to check her chime once more.

"Let go, Sim; I've got you." His low voice caught her. The promise in his eyes held her.

Sim shifted her head, drew in a shattered breath. "I want to touch you, but I don't want to hurt you."

Nate let out a husky growl. The rumble ran through and around her body, teased every nerve ending.

"Sim, you won't hurt me." He picked up her hand, pressed a searing kiss right to the center, followed it with a touch of his tongue.

Electric heat fired to her groin, set her body humming.

She took a choppy breath, mesmerized by the wicked fire of his eyes as he hovered above her, those sculpted lips curved. And then, looking out beneath mussed hair, eyes still holding hers, he did it again.

More fire arced to her groin. She hissed, undulating to get closer to his heat.

"Trust me, Sim. We've got this."

Gazes locked, he kissed his way around her hand, then laced his fingers through hers.

"Let go, baby." He pressed more fiery, heady kisses to her shoulder, ran his tongue along her collarbone.

Sim's head fell back to the bed.

Shivers raced over her skin as he kissed one side of her breast, and then his mouth was right there, suckling hard, pulling on her nipple. Pressure built beneath his hot, wild tongue. And when he bit down, oh so lightly, fire arced from her breast to her groin. Her hips rose again, tried to capture his heat at the point she needed it most.

He chuckled, the deep sound barely there, and then he

moved to her other breast. Laved it too, while his hand came up to stroke, plump, and shape the breast he'd just abandoned.

The fire turned to liquid gold.

Nate's hot breath moved down from her breasts, down to her stomach, dipped into the curve of her belly. Over and over, he pressed hard, hot kisses across her heated skin.

"Let go, baby."

Damn, but Sim wanted to follow his words. The dark, sinful beauty of his voice rolled over her again.

He opened the fly to her jeans, and she lifted her hips, helped him out. Bloody hell, why did they make jeans so hard to get off?

Nate reared back, stared at her sex, her breasts, the curve and sweep of her body. With Sim's legs draped over the end of the bed, she was laid out, just for him. And then he met her eyes.

She held his gaze as he stripped off his jeans.

Oh damn, he was hot. Hard. Thick. Long. Her mouth watered; her sex clenched. Sim was going to have him —in her.

Total feminine approval arrowed through her.

Nate knelt on the floor before her, and then his gaze held hers as he lowered, lowered.

"Sim, I've wanted to do this forever. May I?"

His hot breath struck the top of her sex, and even that puff of air sent a shiver through her. Her hips rose in reaction, and he must've taken that for yes because then his hand was there, gently parting her folds, and he dipped his head lower still.

Sim held her breath. Waited at the edge of an agony of

need and desire, and then he was there. The fiery tip of his tongue ran along her folds, and then he spread her apart with his hands, and licked her up, up, all the way until he reached her nub.

Sensation poured into her. An involuntary keen escaped her.

He did it again. And again.

Every sweep of his wicked mouth sent her higher, higher, and then his hand held her hips down, and he feasted.

Hot velvet lashed her, and the blood swelled through her veins; the pressure built and built with every stab, every sweep until she panted with the need to get all the way.

And then, Nate sucked right on her clitoris, his fingers stroked in to replace his tongue. She flew apart. Sensation after sensation pulsed through her, sent her flying in a storm of feeling and lights and sounds.

Sim somehow opened eyes she didn't know were closed as he rose above her. Adonis back to cover her with his body.

And he did. All the way he climbed up, his massive shoulders blocking out the light, blue eyes edged with feral need, lips gleaming from her. And then he pushed inside.

She gasped as heat, hotter and darker than ever before, sank deep, deep, deeper inside.

Her muscles stretched, the pain of merging with him blended with the unending pleasure coursing over her raw nerve endings.

Holy hell, Nate was hot. So hot he scorched her. And he was big. Bigger than she'd expected.

Sim moved her hips, tried to find relief, but it only

pushed him farther. He groaned as she flexed again, seating him deeper still. She locked her eyes on his.

And he watched her. Desire, and something more, something raw and deep and ancient, filled his gaze.

He was hers.

She was his.

But it wasn't enough. The pressure grew again. She needed to reach that crest, needed him to move. She planted her feet on the bed and raised her hips, took him all the way.

Nate groaned, and his eyes closed, his jaw clenched. Sweat beaded on his brow, on his shoulders, caught in the gleam of the golden light.

She loved it. Loved the way he looked like he was running a massive race, and this feast of a body was all hers to command. And right now, he was letting her call the shots—but she could see what it cost him, his struggle to let her set the pace.

She did it again. Let her hips drop and then surge back up his shaft. Smooth, hot, hard. Her inner muscles clenched, squeezed him every inch of the way as her body set alight again.

More. She needed more. Her toes curled, her eyes closed, her body tightened. With every move of her hips, a flare of fire scorched her over and over.

And the world shifted.

Nate growled, a low, long rumble. He hooked his arms beneath her thighs, lifted her legs up and around him.

The shift sent him to her depths; sensation pummeled through her body. Yes. Yes. Yes. *Finally*. She cried out as every nerve exploded.

And then he hammered in and out.

"Sim, Sim, Sim," he chanted her name.

And then he thrust one last time. Held himself still and deep inside her. His flesh, every inch of him, all the way inside her, scorched every single nerve ending.

He dropped his head into the curve of her neck right as his body tensed.

"I love you," he whispered into her shoulder.

26

Sim's eyes snapped open, and instantly she was aware of four things.

One, Nate was cocooned around her, his arm wrapped around her waist, his body spooning hers, and his warm scent a comforting blanket all of its own.

Two, she'd had sex with Nate. Sex. With. Nate.

The most amazing, multiple orgasmic, out-of-body sex she'd ever had.

Three, Nate loved her.

If she could've slapped herself in the head, she would've. She didn't, only because she didn't want to wake Nate up.

Like, what would she even say? Thanks, the sex was outstanding, but let's face it, romantic love isn't to be trusted. Sex, yeah, that's fine. But love? *Love*?

And four. Sim had been *asleep*. How could she have slept with Tara still not home? And how long had they slept? Serephena might have news about Tara, and Sim had been in here, passed out from sex.

Her gut curdled.

Biting her lip, Sim eased out from under Nate's arm and quickly got dressed. Somehow, she finished dressing without waking Nate; only then did she stop and look at him.

His handsome face was softer than she'd ever seen when he was awake. His barely parted lips tempted her to lean down and remind herself how smooth and tantalizing they were. Bloody hell, she could spend the rest of her life happily watching Nate sleep. Wake up with him. Be with him.

She tried to find the ball of resentment, the desire to leave, that she was used to.

Except, it didn't come. She swallowed hard. *Don't be a fool, Sim.* One amazing bout of sex didn't make a forever relationship. She made herself recall just how much she'd never been able to rely on someone—anyone—else.

Despite that, Sim didn't want to walk away from Nate.

Goosebumps rose on her skin. Her gut clenched. And then she sighed, took the time that she had before he woke to look her fill.

Maybe she could take a picture of this moment in her mind, and if she looked at him enough, she'd remember this forever, no matter what happened between them. The sexy, rumpled, sated, at-ease Nate, with his golden skin and mussed hair. The shadow of stubble on his carved jaw.

If some sculptor wanted to capture the perfect male form, lean muscles flowing beneath golden skin, they wouldn't find a better model than Nate.

He rolled over onto his stomach, and the blanket caught beneath him, showing two dimples just above the curve of his butt. Sim's mouth went dry. That was a place she'd touched—but holy hell, if she'd had the chance, she would've run her lips over those dimples, scraped her teeth along that smooth skin.

Nate's eyes opened. Somehow, he moved from sleep to alert in an instant, and he rolled over again, this time drew the blanket up with him. Just as well, because that amazing body tempted her to go back for more.

But that would be bad. They needed to keep this about friends with benefits only. Sim couldn't afford to get addicted to him.

She licked her lips, tried to replace the moisture that had wicked away at that glorious view.

Nate looked around, but obviously seeing nothing amiss, settled his focus back on her. "Is it time?"

"Yeah, I want to find Serephena. I don't know how long we slept for, but she might have news on Tara. And even if she hasn't, she's mentioned my father twice now. I don't think I'm going to come visit here again, so I should at least try to find out who he is."

Nate stretched, abs flexing, shoulders rolling, stomach tightening.

Heat shot through her. Her core clenched. Suddenly wanting round two. Damn, he was waaay too hot for her body to handle.

She hurriedly braided her hair, using the task to turn away from Nate and keep her face hidden.

Sim raised her arms behind her head, a move that pushed her beautiful breasts forward. She deftly, swiftly pulled the glimmering strands of her hair into a tight braid.

Nate drank in every single move.

"That might be the sexiest thing I've seen you do," he said softly.

Her eyes flew to his. Then down to his groin. Her creamy cheeks grew rosy, and she bit her lip. Was she interested in another round? Not that he had another condom, but there were plenty of other things they could do.

But Sim was made of strong stuff—something he'd always known—and even had she been keen, she turned around, finished braiding her hair.

He wanted to let a sleepy, satisfied smile stretch across his face but held back.

Something was off. Yeah, her comment about Tara made sense. And, of course, Sim would want to take this opportunity to find out about her father. Hell, he was more than curious himself. But he also saw through it.

Because not long ago, Sim had been under him, part of him, given herself to him. But where had that closeness gone? Their physical link. Unease snuck through him. What had happened in the little time he'd been asleep?

Then the unease liquefied, turned to molten determination.

He didn't know how—if—Sim could be part of his life now that he was tied to the World Tree. But he did know he wasn't letting her go without a fight. He'd wanted her from the moment she came to town. And now they'd been together, and it had been ... it had been fucking exceptional.

He mentally girded his loins. Clearly, he had a fight

ahead of him—just when he thought he'd won the battle. Okay, so this was going to be more like a siege.

He had one thing up his sleeve. They'd rocked together. And by the way she kept casting little glances at his body, the heat in her gaze, she wasn't totally against them being together. He just had to show her how they could make it work on all levels.

And he wasn't above playing dirty.

He somehow wrangled his expression into a calm façade. "Okay, let me get dressed and we'll find Serephena."

He threw back the covers and stepped down from the bed. Sim's gaze flew to his groin. He bit back a smile as her eyes widened at his clear desire for her.

"Ah, yeah. I mean no, no, you don't need to come with me," she said with a cough.

Nate snorted as he pulled on his jeans. Hid a wince as he fitted himself into the denim. "Sim, you're mad if you think I'm leaving you out there on your own. And don't even try to argue. You're a mortal in the Underworld. Believe me, I am sticking to you like glue until we get back home."

"So, ah ..."

"What's up?" He turned around, making sure she got a good look at his body—she'd sure seemed to like it earlier—and took his time shrugging into his top, then his jacket.

Sim licked her lips, and then *he* had to turn away because that move made his blood surge.

"What about you? I know you're a Keeper now, but what does that mean?"

Nate sat on the bed to pull on his shoes, the question rolling over and over in his mind. Finally, he sat up, ran a hand through his hair—faced the question head on.

"Truthfully, right now, I have no idea what it means for the years ahead. But I know I'm tied to the World Tree. Once Tara's back safe and sound, then I can work out the rest."

"You did this thing, this Keeper-thing for Tara, didn't you?"

"There's nothing I wouldn't do for Tara, for you. But yeah, current circumstances led me here. Though I can tell you, I would've gotten here at some point, regardless. Because the well-being of the World Tree is vitally important for everyone and everything I care about. I used to think I could do more to look after my family, my town as a cop. But turns out this purpose, it's even more important." A smile curved his lips as that last truth came out.

Nate rubbed his hands over his thighs as he stood up. "Now c'mon, let's go find Serephena."

But when Sim and Nate reached the main cavern, the steward advised them that the Valkyrie wouldn't be back for some time. More food and wine were offered while they waited. They accepted the food but rejected the wine, agreeing it was best to keep their wits fully about them.

Nate explained the World Tree to Sim, and they spoke about witchcraft and spells and the world that Nate had been born into.

Gradually, more and more people filled the common area, and the overhead vents lit the space with more and more light. Nate presumed that meant morning had come to the Underworld. He guessed it was late morning back home.

They must've been in the cavern for a few hours when a heavy knock echoed through it.

Around them, everyone stopped, looked toward the

gigantic doors at the far end. The guards swung their spears toward the door and unfurled their wings with hard snaps.

Another knock sounded.

Nate threw a glance at the surrounding people; they were alert but not panicked. A shiver of awareness hit Nate's spine, and he brought his magic up, grabbed Sim's hand as he stood up, and hauled her into his side.

"What's going on?" She too glanced around them, and her face tightened.

Nate shuddered as another shiver of awareness hit him, and he turned in time to see Serephena shoot into the cavern behind them. Her wings arrowed behind her, her face was grim.

Serephena looked once at Sim then landed right in front of the doors, but she held no weapon. Nate had no idea what her offensive skills were or even if she was going to need them, which seemed a possibility.

Nate whirled to Sim. "If I say run, you run like hell to the back of the cavern, the same door we went through to our room, but turn right, and head for a spiral staircase. Wait in that stairwell for Thrane, no matter how long it takes."

Serephena's voice rang out as she called for the doors to be opened, and the massive arches swung wide.

A tall, masculine figure with long hair stood in the doorway. The male was winged, with two massive spreads of silvery-white feathers arched at his back.

Nate flicked a glance at everyone around them. The tension had lessened, conversations and tasks resumed. Several people murmured "moyarn".

Moyarn. Nate rocked back on his heels. Not a word. A name. Thank fuck. He let out his breath and relaxed.

As Serephena and Moyarn spoke—they were too far away to make out their words—Nate absently rubbed Sim's palm, heat rising to mingle where their skin connected. And his body responded. Damn, he was going to be walking around with a permanent hard-on the way he was going. But now that he knew how Sim tasted, how hot and tight she was, how perfectly she fit him, how she sounded when she came, how she looked when her body convulsed beneath him—ah hell, of course he'd have a permanent hard-on.

"Who is that? What's going on?" Sim asked.

"That's Moyarn, an ex-Angel from the Higherworld." he explained.

"Who?"

"Moyarn. I know it's an unusual name. It's a long story, but this is good because Moyarn can get a message to Nan."

"What? How?"

"Well, the ex-Angels have an agreement with Nan's twin-sister, Elaine, who lives here in the Underworld. And Elaine can communicate with Nan through their twin-bond. *That's* how we're going to get a message back to the Mortalworld about Tara."

Sim slowly took her hand from her mouth and just as slowly sank to sit on the bench seat behind them. She pulled him with her.

"Nate, I think you don't need to tell me anymore. Maybe just let me process what I've found out so far."

"It's been one hell of a day, huh? No one could blame you for wanting to take a pause on all of this. Listen, why don't you just sit here. I need to talk to Moyarn, but I'll be right over there, and you'll be able to see me the whole time."

Sim glanced over to where he gestured. Steel entered her gaze, and he swore her chin practically set like stone.

"No, I'm coming with you," she said. "If this is about Tara, I need to hear firsthand."

Nate sighed. Sim had to be the most stubborn female he'd ever encountered—and that was saying something given his family. He held out a hand. Might as well stay close since she wasn't sitting this one out.

Eventually, Sim took it. And another blast of heat radiated from where they touched. But it also waned, something he read as a kind of weariness. Shit, that was coming from Sim, through her touch.

He searched her eyes. She didn't seem aware she was doing it.

Protectiveness filled him. He cradled her hand in his and ignored the curious look that she shot him.

27

S im nearly withdrew her hand from Nate's, but his warmth once again leaned into her strength; and right now, she needed all she could get.

This world she'd fallen into was stranger than she could ever have imagined.

But Sim had also found her rhythm faster than she would've thought possible. Maybe because her focus had been solely on finding Tara, she'd taken in all the strangeness without question.

So Sim took another breath and prepared to deal with Serephena once again. And whoever this Moyarn was. At least Nate didn't think they were in danger.

She'd thought to get some space from Nate, get things back to where they used to be. Except for his heat, his scent, they'd marked her. She still clearly recalled the slide of his body against hers, how he filled her up. Set her on fire.

A low vibrating hum gathered inside her, and she battled back the urge to turn around, lead him back to that chamber.

Nate coughed, and his hand clenched on hers.

Sim glanced up at him, but he stared straight ahead. If she hadn't been so attuned, she might've missed how his jaw ticked.

But he didn't slow down, just walked faster, pulled her along with him. And that's when Sim got her first up-close look at the other man.

She swallowed a gasp. How in the world could anyone be so beautiful? She looked between Nate, Serephena and Moyarn. Internally, she shook her head—these people were made on a different scale to everyone else.

And Moyarn was regarding her, just as she had him.

"Hi," she said with a tentative smile.

He smiled back, genuine appreciation in his eyes. Eyes such a striking violet hue that Sim swallowed another gasp.

And then both Nate and Serephena moved between them.

This protectiveness was unnecessary. Moyarn clearly wasn't here to harm her. Serephena's move surprised her. But hey, maybe the Valkyrie just took good care of her guests.

But Sim's chime rang slowly, slightly off-pitch, and that was enough for her to know her guess wasn't right. She tilted her head, tried to work out what was going on.

And Moyarn must've wondered too because he cut his eyes from her would-be protectors to her.

She shrugged. His guess was as good as hers.

A brief smile lit his eyes before he looked back at Serephena. A new tension hit his face, and the smile slowly faded, replaced with a powerful intent wholly focused on the Valkyrie.

"Lord Ursiel." Moyarn dipped his head at Serephena.

Serephena's wings straightened even farther, their midnight lengths almost vibrating. Why, Sim had no idea.

"Moyarn. You are here in my domain. Why?" Ice dripped from Serephena's words.

"You asked my lord for assistance. Therefore, I am here," Moyarn added with a little flourish at the end.

Sim frowned, not trusting Moyarn's mild tone at all. Clearly, neither did Serephena, which made her a smart woman in Sim's eyes.

"Your lord could have sent anyone. And I recall your last visit here ended with a directive to never return. Yet here you are."

"Yes, well, when my lord received your request, her understanding was that it would pave the way for a safe ... visit."

"Your lord presumed much." Serephena's chin rose into the air.

Moyarn just shrugged one impressive shoulder.

Finally, Serephena furled her wings with a snap, pivoted on her elegant toes. "Come, I do not want to waste time."

Sim shot a look at Nate, but he and Moyarn were talking, and so instead she followed Serephena to the closest of the trestle tables where the Valkyrie took a seat.

The bench seats were perfect because they allowed the Valkyrie's wings to rest unimpeded.

"Here, Simone, sit beside me."

Sim slid on the bench beside Serephena, and Nate and Moyarn joined them on the other side of the table. Sim faced the surreal violet eyes of Moyarn.

"Hi, again," she said with a smile.

"Hello. So, you are Nate's witch?"

Sim checked Nate out. He looked at her innocently, but he didn't fool her.

"I'm a witch, yes, and my name's Sim. But we don't have a lot of time for pleasantries. Can you help us?"

Beside her, Serephena shifted on the bench, and a genuine smile spread across her face.

"Of course." Moyarn's lips curved upward. "Nate has explained your situation. My lord will pass the message that you are ready to leave."

"Is that it? Why did you have to come here?" Serephena asked.

"Your correspondence to the Lord of Light indicated that the child you scried for is with the Angelkin in the Higher-world. That is one area where I may help you."

"You? You're an Ex. Why would they listen to you?"

"I still have contacts. But I still can't fathom why they would take a mortal child. And I can ask my contacts to find out."

"That's what I want to know. After I get her back." Sim rubbed her arms as a chill bit through her. Even knowing Tara was okay, she couldn't truly settle until Tara was home. "How long will it take you to get a message to them?"

"Perhaps two to three hours. I'll return once I have an update for you." Moyarn gazed squarely at Serephena. "Is there anything else I need to be aware of?"

For a long moment, Serephena and Moyarn traded stares. Then she flicked a glance at Sim. Something tightened in Sim's gut.

"What? What else is there?" Sim asked.

Serephena sighed, settled her hands on the table before

her. She appeared relaxed, but her fingers were clasped so tightly her knuckles lost all color. Finally, the Valkyrie unclenched her hands.

"Moyarn, there is one more thing. Please inform your lord that Simone is a daughter of Benedict; therefore, she and her kin come under my protection."

"I go by Sim, actually." She cleared her throat. "And that's what I wanted to talk to you about. This Benedict that you keep saying is my father. Who is he exactly?"

Moyarn slowly turned back to Sim. His violet eyes crystalized; they were like looking through pure amethyst. One of his hands snaked out and grabbed hers.

"Hey, stop that." Sim tried to pull back.

But Moyarn held on tight.

"Moyarn. Hands off," Nate growled. He grabbed Moyarn's wrist. "I said let her go."

Moyarn hissed. His arm tensed, but he didn't let her go. Instead, he slowly uncurled her fingers and pressed her hand to his own.

A shiver tingled where their hands met. Like how her intuitive chime rang in her chest.

"What is that?" Sim breathed.

"That there—that sensation in your palm—is how the Angelkin recognize each other." Moyarn's eyes widened, and he released her hand. He cut Nate a look. "I would not hurt her."

"Sim said stop, and you didn't." Nate bared his teeth. "That's all that matters. We might need your help, but you're never allowed to scare her."

Sim sent Nate a small smile. He just kept doing it, looking out for her. She almost sighed. Keeping things light with Nate was going to be one of the hardest things she'd ever had to do. She forced a calmness to her voice that was the opposite of the tumult of emotions racing through her mind. "So who wants to tell me what's going on?"

Nate, Moyarn, Serephena all looked at each other.

"Now," she added as she planted her hands on the table.

"They will fight for her if she does not wish this," Moyarn said to Serephena.

"Any idea what they're talking about?" Sim traded another look with Nate.

Nate slowly nodded, and his eyes had turned flinty again. Sim chewed her lip as she looked between all three faces.

"Okay," she said, "no one's actually telling me anything. I need to know what's going on, and of you all, I trust Nate. So, Nate, spill."

Serephena rolled her eyes, but chagrin clearly marked her expression.

Nate picked up her hands. His warm, calloused palms held hers, the pad of his thumb gently stroked her, around and around in slow, comforting circles. But she didn't want to be comforted. She wanted answers. She glared at him.

"Okay, okay." Nate dropped her hands. "I think Serephena and Moyarn are arguing over who can have protection of you. I know—it's weird. But, Sim, if your father is ... was ... an angel, that makes you a half angel, if that's such a thing. Maybe the Angelkin would let you live with them, and Tara too, if you wanted."

"Me?" Sim cut a look at Moyarn, who nodded.

"Yes," Nate continued. "You. And it makes sense. Look at your magic. It's completely different to mine, and Nan's, even India's, right? Because it's through your touch. Your hands are where your magic is. And that's an Angel trait. Their abilities come from their touch."

"Even if that was true about my father, why would I stay with these Angels? Some family I've never met, who've ignored *my* family for twenty-six years, who flew down to earth and stole my baby? They can keep their bloody *protection*. Moyarn, you offered to get word to where Tara is. I'd appreciate it if you'd do that. Now."

Sim lifted her chin and folded her arms. Dared any of the three to challenge her.

Serephena stood in one graceful shift of her body. Tension clearly flitted about the Valkyrie's mouth, and even her electric eyes had turned turbulent.

"Your Keeper has it right, Simone," Serephena said.

"It's Sim."

Serephena didn't budge, either. "Your sire, Benedict, was an Angel. He joined the Keepers to help protect the World Tree in the Higherworld. However, when our Tree here came under attack some thousand years ago, Benedict led a wing of warriors from Higherworld to help us. While he was here, he met my mother, one of the original lords of the Underworld. She settled here when the World Tree first created the three worlds."

Sim's chime resolutely rang once. Truth. Serephena's mother had been with Sim's father. *Bloody hell.* Sim's mouth dropped open.

"Are you saying—"

Serephena nodded.

"You're ... we're ... half sisters?"

"Yes."

Sim's eyes widened, and she stepped back, took in Serephena. Physically, they were different—not just the winged part, but their builds, their hair, their eyes. And yet ...

"That man in my memories?" Sim asked. "That was him?"

Serephena nodded.

"Where do you fit into this?" Sim swiveled to Moyarn, who still sat at the table.

"I came with Benedict all those years ago. I stayed, but he eventually left. And I can tell you that as kin to the Angels, you would be welcome in their home anytime. You could claim protection from their clan if you chose."

"Why do you say that like it's not a good idea?"

"The Angelkin can be single-minded when it comes to their agenda." Moyarn's gaze grew shuttered. "That's why I, and others, stayed here. We're known as the Ex's."

"Like a fallen Angel?"

"Not exactly. But when we left the Higherworld for good, it was permanent."

"What does an Angel do?"

Moyarn went to speak, but Serephena cut him off, lip curling. "They run around our world trying to make sure we do good."

"It's an old argument here in the Underworld," Moyarn said dryly. "But the truth is, those of us who stayed here did so because we saw this world as a world of opportunity and a place where we can be of use. In the Higherworld, the Angelkin were—are—a breed apart. Here, we are part of the whole."

"Listen, right now, my only focus is getting Tara back. I'm

not losing sight of that just because my father ..." She cut Serephena a glance. "*Our* father turned out to be, well, you know. But right now, all that matters is Tara. So I need to get home."

"How will you leave?" Moyarn asked.

"We have to work out the details," Nate said. "When Thrane returns, we're going to work out how to get Sim to the World Tree here."

"Keeper, do you know our World Tree is on the other side of this mountain range?" Moyarn said. "It will take days to get there by foot. But I can fly Simone—it is not far off my course when I return to my lands. Unfortunately, I couldn't carry you both that distance, but as you said, you can cross back with Thrane, and Simone can meet you in the Mortalworld."

"Uh, no way," Nate said. "It's too dangerous for Sim out there."

"Nay, Keeper, I will keep your witch safe during our flight."

"Not his witch." Sim rolled her eyes. "But it's a way home. I'll take it."

28

Long after Moyarn had left to pass on the message about Tara, Nate held back a grimace as Serephena returned to whatever duties she did as a Lord of the Underworld. Of course, Sim and Serephena had wanted to get to know each other, and he'd tried not to intrude on what little time they had.

But *finally*, he had Sim alone—well, as alone as they could be in a cavern full of Underworldians, or whatever you called them—at least until Moyarn returned.

But Sim's gaze was a million miles away. Their brief time together earlier, where they'd been so in tune, so close, seemed a thing of the past already. Nate's gut churned. He wanted more than a moment with Sim.

He wanted forever. For as long as they had together, anyway.

What if she didn't want a relationship with him? Sim had always kept him in the friend zone until now. And yeah, she'd been into the sex, but what if that was all she wanted?

"Hey, Sim, see those giant, high-backed overstuffed armchairs against the far wall?" He waited until she nodded. "No one's using them, so want to wait over there? Moyarn could be another half hour yet, and my butt's gone numb on this bench. Those chairs look like a much more comfortable place to wait."

He let Sim lead the way, only to run into her back when she halted.

"Huh. They're a lot wider than normal armchairs," Sim said. "Maybe to accommodate wings?"

"Maybe, but I don't care. My butt is going to appreciate these cushions." He stepped around her and dropped into the nearest chair. "Oh yeah. That's better."

Sim's lips twitched as she sat on the chair beside him. She was responding to him ... that was a win.

"So, you're going on another adventure," he said. "This one without me."

"Yeah, looks like. These last few days have been one new experience after another. But I'll take every single one needed to get Tara back—even fly with an Angel." Her eyes went wide. "Can't believe I just said that."

"Sim, India and Thrane have both spoken about Moyarn. He's a decent guy. Angel. Male. Whatever you call him." He was also a damned attractive SOB who was going to be carrying Sim in his arms while he flew them across the Underworld.

"Then why are you all grumpy? You're not filling me with confidence here, Nate."

"What?" Nate scowled, folded his arms. "I'm not grumpy."

"Sure you're not," Sim said, shaking her head.

"No, I mean it. I just..." He blew out a hard breath. Fuck, how to say this? "Sim, it's just that he's going to be carrying you against that wide chest. Flying with you. Keeping you safe."

"Oh." Sim's eyes widened, and she blinked. "Are you jealous?"

"Pfft. Jealous of the smoking hot angel doing what I want to do? Why in the world would you think that?"

"Oh. I get it." Sim moved forward in her seat until her knees were touching his. "Sure, Moyarn's got this god-like vibe going on, and yeah, I guess he'll be carrying me against that stupidly wide chest ..."

Nate couldn't contain a snort.

"But I'm not along for the ride because he's hot. I'm there to get home to Tara."

"Sorry, Sim. That was a dick thing to get worked up about. You're right. We're getting Tara back. And getting you home. Those are the things that matter."

She leaned close. Secrets played in her gaze, and he searched her eyes. What was she thinking? What did she want?

She pressed cool sweet lips to his. His heart leaped, just like another part of his body.

And then she sat back.

"What was that for?" Nate asked.

Sim's gaze dropped for one moment, then rose to meet his head on, flashed with fire. "Does there need to be a reason?"

A growl rumbled through him. People—beings—

surrounded them, but he didn't care. He pulled her up onto him. Kissed her hard and fast, pushed his tongue into her mouth. She pressed back into him, making him cheer inside. Hell, he wanted her. Now.

"Really? You two have to do this now?" Thrane's voice echoed behind them.

He drew in another harsh breath, backed away enough to rest his forehead to Sim's, took in her red lips, parted still. "Thrane, your timing is shit."

Thrane chuckled.

Desire simmered in Sim's eyes. Thank fuck, because the knowledge that she wanted him was one of the few things that gave him hope.

He grinned. "Why do people keep interrupting us?"

Nate and Thrane delayed their departure from the Underworld to time their crossing as close to Sim's as possible. They arrived back at the World Tree in the Mortalworld as the late afternoon sun gilded the forest. There was no sign of Sim.

"Shouldn't Sim be here by now?" Nate shuffled his feet in the leaf litter. His heart raced. "Moyarn left over two hours ago."

"She'll be fine. Moyarn's an ancient. Trust me, he can take care of Sim."

"But what if something went wrong? What if she's crossed somewhere else—"

And then Sim appeared, wide-eyed and pale, right before them. There'd been no gradual appearance, no misty form. Just wham. Present. Nate's breath whooshed out.

"See?" Thrane clapped him on his back. "Told you Moyarn would get her here."

"Yeah. I wasn't worried at all." He ignored Thrane's stare and said to Sim, "So, how was the ride?"

"It was something else. But I'm just happy to be home."

Home. The tang of the loam. The sweet icy air. Yeah, this was home. His chest expanded as that knowledge filled him. This forest was his place, his right place.

A gentle knock tapped on his mind, but this time, he didn't hold it at bay. Instead, he let the Tree in.

Tara's face came to mind at the same time as ice swept through his veins and the hairs on the back of his neck pricked. And a red boot replaced Tara's face, striding over the ashes of millions of charred, wrecked bodies.

Adrenaline surged through Nate, and he turned to Sim. "Tara's coming here now."

"What?" Sim gasped. "Nate, how do you know?"

"The Tree told me. But she's still in danger."

"What did you see?" Thrane demanded.

Even as Nate explained, Thrane touched the Tree, then withdrew his hand moments later. "You're right. Tara's on her way. And I got the same impression; we need to watch over Tara."

"What's with the red boot?" Nate asked. "That's twice the Tree has shown me that image. It must mean something."

"I didn't receive an image of a boot, but I had the same sense of danger that I get when the Order is here."

"Fucking hell. Why are the Order involved with Tara?"

"What makes you think they are?" Thrane asked.

"I'm still deciphering how the Tree communicates, but the image and sensations I saw were about Tara. You saw Tara too, but your sense of the danger related to the Order. Either we have two separate risks, and only one is to do with Tara, or Tara is the link between them."

"What?" Sim grabbed Nate's arm. "You think this is about Tara?"

Nate nodded. Sim shivered, her arm brushing his.

"Here, take this. It's bloody freezing," he said, shrugging out of his jacket and handing it to her.

"That wasn't from the cold. I want to know what the hell is going on with Tara."

"We will. When these Angelkin bring her back, we're going to find out everything. We need to know the why so we can work out who. Then we'll know how to keep Tara safe."

Sim stared up at him and nodded. Her trust was a delicate thing. But it was present. And it made Nate want to cheer.

The Tree whistled through his mind, a long, sweeping song that had him look at it.

And then, just as suddenly as Sim had appeared minutes earlier, Tara and another woman were there, right at the base of the World Tree. The woman stood behind Tara, one hand resting on her shoulder. Tara's gaze went straight to Sim, and a smile lit up her little round face. She was in her pajamas still, and her feet were bare. The woman was looking around the forest, blinking.

Nate's heart jumped, and he blinked, too.

Sim, who'd been looking in the opposite direction, whirled around. "Tara!" She launched in a stumbling leap, fell to her knees, and wrapped Tara up in her arms. The woman at her back remained calm, but her eyes softened as she removed her hand.

Nate's breath sawed in, his knees went weak, and he had to swallow the bloody great lump that rose in his throat. He clenched his jaw to keep it that way.

Tara was okay. Seeing her here, in her mother's arms, made everything worthwhile.

A tremble went through him at the thought of what might've been. His knees almost buckled, but he held himself up and stepped over on wobbly legs, tentatively rested one hand on Sim's back.

She didn't let Tara go, just turned her head to look up at him. Tears streaked down her cheeks. Sim's eyes whirled with a tumult of happiness, anger, relief, fear.

Fuck. When her emotions were like this, she'd cut him and her mother. He darted a look at where her hands held on to Tara, but while Sim's arms banded around the little girl, her hands were clenching her own forearms.

Nate blew out a breath and rubbed Sim's back. "Come on now, it's too cold to stand here, and Tara's barefoot." He turned to Thrane. "Can we get a ride up to Nan's? And can we use your jacket for Tara since Sim's got mine?"

Thrane handed his jacket over to Nate, but his gaze was firmly on the unknown female.

This was an Angel? Nate bared his teeth in a grim smile.

"We need to get Tara out of the cold." Nate slipped Thrane's jacket around Tara's shoulders as best he could, with Simone still holding her tight before glancing back over his shoulder to the woman. "I'm Nate, this is Sim, Tara's mother, and this is Thrane."

"Hello, I am Amadis, of the Angelkin."

"We need some answers from you. Can you join us where we're going? If not, I'll stay here while Sim takes Tara up to the farmhouse."

"I will come with you to see the child home and safe."

"Safe?" Sim growled as she lifted her head. Fire rose to burn, hot and furious, in her eyes. Thank fuck she wasn't touching anyone because Nate swore she'd have singed anyone that came into contact with her fingers, based on the firestorm of anger in her expression.

"You're concerned about my daughter's safety now?"

Less than an hour later, Nate let out a massive sigh as Thrane turned his truck into Nan's property. Nate sat in the back seat with Tara between him and Sim. Amadis sat in the front, the drive giving him ample time to consider how the Angelkin fit into the puzzle. When they reached the farm-house, and Thrane pulled his car to a crunching halt on the gravel, Nate knew his first line of questioning.

But first he messaged Kat to let her know Tara was home and safe.

Then he took a careful look at Sim's feet. After their trek through the forest, hypothermia was a genuine worry. She'd tried to wear his shoes, but she'd tripped too often, making it more dangerous. They'd settled for his socks for some protection. But by the time they'd reached Thrane's truck, her feet were blue, and she'd had barely any feeling in them.

They'd turned the heater on in the car to warm Tara up,

and Thrane had run inside to find warm socks for Sim. But frostbite was still a risk.

"I'll come around and help you out," Nate said to Sim. Tara had fallen asleep just as they'd reached the farm. "Do you want me to carry Tara? And then we need to see to your feet."

"A hand to get out would be good, thanks." Sim gave him another small smile, and her eyes rested with utter love on Tara for a moment.

Sim transferred Tara into his arms without waking her, and Tara then snuggled into his chest. A surge of contentment swept through him.

Sim looked at Nate, a puzzled, no, more like bemused, look on her face. He raised his eyebrows. She smiled, the tension slowly receding from around her eyes. "Nothing, just thinking that you do care for her, that's all."

"Yeah, I do. But not just Tara." He held Sim's gaze.

She smoothed a hand over Tara's hair, and her lips curved, but she said nothing. Nate bit back a sigh. Still a little way to go.

"Nate," Thrane said. "India and I need to talk with Amadis. We'll stay outside until we're done."

He nodded and followed Sim to the farmhouse. Nan and his mum met them at the door and ushered them inside.

"Bring Tara inside," Nan said. "We've got the spare room set."

"Thanks, and we'll need something for Sim's feet as well," Nate said.

In the spare room, the bedside lamp cast a low, warm light as Sim, standing by the bed, pulled back the quilt.

"They've already turned on the electric blanket," she whispered. "Here, put her down."

Nate carefully laid Tara on the warm sheets, then stood back as Sim drew the quilt up and over Tara.

She pressed a gentle kiss to Tara's forehead, then rested one hand on Tara's little round cheek. Nate was about to turn away, give Sim a moment, when her breath caught and her shoulders shook.

No way he could leave her like that and, steeling himself for whatever backlash her emotions dealt, he reached out, drew her back into his chest so she could still watch Tara.

Nate wrapped his arms around her, and when she grasped him back, they held on to each other. Tight.

And then Sim cried. Silent tears glistened in the dim light as they tracked down her cheeks, and she half turned into him even as she kept her gaze on Tara.

His own eyes stung, but he held himself still. Held her. Was held. And a connection he'd not expected reached out from her, through her hands, and called straight to the heart of his magic.

Their magics connected.

And Nate stood there, content with that knowledge.

After several long minutes, Sim's shoulders stopped shaking. Her hands loosened on his. She twisted to him, her eyes going to his, then dropping to his lips. Mingled magic infused the air.

There was never any doubt about what he'd do next.

Desire rose in a rapid spike, harder and faster than ever before. Only the fact that Tara lay sleeping steps away stopped Nate from unleashing the need, the want. Instead, he brushed Sim's lips. Once. Twice.

His pulse took flight, his body went hard, and he drew in a harsh breath and restrained himself from taking their kiss any farther.

"I want to kiss you so much," he whispered. "But we need to see to your feet."

29

It took everything in Sim to force herself to leave Tara. Leaving the bedroom door ajar, she followed Nate into the living room.

Tara's safe. She's back. She's safe.

Nan and Vera both stood at the kitchen bench, their faces drawn. There was no sign of Thrane, India or the angel, so they must have still been outside. Nate dropped into one of the dining table chairs and scrubbed a hand over his stubbled jaw. His gaze cut to Sim's without warning. Desire simmered just below the surface.

Nate was normally a closed book, so good at projecting the country-boy charm she had to work really hard to figure out what he was thinking or feeling. But one thing she could read was his desire.

Beneath his stare, a hot tingle arrowed through her, her nipples tightened, and warm, delicious heat pooled slowly. Her chime rang once, long and soft.

What the hell? She blinked, cutting the connection between their gazes. That tingle and her chime subsided.

The sound of the coffee machine brewing broke her focus. She looked up.

Vera and Nan both watched her with curious gazes. Like they were waiting for her to say something. Damn. She moistened her lips. Had they spoken?

"Ah, sorry, I missed what you said."

Nan cleared her throat. "Vera asked if you'd liked a tea or coffee, dear."

Heat prickled up Sim's cheeks, but she just sighed. She probably had no hope ever of hiding anything from this family, so she went with it.

"Vera, I would kiss you for a coffee."

"No need, hon, but I'm sure someone else would be happy for the honor." Vera smiled, glanced at Nate.

"Mum, not very smooth." Nate groaned.

"Well, you're my son, and I'm happy to help you out."

Sim's lips curved, and she shook her head—more at herself than anything, bemused that she could even laugh.

"I don't think you need to worry about Nate, Vera," she said. "He's doing a fine job on his own."

"Okay, that's enough of this," Nate growled. "*Mum*, remember we talked about this? How about we change the topic?"

"I was happy to have a light moment, to be honest," Sim said.

"You're right, Morris," Nate said, "and we could all do with one. Let's grab a hot coffee, and then we can regroup. But first, I need to look at your feet."

"Frost nip?" Nan's gaze homed in on Sim's feet.

"Nip? Nate called it frostbite before."

Nate walked into the kitchen, rummaging through a low

cupboard before coming up with a plastic bucket. "Yeah," he said, "frostnip is the first stage. So you've got two choices. You can sit here and rest your feet in a bucket of warm water, or you can have a bath. But the water can't be too hot, so you might find a bucket more comfortable."

"Ah, my feet feel fine now." Sim wriggled her toes. "I think Thrane's socks have done the trick."

"Uh-uh. You didn't have any feeling when we got in the car. Trust me, we need to look after your feet properly."

"Well, if you really think it's needed, let's go with the bucket." Sim went to stand.

"No, stay there. I'll fill this and bring it to you."

Sim looked at Nan and Vera, but they were both busy making tea or coffee, maybe both.

Nate came back around the kitchen counter and knelt at her feet. His mussed blond hair fell all over the place, concern clear in his eyes. He lifted one of her feet and peeled off the borrowed sock.

As soon as Nate's warm hands were on Sim's skin, sparks of heat ignited through her. His hand went to her other foot, again he peeled back the sock, and again his warm touch set off another arc of heat.

Hell, she wasn't cold. She was on fire.

And suddenly, they were in their own cocoon, with the rest of the house, the family, obscured. Just the two of them. Sim blew out a breath, tried to control her thoughts when all they wanted to do was run back to him. Nate dipped her feet into the bucket. The warm water had nothing on the heat of his hands.

His eyes tightened, and he cleared this throat before murmuring, "Are you ready for that coffee now?"

She swallowed hard, and suddenly unable to form words, nodded. Nate was the one who broke their stare. Just as well because she'd had no hope of doing that. He blew out a hard breath but schooled his features.

"Right, I'll be back in a few minutes," he said as he stood up, headed into the kitchen.

Sim let the conversation between Nate and his family flow around her without paying too close attention. With Nate's hands off her skin, her pulse returned to normal, and her focus returned to what needed to be done next.

Answers about Tara.

Someone had messed with her daughter. She was going to find out who, and then she was going to make sure that never happened again.

Nan and Vera pulled together a meal for all of them, a double boiler full of pasta and a giant pot of Bolognese sauce, and Sim offered to help but was told no. Instead, they refilled the bucket with more warm water, even though Vera inspected Sim's feet and declared they looked fine.

Sim was still sitting with her feet in the bucket when India came inside, followed by Amadis and Thrane.

It was the first time Sim had looked closely at the angel. She had silvery-white hair in a funky cut. Her face was perfection, with possibly the most exquisite features Sim had ever seen. She looked like she was early twenties—max. And how could someone who'd steal a child have such a tranquil expression?

"Where is the child?" Amadis asked, looking around.

"Tara? You're talking about my daughter?" Sim's hackles spiked, and she jumped up. "How about you answer my question? What do you want with my baby? Why? Why did you take her?"

The woman tilted her head, her perfect brows furrowed for a moment. "The Angelkin council ordered to see to the safety of the child. Therefore, I took her to our lands in the Higherworld."

"That's not good enough," Sim growled.

And then Nate was there. He eyed her hands before he placed his on her upper arm. He'd done that a lot. And the touch gave her a little breathing room from her anger. Her fingers even uncurled. When had they clenched?

"Well, Ammy," Nate said. "We need answers. You say you're here to see to Tara's safety, but the only way *we* can keep her safe is to know why she was taken."

Amadis looked around the group. "If that will help you keep the child safe, then I will answer any question of which I have knowledge."

Thrane took a seat. "Why don't we start at the beginning? Nan, Vera, you met Amadis earlier, but she didn't stay inside for long. Just to be clear, Amadis is an Angel, and yes, she has wings."

Sim scowled. Wings? She was pretty sure she'd have noticed that.

"It is true," Amadis said. "However, Angel wings are glamoured in the Mortalworld. Humans cannot see them unless I choose to reveal myself."

"Did you just read my mind?" Sim tensed up.

"No, I simply read your expression."

"And what's a glamour?"

Amadis tilted her head again. "You're a witch, yet you don't know a glamour?"

"I've only been a witch for a short time."

Nate cleared his throat. "Technically, that's not true, Sim. You've always been a witch, but your ability to consciously use your magic has only recently triggered."

"Consciously?"

"Remember that feeling you had to go into that lotto store and buy the winning ticket? We think that when you've had these 'feelings,' that's been your witchcraft guiding you. You seem to be sensitive to the events of the future, but that used to be instinctual. Now, you're guiding your magic to an outcome. Does that make sense?"

"But why? What changed? And what's it got to do with magic coming from my hands?"

"That is our way," Amadis said. "I understand your father is Benedict?"

"Is? I think you mean was. Apparently, he died fighting in the Underworld." A lump rose in Sim's throat. But she swallowed it away. She'd never known the man; there was no reason to get all emotional over him now.

"You are correct that he died, but death is not the end of us. It is merely a change in our state. Your father moved from a corporeal being to one of energy. He still exists, simply not in a way that you, nor I, can perceive. In fact, your father has been contacting your child through her dreams—I understand Tara is far more receptive to his visits than you."

Sim stared at Amadis—was the woman for real? Then she looked at everyone in the room. "You all seem a little too unshocked at hearing this."

"It's true about death only being a physical state," India said. "The part about your father ... sorry, hon, I can't tell you anything more about that. But we know this is a lot to take in."

"You know, people keep saying that this is a lot to take in. But here's the thing, I don't care. All I care about, all I want, is to find out why Tara was taken." Sim stared at Amadis. "So, tell me everything you know about Tara."

Nate shifted in his seat beside her, eyes sharpening. "Ammy, is there a way Sim's Angel heritage could've had something to do with her magic suddenly changing?" he asked.

"I'm not interested in my magic, Nate. This is about Tara."

"What if they're connected?" He rubbed a hand over her arm.

Damn. She shot him a look. "Then yeah, I ... we ... need to know."

"Simone, worry not. I will answer both of your questions as best I can. Your witchcraft being ignited is the easiest question to answer. Yes, it is possible a significant event may have triggered your witchcraft to manifest into a conscious state. Did you undergo a trauma?"

She chewed on her lip for a moment, absently rubbed the heel of her palm over her chest. "Well ..." She recounted what had happened—it seemed like a million years ago— the day her magic had seemed to start. "But apart from the one moment where I thought I saw someone, no one else was there, and nothing physically hit me."

"Sim," Nate said. "You said that before. You thought you

saw someone, right? But when you woke up, you were alone."

"Yeah, I must've imagined it."

"But what if it *was* someone?" Nate whirled to Nan. "Could a person have triggered Sim's magic?"

"Possibly. There are some beings with enough power to activate dormant magic, but not many. And certainly not many in this world." Nan looked at Amadis. "Could an Angel?"

"Our elders would know how to trigger power. But that is not our way."

"Great," Sim muttered. "Well, it looks like I've been in the presence of a superbeing. Okay, so if this is right, what does that have to do with Tara?"

"Some hours ago," Amadis said, "I received a call from our warden that I had a task to complete. That is the purpose of Angels." She paused, her eyes flashing for a moment. "The quest assigned to me was twofold, as I mentioned earlier. The first was about an Angelkin child in the Mortalworld. I was to ensure the safety of the child."

"But how did you take Tara?"

"I flew to her bedroom window. Initially, I transferred Tara to Kin lands in the Higherworld. However, not long after, the instructions changed to bring the child to a place of safety in the Mortalworld, specifically this House of Witches."

Sim couldn't contain a frown as she eyed Amadis's slim, close-to-tiny frame. *She* was going to keep Tara safe? She snorted but said nothing more on that score because Amadis had said something way more important.

"Okay, what is this danger to my baby?"

"Dangers."

"As in more than one?"

"Yes. One of malevolent intent, and one of innocent risk, though no less deadly. The Angelkin became aware of these dangers and could not allow such a risk to one of our kind at such a young age, and so they dispatched me to safeguard her until they assessed the dangers."

"So there are two dangers?" Nate leaned forward.

"There was. The risk of unintentional harm has ended. The risk of intentional harm persists. However, the Angelkin deemed the property we are in now to be safe, hence here we are."

Sim's gut dropped. Her gaze dipped to her hands.

"*I* was the danger?"

30

Tara was asleep, her round little cheeks soft and pink in the muted light cast by the bedside lamp. Sim sat on the end of the bed, staring at her baby's face—unwilling to look away in case she wasn't there when she looked back.

Tara rolled over, and when the blankets slipped away, Sim reached out, tucked them back in tight. She reached out to stroke Tara's hair—and froze.

Freckles dotted the back of Sim' hands and she turned them over. Her eyes traced the lines worn into her palms.

She'd been a worker from as soon as she could earn a dollar, cleaning, waiting tables, making coffees. Her hands were worn but pretty good for a twenty-six-year-old. And now, they'd caused harm.

Could she really have been a danger to her baby?

She'd *never* harm Tara. But what if her witchcraft ... this magic ... had happened when she'd had no clue it was going to? What if she'd been hugging Tara, or doing her hair, or getting her dressed, and something had happened?

Shudders trembled through her, and her hands shook.

This magic, this thing she hadn't even asked for, could've hurt her baby.

So maybe, just maybe, the Angelkin had stepped in for a good reason. But they damn well should've told her. To simply step in and take Tara, without even saying why, was unforgivable. And while she might understand the reason behind it, she'd never have agreed to their method.

Which led her mind to another burning question.

"Who *wants* to harm Tara?" Nate whispered from the doorway.

Sim rubbed her arms both from the cold and to ward off the inner chill at the thought of someone wanting to hurt her baby.

Sim stared at Tara for one more moment. *Tara was here. She was okay. She wasn't going anywhere.*

Sim turned around. The dim light of the hallway cast a warm, mellow halo around Nate, gilding his hair, making *him* look like the angel.

"Now *you're* reading my mind?" she said.

He smiled, but his eyes were full of questions.

"Nah, just saying what we're all thinking." He backed out into the hallway, let her pass by. "The fire's on in the lounge if you want to come through?" Nate said.

Nate and Sim walked into the formal lounge. Golden flames crackled and popped in the fireplace. Sim's nose tingled at the tang of wood smoke.

"Where is everyone?" she asked, holding her hands out toward the fire before turning her backside to the flames.

Nate sat on the couch nearest to the fire. "Nan and Mum are casting a protection spell around the house yard. Your mum is asleep in India's old room—India and Nan brought her back. Thrane and India took Amadis back to his place so she can do her next quest, whatever that is, and India will come back here later.

"And Sim, you'd left the room, but Amadis said something else you need to know. Apparently, there are rumors among the Angelkin about the soul of a witch trapped in the Higherworld."

Sim gasped. "June?"

"Maybe. Amadis said the rumors are that the witch is looking for an Angel. But maybe the rumor's real—maybe it's your mother's soul. She could've been trying to find your father, not knowing he'd died, and lost control of the spell. I asked Amadis, and she said when she returns to the Higherworld that she'll look into it for us."

"Nate, if you're right, if June's ... Mum's ... been there this whole time. Oh my God." Sim swayed toward him, and tears burned her eyes.

"Yeah, I know." He cradled her to him.

Many minutes later, Sim's eyes were gritty from crying, but at least the tears had stopped.

"What's a border spell?" she asked.

"It repels anyone you don't want to enter. Because we need to make the spell big enough to cover the house and the cottages, it takes a lot of sustained energy. I'm going to take over the spell from midnight till morning. We've called in the entire family to help. But it doesn't keep people in, so Tara needs to know she can't leave the house and the yard until we say so."

"Nate, you're ... you've all ... gone to so much trouble for Tara. For me." Sim searched his eyes for the answer that made any of this make sense.

Hunger. Need. Connection blazed back at her.

He picked up her hand, turned it over in his own.

"You're part of this family." He must've seen the rebuttal that leaped to her lips. "No, not just because you and I got under the sheets together. Regardless of what happens with you and me—Tara, you, your mum, we're all community. And here in the country, that means we take care of each other."

A lump worked its way up into Sim's throat, and she battled it back down. Nate's face rang with honesty. His eyes held hers. Sure, and true.

Nate meant it. He and his family would be there for her. She'd never had that. Never been able to lean on someone else, give someone else her trust in that way.

And then his lips were on hers. Heat fired through her as his lips shaped and caressed hers, over and over.

Damn it, she shouldn't do this again. This bond kept growing stronger, reeling them closer. Having sex again wasn't going to make it any easier.

But all that went out the window when his hands framed her face and his mouth worshiped hers. His tongue slid between her lips, tempting. Tantalizing. Until she met it, let him inside.

Her low moan whispered through the room.

Flames crackled and hissed and popped as they licked over the timber in the hearth, but it was nothing to the fire that ignited when Nate's mouth ran down over her cheek, around to her ear.

He bit the delicate skin of her lobe.

Sim gasped as a spiral of fire arced from where he

nibbled on her ear straight to her core. Her breasts swelled, their tips tightened. Heat pooled between her legs.

Damn, she wanted him.

The voice of reason fell away as his hot breath ran across her neck to her other ear. Another bite. Another nibble. Another shot of heat coursed through her.

Demanded more.

She turned her head, brought his mouth back to hers. And she kissed him. Ran her lips over his, tasted him right back. A shiver coursed through his body. Because of her. *She* had made his body tremble.

She drew in a breath, inhaled the musk and fresh spice of his skin. She wanted this. Wanted him.

Maybe they could work out a way to have this thing together, and no one would get hurt.

Latching onto that thought as all the permission she needed, Sim pressed harder against Nate. Heat coursed through her. But she needed more.

She drew back. "Nate, I need ..."

He kissed his way back down her neck, sucked hard right where her pulse jumped. She hissed, then moaned as the forceful suction drew another spiral of fire from his mouth to her core.

"Nate, I'm on top this time."

He paused, lifted his head. His silky hair brushed against her chin, and when his blue eyes looked down at her, their glittery fire sparkled brighter than ever.

That bond snapped back to him, and without thinking, she cupped his jaw. Nate hissed at the contact, and Sim jerked back. Oh damn, her hands—

But then he grabbed her, brought her palm to his mouth.

"Sh, I'm okay. Better than. Your touch is like fire. I loved it. I can tell how you're feeling because it's right there, right here."

He kissed the sensitive skin right in the center of her palm, then drew one finger into his mouth, and with his piercing blue eyes dancing on hers, scraped his teeth along the sensitive inner edge.

A shiver ran through Sim at the sight of Nate's firm mouth on her skin, at the heat and promise and mischief in his eyes, at the hot sting of his teeth.

"Really?" Sim asked. "Are you sure you want to go there?"

His mouth curved. "Oh, yeah." But then he stopped, and his gaze cut to the doorway behind them. "What about Tara? What if she wakes up?"

The bubble of happiness inside Sim expanded. Man, this guy was just too good. She shook her head, unable to contain her smile.

"Tara's out solid. And even if she wakes up, she'll come out, and we'll hear her." She looked around the room and hopped up and grabbed the throw rug from the other couch. "And we have this."

"What about your no-kissing-in-front-of-Tara rule? If she comes out, this might let the cat out of the bag."

"Why does it sound like you're trying to find reasons for this not to happen?"

Nate grinned, held up his hands. "Oh no. No way am I looking for that. Just making sure it happens the way we both want."

"Well, what about Nan and your mum?"

Nate dropped back into the curve of the couch, his body sprawled like a lavish feast of long, lean, muscled limbs.

"They're staying put until midnight when I'll take over. And no one can see us from here." He grabbed his mobile phone, glanced at the display. "My alarm's set for quarter to midnight, so I've got three hours."

"Won't you need some sleep?" Sim asked.

He laughed, the sound tinged with gravel. "Honey, if you're talking about coming over here and hopping on board, trust me, that's going to give me all the energy I need to get through until the morning."

"Well, if you think you can manage ..."

He growled.

That damned bubble inside her expanded even farther.

"Whoa, boy. No need to get all cave dweller. Trust me. You're going to like this. But first, I'm just going to draw the drapes. Just in case ..."

She stepped back over to him moments later. And with the fire behind her, Sim drew her borrowed sweater over her head.

Nate shifted as if he was going to move.

"No, stay there. I want to strip for you."

Sim didn't need a mirror to guide her; she used the flush that hit high on Nate's cheekbones, the way his mouth tightened and pulled into a hard, firm line. The restless movement of his long, lanky legs. The burning light in his eyes, frank and hot.

She pulled her jeans down, kicked them the rest of the way.

Standing there in nothing but her underwear, Sim should've been cold in the winter's chill night air.

Only, with the fire at her back and Nate's fire at her front, she was anything but.

Because this massive male before her, all feline grace, somehow both lazy and lethal, regarded her like she was a rich dessert that he craved to devour.

He ran hot eyes down her body, back up again. He shifted on the couch, adjusted his pants.

"I take it you approve?"

"Honey, I am so fucking hot for you right now. I could come with a touch."

The gravel in Nate's voice sent a shiver through her. She didn't think twice and slipped off her underwear.

Nate's eyes turned hotter still. He licked his lips.

A feminine thrill coursed through her. Oh man, she was ready for this.

She stepped between his legs. His thighs brushed hers, and the friction of his jeans on her bare flesh sent goose-bumps all over her.

"Are you cold?" Nate asked.

Of course, he didn't miss a thing. Sim shook her head, and a slow smile curved her lips. "Uh-uh. Not cold, sensitive."

"Ah." Understanding dawned in his eyes, and he raised one calloused hand, cupped her breast. Heat and friction and a coiling, tugging need gathered inside her.

Nate sat there, decadent, like a fantasy lover, and the approval in his eyes heated her even more.

Her breasts swelled. Her hips rolled forward. Desperate for more contact, more heat. More Nate.

Nate shifted down, and with his other hand, brought her body into his.

His hot breath hit her belly, and with his wicked gaze on hers, he swept his hands over her breasts, then down, down farther over her body, a trail of fire flowing beneath his touch.

He shifted lower, farther still. His eyes cut to her core.

"You're fire all over," he murmured, licking his lips.

She ran a hand through his hair, guided him to her. The touch of his breath on her skin made her core clench.

He chuckled and then feasted.

Sim tried to control herself. Tried not to cry out, but the lash of his tongue up and over her, the rasp around and around her nub, hurled her into a storm of fire. Her body clenched again and again with each velvet stroke and rub until, in a burst, her body released, and she cried out, her eyes closed as sensation after sensation rolled through her.

Panting, Sim opened her eyes—startled to see his mouth still on her.

"More," he growled. And then his tongue stabbed inside her.

Her head dropped back. Her body flew. Sim would've fallen if not held in his large, capable hands.

With every plunge, he feasted like a man possessed.

Her skin prickled, her nerves sang, and she came again.

She barely registered Nate's withdrawal, barely noted the shift of his legs, the scrape of his arms on hers. A moment later, maybe minutes, he drew her back, but this time he was naked, and rolling on a condom. Then he pulled her down, down, until his cock brushed her folds.

Sim forced her heavy eyelids open, tried to catch her

breath. But it was useless because he pulled her astride his hips. Her thighs spread, and the hard, hot silk of him stroked her inner folds.

Nate surged forward. She lost her breath again, finally caught it, and a low moan vibrated through her at the fullness, at being impaled, at the way he hit every single nerve deep, deep inside.

She shifted, tried to get some space from the incredible, unending feeling of him seated totally inside her. She blew out a short, choppy breath, opened her eyes.

Nate's eyes were closed. Tension pulled his eyes, his mouth, tight. A fine tremble rippled across his chest, muscles clenched hard.

Damn, he was fine. Finer than anything she could ever have imagined. And right here and now, he was hers.

Sim leaned down, needing to press a kiss to his firm, sculpted lips. But the move pressed him higher, harder inside her.

Nate gasped. His eyes snapped open—like blue fire, laser bright. They glittered up at her.

"God, Sim, do that again." He took a short, hard breath. "But, honey, I'm not going to last long."

A thrill coursed through her, and she laughed, then did as he asked. Sim moaned as once more his shaft pressed harder along her internal muscles, and then she kissed him, swallowed his groan. She tasted the salt and musk of herself on him.

He groaned again, low and long.

She smiled.

The pleasure he'd given her with his mouth had been his doing. Now, she'd be the one to give him the thrill.

She lifted high; her body clenched, already missing the loss of pressure. But then she swept back down.

Again, she swept up and down, and with every sweep, his body hardened, muscles coiled tighter, breath came faster and faster. And then Nate growled, a long lethal sound. His arms banded around her; his head burrowed into the curve of her neck. He kissed her there, sucked her skin into his mouth.

She lifted and slammed, urgent, faster, and his hips rose to meet hers.

They raced that way until he thrust so hard everything stopped. All her inner muscles convulsed in one massive burst of sensation.

Nate shouted into her neck. His massive body shuddered beneath her, the corded veins in his neck strained, and inside her, his flesh pulsed, over and over.

31

Nate eased himself from beneath the throw blanket and, scrubbing his face, shifted to sit on the couch. Sim was still sleeping, her head cushioned on her arm.

With him gone, she rolled onto her back.

He grabbed a cushion from the floor, gently maneuvered it underneath her head, then pulled the throw over her. Even though they'd dressed after making love and snuggling back beneath the blanket, it was too cold not to have the cover.

And then he just looked.

The tension that had tightened the lines around her eyes and pulled at the corners of her mouth had eased. Now her soft, full lips curved as if her dreams were pretty damned nice.

The sweep of her deep russet lashes fanned over her creamy skin, a spill of freckles scattered over her nose and high on her cheeks.

He gave in to the urge to rub one knuckle over her skin.

Warm silk. With a smile, he just as gently brushed those full lips with his.

Man, she was amazing. As he sat back upright and looked around for his shoes, he couldn't help but shake his head at himself. The truth was, he was a goner for Sim. He knew it, and he had the feeling she did too.

And it wasn't just about the sex, although hell, when sex was this good, it was a major thing. He couldn't remember ever feeling this way with another woman. All he needed to do was work out how to live without her ... one day. But that was his choice. He couldn't imagine not having Sim in his life. But how could she fit into his new world?

Nate sighed, ran a hand through his hair. Man, things had gotten complicated.

With that, he stood up. It was bloody cold, though, and he quickly pulled on his shoes and then added some timber to the hearth and stoked the flames.

"Is it time?" Sim asked, the blanket falling away as she sat up.

She sleepily blinked, and her hair, released from its braid, curtained her shoulders. She was fucking perfect. His heart damned near exploded right there.

He tried to speak but had to clear his throat first. "Ah, yeah. Going to put the kettle on, though, in case Mum or Nan want something hot when they come in."

"We should've brought them something. Instead, we were in here ..." Sim's cheeks reddened.

"Making love?" He chuckled, couldn't help but lean in and buss her again on the lips.

She swatted his arm, and he laughed further.

"Don't worry, Morris, they won't know a thing. And they each took a thermos with them when they went out."

"Ha, your mum sees everything. Let alone Nan." Sim stretched, then swung her legs around. "Can I make you a thermos too?"

"I can do it."

"Uh-uh, you've been taking care of me. Let me do something for you."

Nate smiled, nodded. Inside, his heart cheered.

"And then I need a coat. Because it's freezing."

"I'm going to grab mine and some gloves, and I can get you one of Nan's. Here, get close to the fire. I'll be back in a minute."

He darted into the family wing, checked on Tara. Sure enough, she was sleeping peacefully. Then he grabbed what he needed.

When Nate came back, Sim had left the fire, of course—the stubborn thing—and was already in the kitchen with the coffee machine on, chugging out the hot, bitter brew.

He shrugged into his coat.

"Right, I'll head out." He handed over the spare jacket. "Here, this'll keep you warm."

Sim hugged the jacket to her chest.

"Thanks. Are you sure I can't help with the spell to protect the house? I am a witch."

Nate's lips curved upward. "And you're one very sweet witch for offering to sit out in the cold. But no, unfortunately, your craft doesn't quite work the same way as ours, and we can't risk the spell being inaccurate."

She sighed and hugged the jacket closer. "Well, I can at least make sure Nan and Vera are comfortable when they come inside. Then I'm going to sit in with Tara for a bit. But after that, I can come out and keep you company?"

"If you're up, and you feel like freezing your tail off, then come out and say hi. But it's not needed. Trust me, we've been here before, and the spell takes a lot of energy. It's like when you run, you naturally warm up."

"Tell Nan and your mum I'll be making tea or coffee if they want. And, Nate, thank you. Again."

He left the house and found Nan in a chair several feet from the front door. She had her winter coat on, plus gloves and a beanie.

But she didn't have a blanket, and he knew why. Nan wanted to be warm but not so comfortable she'd risk becoming sleepy and possibly lose the spell. She'd been sitting out here for four hours.

Now this was a woman to be respected. Even in her seventies, her will was indomitable. She was every inch the matriarch of this clan.

And Nate loved her so much.

She looked up as the door swung shut behind him. Wrinkles, well-worn into her cheeks, creased farther with her smile. "Nate, is it time already?"

"It is. The kettle's on, and Sim said to tell you she's making tea or coffee."

Nan took off one glove and held out a hand. He stepped over and picked it up. Instantly her magic, the force, the pull of the spell Nan had created, invited him to join it.

Nan's spell swept over to Vera—and then his mother's energy brushed against him as she leaned her will to the spell, sending it back to Nan to supplement Nan's energy. But the spell wasn't as sure as it had been four hours ago, which meant Nan and Mum's strength were flagging. He'd come at the right time.

Neither needed to risk burning out. Not when Nate was there, and India would be along shortly, too. "I'll come in now, Nan."

He sent his magic to join Nan's first. The tug of the spell wound through his body, picked up his energy, flowed from Nan to his mother—but then his magic rose to the top of the spell.

His eyes widened—so did Nan's. Fucking hell, he was the strongest witch present. This would change the dynamic of their family magic forever, but they'd have to work out *what* that meant later.

Right now, he concentrated on picking up the spell, murmuring the words over and over until the magic was his.

He let Nan's hand slip from his, and then it was just him and his mother.

Nan stood up and offered him her chair. But he shook his head, relishing the feel of his power as it rushed through him. He smiled his thanks but didn't risk any words just yet. Keeping the spell intact was the more important task.

"I can see you've got this, dear. I'll head in. These old bones don't handle the cold like they used to." Nan patted his arm gently.

His lips twitched. Nan was possibly the strongest seventy-five-year-old he knew. And then he got down to the business of protecting the people he cared about.

The sun was barely tinting the horizon when the first of his uncles arrived. They had held him at the barrier, and only when Nate had recognized the magic of his uncle Jack, a touch he'd known since birth, had he allowed the wind to lessen at the very spot and let him enter.

Nate gratefully let Uncle Jack, the second oldest of Nan's four children, take over. The spell wobbled for a few seconds, but he waited until his uncle had a hold of it. He said a quick thanks, then squelched across the yard to check on India.

She was better off than him because she'd been sitting under the covered porch as she held the spell. Her magic was so strong and different from the rest of the family's—at least until last night for Nate anyway—that it was harder for her to join and hold an incantation, and she looked exhausted from her efforts.

But she still smiled at him. He gave her a sympathetic grin back.

"Will your magic be able to work with Jack's?" Nate asked. "Do you need me to take over for you?"

"Please."

She said nothing else, and he knew then the effort India was making to keep her magic under control.

"Okay," Nate said, "I'll come into the spell now."

But when he held India's hand, the first time he'd touched her since becoming a Keeper, their magic worked seamlessly together, and she easily handed the energy of the spell to him. Much easier than even Nan had last night.

"Wow. That's never happened before." India looked up at him in surprise.

"Is it because of the Tree?"

"It is." India looked toward the Tree and then back to him, her eyes suddenly bright. "How amazing. And I'm so happy that you've joined us. You'll make an amazing Keeper, Nate."

He just smiled as India headed for the house. His cousin was pretty amazing herself.

And then he got back to concentrating on feeding the energy of the spell. But it would wear the family thin if they had to keep their magic up like this for too long.

Nate needed to find the threat to Tara and end it.

Minutes later, the front door to the farmhouse opened, and his mum walked out into the morning air, her breath causing puffs of air to form with every step. She handed a thermos to Uncle Jack and then walked straight across the yard to him.

"Nate, you must be exhausted."

He smiled down at his mum, and with one arm, pulled her to his side. She wrapped hers around him, and they just stood there, looking out over the garden, barns, and the stables in the distance.

In their little world within a world, all was still. But around the buildings, the wind silently roared around and around, endless.

It was peaceful, yet eerie. Reassuring yet terrifying that they even needed to do it.

After a moment, his mum eased from his side, looked up at him with her clear, serious gray eyes. "Nate, we can all see how much you feel for Sim and Tara. I just want you to know you deserve to be happy, and I hope that this is what it takes. I love you."

Nate took a deep breath, exhaled carefully so as not to

lose his focus, but it was hard when his mum had just filled his heart. He pulled her into him for a hug and kissed the top of her head.

"Well, now that I've said my piece," Mum said, "I'm here to relieve you."

He narrowed his eyes. She'd been up till after midnight. He shook his head.

"Uh-uh, don't say no," she replied. "Your father is coming back early, and the rest of the family is coming too. We'll all be here to help, and that means you need to fix this problem. So, my boy, time to share this spell. And then be a detective. Our witch-detective."

Nate sighed, but he knew his mother was right. If the entire family were here, they could share the load, prolong the spell. And he needed to find, then remove, the danger to Tara.

And Luc was the very first person he was going to check out. He reached out with one hand and shared the spell with his mum.

Nate raced up to his apartment above the stables, and after a fast shower, he changed into a pair of dark navy cargo pants and a warm sweater. He jogged back to the farmhouse where he found Sim and Tara sitting at the small dining table.

Sim looked up, buttering a slice of toast. "You're up? I thought you'd grab some sleep."

"Not yet. The family will hold the spell, so I need to get to work on you know what. Want a coffee?" He plunked two slices of bread in the toaster and flicked the lever.

An odd look crossed Sim's face before she glanced down at Tara. "Honey, Mumma's got to have a quick talk to Nate.

You eat your brekkie, okay?" She ran a hand over Tara's hair and then walked over to him in the kitchen. She grabbed a pod and a mug. "Here, let me make you a coffee."

Nate rested one hip on the counter. Sim's hair was back in the usual braid. She was here, once again, doing a little something for him in this place where all his memories were of family and love. She was the first woman he'd ever brought here, and he couldn't imagine it being anyone else, ever.

At that moment, Sim looked back at him, her eyes warm, mouth soft. Man, he wanted to lean down and kiss her, but he had to keep in mind her concern about Tara, so he settled for resting one hand on the small of her back.

She licked her lips.

He had to stifle a groan. She was testing him, and she wasn't even aware of it. He cleared his throat.

"So, ah, what did you want to talk about?" he asked.

Sim shot Tara a quick glance and then moved closer to him.

"Here, drink this before it gets cold." She passed him his mug. "You're going to find out what the second danger is, aren't you?"

"I am. And then *I'm* going to end it."

Sim searched his eyes. "How?"

He took a sip of his coffee, suddenly cautious. How was she going to react to his suspicion? But she deserved his honesty.

"I need to start with Luc. And I'm saying this with my detective hat on. He's the only unknown here."

Sim's eyes narrowed, and her hands rose to sit on her hips. "Why—" Sim lowered her voice. "Why Luc?"

A coil of unease stirred in his gut. But he stuck to his plan.

"To know why Tara's in danger, we need to understand Tara. And we already know her through you. She's the daughter of a witch, the granddaughter of an Angel. But we don't know her through Luc. And he might not be a witch, but I can tell you there's something off about Luc."

"How do you know he's not a witch?"

"Because I probed him for magic—"

"You what?"

Nate blew out a breath. "Sim, the man shows up on your doorstep at the same time this all happens. Of course, I checked him out. Plus, he's in my town. Around my people. I used a spell to confirm if he was a witch or not. He's not, by the way. But that doesn't mean there's nothing else we need to know."

"You shouldn't have done that without telling me."

"What? I have a job to do. And that's not even considering that I'm invested in this."

"That's not the point. You should've told me."

Nate jerked a hand through his hair. "Listen, I'm just saying that I need to check Luc out."

"You mean we." Sim stalked back to the table, picked up the butter and Vegemite, and came back into the kitchen. She buttered—well, more like stabbed—his toast. "*We* need to check Luc out."

He eyed her warily. She was angry, and she had a knife. Not the time to provoke her.

"Ah, yeah, okay. *We* need to check him out, but I can get started on that, and then yes, I will let you know everything I find." He waited, and finally Sim slapped his toast on a palm and shoved it in front of him. He surveyed the mangled toast. "Thanks."

She finally looked up at him, and her eyes had turned to molten fire. Not the good kind. He took a step back.

"How long before you leave?" she asked through gritted teeth.

"Ah, a couple of minutes. I need to let Nan and Mum know my plans. And I'll call Thrane on the way into town."

Sim nodded and walked—less stalking now—back to Tara. "Come on, honey, keep eating your toast."

Nate stood still. What in hell had just happened? They'd been talking fine one moment, and the next she was all pissed off. And he was definitely reading her right. Her cheeks had two high blooms of color, and her mouth pursed in a tight line. If she'd had a hand on him, he'd have been singed.

Which sounded hot and slightly scary.

But Nate knew what had to be done. And, of course, he'd tell Sim once he found out what they needed to know. It wasn't like he'd keep the details back from her.

"Okay, well, I have to find Nan. Do you know if she's still asleep?"

Sim didn't look up as she answered. "She just left before you came in. But she said she was going to have a shower and get dressed."

"Okay, I'll go let Mum and Nan know."

"Okay."

"Okay, then."

Sim was pissed. He wanted to go over and ask why. And then kiss her. Hell, kiss her and then ask why. But he was smart enough to know this wasn't the time or place. Though he did walk over to Tara and ruffle her hair.

"See you soon, monkey."

"Nooo, Nate, I'm a puppy."

"Oops. See you soon, puppy." He looked up to catch Sim's grin—but she just looked back at him, her eyes cool now but no less cutting.

"I'll see you soon, too," he muttered.

"Yes, you will."

"Right." Unsure of what else to do—say—he left the living room. Sim needed to come with a warning sign.

After Nate relayed his plans to Mum, he returned to the kitchen and found Nan there alone.

"Sim mentioned you're heading into town," Nan said.

"Yeah, I need to get this figured out quickly. I love that you're all here to help, but this can't go on for long."

He said goodbye to Nan and headed out to his ute—and pulled to a stop. Sim, handbag over her shoulder, stood in front of it.

32

"Why do you look like you're going somewhere?" Nate asked Sim.

"Because I am." Sim lifted her chin. His stomach dropped. He knew that movement all too well.

"Shit," Nate said under his breath. "Listen, I know you weren't happy before, but I meant what I said. I will tell you everything I find out." He went to rub her arm, but she stiffened, pulled away. He dropped his hand. "I have to hurry. My family can't hold this spell for that long. You get why I'm doing this, right?"

"No, Nate, I do not get why you're doing this." Her chin lifted even higher, if that was possible, and her eyes flashed.

"It's because my family can't hold this spell for that long."

"Not that. Of course they can't. I meant, no, I don't get why you think it's okay to do this without me."

"Sim, we're talking about a danger bad enough that the fucking Angel people, or whoever the hell they are, came and took Tara. This isn't something you experiment with."

Sim's hands curled, and was that steam drifting from her fingertips? But he couldn't back down. No way was he letting her put herself in danger. Why didn't she get that?

"Playing around? *Playing*? How dare you say that? I'm the one who woke up to find her gone, and *that* is why I'm coming with you. Because of Tara. She's mine. Mine, Nate!"

"So what, I can't try to protect her, and you too?"

"Not without my input, no. I've tried to tell you this over and over, but you don't listen. When it comes to Tara, I have the say. I have the right to make the calls. You can't try to keep me out of this."

"I'm not trying to keep you out of it. I'm trying to keep you safe. And I will tell you what happens."

"Right, because you've already made one decision without telling me, but oh no, you won't do that again. No way, Nate. I'm coming into town, and when you find Luc, I'm going to be there when he answers who ... what ... he is. And then I'm going to do the other things that I need to do. Like get clothes for Tara and me, make sure my business is okay. You know, things like that. And don't drive off without me; you said anyone could leave. Believe me, I am going into town, with or without you." Sim crossed her arms over her chest, stared him down.

Nate cursed again. No way was he putting Sim in physical danger. He tried one last thing. "What about Tara? Surely she needs you here right now?"

"She's fine, and completely unaware of all our worry and fuss. You've said she's safe here, and I believe that."

"So you want me to drive you in, but that's it?"

"This is why I need to look after myself. No one else gets to decide the outcome for my life."

"Exactly what are you saying here, Sim?"

She winced, but she didn't back down. "Just take me into town, Nate. You know what I'm saying. Relationships and I don't mix."

"So I'm good for sex, but nothing else?"

Sim's eyes narrowed, and she uncrossed her arms, stabbed a finger toward him.

"I told you, Nate, this is me. And I didn't ... don't ... want to hurt you. God, I can't even explain it, but I know it. And that's why I'm not good in a relationship. And everything you've done this morning just reminded me why I'm right."

As her words sank in, the ball of lead that had gathered in his chest exploded. Sim was walking away. From him, from them.

What the fuck was she thinking? He tried to speak—but a giant fucking knot filled his throat, and he couldn't get a sound past it. He just looked at her hard. She couldn't mean it.

But her lips were pursed. Her face icy. Clearly defensive, yet ready to fight him. The hell with that.

Nate jerked open the driver's door. "That's just weak, Sim," he said, finally able to speak. "You can do whatever you want. And if you were strong enough, you'd fight for us, not back off just because we've had an argument. Get in the ute. Since you're going anyway, you might as well come with me."

~

When Nate turned into the hotel car park an hour later, the stony silence in the ute was cold, oppressive. But he had no fucking words, and even if he tried to say something, it wouldn't have helped because he was angry.

Fuck, angry wasn't half of it. Absolutely fucking furious. And worse—his heart was shredding, like one slice at a time was being carved off, leaving him torn and bloody inside.

And the tiny part of his brain that could think through all of this knew that swearing his head off at Sim for making the worst decision ever wouldn't help.

Nate pulled his ute to a stop out the back but didn't turn the engine off. He blew out a hard breath, steeled himself to talk rationally.

"I've got to call Kat. Get an update on Luc." He took out his mobile phone and made the call.

Kat confirmed Luc was not at the hotel. She'd stayed overnight and knew he wasn't there.

"Thanks, Kat. Sim's here now, and the brekkie crew is here too. You can head home."

He leaned back in the seat and finally turned the ute off. For a moment, he stared at the redbrick wall of the pub suddenly, utterly exhausted.

"Nate, I'm heading inside," Sim said, voice low.

Her shoulders were rigid, the clear depths of her eyes chilled like whiskey on the rocks.

"Sim ..."

"No. There's nothing more to say."

"How about this?" Something dark and nasty threatened to leach into him. But he forced the anger aside and instead let out the truth of his feelings. For what they were worth. "I've been in love with you since the moment you came to town. Me. A cop, a witch, a Keeper now, too, who will do everything in my power to keep you safe ...

"And yeah, sometimes I'm going to make mistakes, but that's just it. I'm also still a human, or I was, and we make them. I also take chances. I was shit-scared you'd never really see me, want me, but that didn't stop me from trying.

"And if you can't take the whole of who and what I am, then that's not good enough for me. So go, head inside and do what you need to; I'm going to find Luc."

"When you find him—"

"Yeah, yeah. You have to be there. Got it." He blew out a harsh laugh.

Sim's mouth opened—then closed.

Thank fuck she finally got out of the ute. Only then did Nate breathe. A shattered heave in and out of air. Eyes burning, he followed Sim as she stalked away and through the back door of the building.

Sim didn't turn back.

His phone rang, but he let the call go to voicemail. No way he could've even answered if he'd wanted to, given the burning, hard ball lodged in his throat. Hell, he could barely breathe.

But Nate got himself under control and listened to the voicemail. There'd been another incident with the florist, apparently some kind of physical attack. He dropped the phone into the middle console and then leaned forward, banged his head on the steering wheel.

Bloody hell, what the fuck had just happened with Sim?

They'd been doing great. They'd been going to make a relationship work. But apparently, that was only his dream. And while he thought fear had driven her, what if she just wasn't that into him?

Sex was one thing, sure. A bodily imperative. An itch

you had to scratch. But what if he was the only one who'd fallen in love? Had Nate read her wrong this entire time?

Another shred ripped from his heart. He cursed again, over and over. Then started the ute. He didn't have time to sit around feeling sorry for himself; he had to talk to Luc. And on his way, he'd stop in at the florist, check what the hell had happened there.

Sim closed the door of the hotel behind her and leaned back on it—for a moment, seeing nothing other than Nate's face as he opened the truck door for her.

His eyes dull, his mouth grim. Pain twisting his face.

His hurt pierced her inside as if it were her own. She *hated* that she'd been the one to make him feel that way. But damn it, this is what she'd been saying all along. He'd made a decision that *she* should have been aware of, but no, instead of consulting her, he'd made the call, and then, oh, of course, when she found out, he was all sorry, it won't happen again.

But that was the trouble. Nate was a protector; it was who he was. If she were in a relationship with him, he'd always be putting himself in front of her. For her, for her family.

He kept saying she was scared, scared to give him a go. Of course she was. Because that's how it would be with him. And then, what if she came to depend on him, and one day he left her? Because that's what had happened with the other males in her life.

Something wet rolled down her cheek. Damn, she was

crying. She scrubbed the tear away. She didn't want to cry. Didn't want to feel sorry for herself.

This had been her call. But he'd been the one who'd made it happen. He'd been the one to think it was okay to decide how she, how her family, was going to be. And then he'd gone and gotten angry at her. What in the hell was up with that?

Anger surged, replaced the sadness, and she pushed away from the door. Sim was going to check on the hotel, pack a bag for June, Tara, and herself, and somehow figure out how to run her business remotely.

And find Luc. Because while she didn't like Nate's method, he was right that Luc was the best place to start.

And if Luc didn't give her any insight, that helped— heaven help her.

In the kitchen, her short-order cook, Stu, was well into his prep for the day. He had his headphones on and was singing away while he worked. She didn't stop him for long and got out of there quickly. Frank was already through prep for the bar, which opened in about half an hour.

At the front desk, Sim looked through her accommodation listings on the computer. Thank the stars it was a Monday because they didn't have any check-ins, and with Luc absent, there was no one in the rooms, which meant she didn't have to worry about guests. No small mercy.

And Frank would handle any walk-ins if they got any. But Sim couldn't ask Frank to look after the place day and night. She might have to leave Tara at the farm, at least until this ordeal was over.

Up in the apartment, she pulled out an overnight bag and walked into Tara's room. The bed covers were turned back, just as they'd been when she and Nate had been searching for Tara.

Dear God, was that only yesterday?

Tara left a trail of toys wherever she went, and her bedroom was no different. And they were all kinds of toys, hard blocks, soft animals, anything and everything to do with puppies. They filled the little bookcase; they leaned up against one wall, covered the end of the bed. Sim sat and picked up the current favorite. It was another puppy, sturdy yet soft, which made it great for cuddling, with big floppy ears.

Why on earth would anyone want to hurt a child? A child who played with toy puppies and loved to color in with crayons? It was bewildering.

Just the thought sent her heart racing. Suddenly, it was nighttime, and all she could see was Tara's room from the night before. Bed covers pulled up. An empty room. Pressure clamped around her chest.

Sim stumbled to stand. The flashback faded. The room as it was here and now came back into view. But the fear stayed. Ice speared through her, choked up her inner chime. Obliterated everything else.

The icy blades kept pouring into her, and finally they erupted, heaved out of her in a sob. And once the tears started, they kept coming and coming. She sank back to her knees, surrounded by her child's toys, and cried. She tried to get control. But the tears kept coming, and the sobs racked her chest. Powerless to stop them, she wrapped her arms about herself, let them come.

Safe. Tara was safe. She had to tell herself that over and over, but eventually the words permeated the fear.

And that was the problem. Fear had overwhelmed her entire being. Fear for Tara. For June. For herself and this magic that had taken over their world. Fear about Luc's entry into their lives. Fear about Nate ... of having him, losing him—of losing his love. Fear of loving him.

Loving him.

The word jarred, caught her, blossomed just enough warmth into her that the daggers of icy fear paused, and her sobs ceased.

Love? How in the hell had that happened? Yes, Nate was an amazing man. And the stars knew he took her breath away every time she looked at him.

But beneath that, he was kind. Loyal. Protective. And yeah, he could be an absolute pain in the butt when he thought he was right and just did things his way.

He was complicated. And he adored Tara. And he was amazing with June.

Damn, no wonder she'd fallen in love with him.

Suddenly the fear didn't just pause, it receded. And Sim breathed again. With that inhale, her choices became obvious. Let the icy shards come back and fill her heart, and that would be all she'd ever know. Or push them away and give the warmth that came with Nate a chance, give *them* a chance.

Because who was she helping by staying alone? Not herself. A world without Nate in it wasn't the world she'd ever be happy in. And Tara either. She adored Nate, maybe more than he did her.

Sim took another breath. Looked within herself to find the woman she was. The woman she wanted to be. She'd always been strong, at least that's what she'd told herself.

But was she being strong if she pushed away this chance with Nate? Or was she taking the safe road because taking a chance on Nate had risk? And yeah, she couldn't actually make Nate stay with her; that was outside of her control.

But the thing she could control was to enjoy every moment the two of them—all of them—could have together. *Taking* the chance. That was her control.

Damn, she needed to call Nate.

She unwrapped her arms and pushed to her feet.

A sound, kind of like a crash and something smashing, echoed up from downstairs. Sim stopped. Listened again.

Nothing.

And then ... A yell. Definitely a yell.

Her chime clanged, hard. Insistent.

What the—? She raced out of the bedroom. As she reached the stairs, another crash resounded through the building.

Her chime rang harder.

Without pause, she kept running down two flights of stairs to the ground floor and into the public bar.

Skidded to a halt. Tables and stools were flung on their sides. Frank!

Frank lay on his side, eyes closed. A pool of blood welled from beneath him.

A sound came from behind her.

Sim whirled as a blond woman appeared in the doorway, flipping a knife over and over in her hands.

Then she threw the knife at Sim's chest.

33

Nate knocked a second time on the door of the florist store. Still no answer. He peered through the glass window. No signs of any activity. Of anyone.

He turned the handle of the door and it opened without pause.

The hairs on the back of his neck prickled.

Was this a hoax or something else? The morning light lit the interior, and it was almost the same as the last time he'd been there. The only difference was one stool lay on its side.

Nate carefully stepped around the stool and moved behind the counter. No cash register, no stock. Just a dusty benchtop. He eased over to the interior door.

It swung open easily under his hand.

The room beyond was pitch black. Even the meager light that spilled from the shop didn't light up more than the doorway. From his memory, when the previous owner, Matt, had worked here, there were windows in the storeroom. They must've been covered.

Nate searched around, tried to find a light switch.

Instantly, a frisson of awareness met his fingers. The farther he moved his hand, the stronger the awareness pushed until it became a solid wall of pressure against his arm.

He withdrew straight away. He knew that sensation.

Magic was here. Right now.

Instantly, he gathered his witchcraft, pulled it together, and murmured the spell for witch light. A bright orb grew in his hand, and he willed the magic-light into the dark. The orb cast enough of a warm glow for him to see the glass doors of two dual-door fridges.

But there were no flowers stored inside them.

Bodies packed the fridges, limbs at all angles, eyes open, staring. Wounds gaping and skin tinged an icy blue.

Nausea rose sharply in the back of his throat; he willed the bile down and sent the ball of light closer.

The first body was Matt, the florist. Neil, Matt's partner, was behind him. Another body, with a face he didn't recognize, was stuffed in the second fridge.

Adrenaline surged through Nate. His lips flattened. People he knew, the people of his town, murdered. Their bodies shoved into the storeroom fridges. The affront of not just the killing, but the callousness of the disposal of the bodies, had his hand clench and unclench.

He'd failed. Somehow these killings had happened, and he hadn't known it.

And he couldn't even help them yet because this was a crime scene. He needed to protect it.

Nate pushed more power into the light spell, sending the orb to the other side of the room. This time, every single hair on his body rose in unison. A shiver racked him. His blood, boiling only a moment earlier, iced over in an instant.

Bone by bleached, mangled bone, his witch light unveiled a macabre structure. An altar.

A new vision slammed into him, wrenched his mind from here and now to another place.

The blood-red boot stepped down from the altar, stiletto heel stabbing through piles of corpses below. Some bodies rose, strained with all their might to lift a hand in plea, but the boot smashed back down. Ground through bones and flesh to tear into the earth.

Over and over, the scene played, caught in a loop that Nate couldn't escape. He tried to withdraw from the vision, tried to move his body. Tried to draw his magic. Anything at all. But every part of his body, of his being, was trapped.

A shout hurtled up his throat—

And then a new presence entered his mind. The weight and pure energy that was the World Tree anchored him, let him detach from the vision.

Thank fuck. Without the World Tree right then, he may never have escaped that vision.

A familiar warmth blew through him—the Tree again. It was communicating with him. He took a deep breath. Behind the warmth, a new image formed in his mind: an animal trap hidden beneath a litter of leaves, snapping shut hard and brutal around the paw of an animal.

The image dissolved and all that remained was the touch of the World Tree, right there in his mind. Nate swallowed hard, sent the roiling churning of his gut back down. He needed to communicate with the Tree, but while it could show him images, how in the hell was he meant to talk back?

"Are you saying ... telling me ... that the magic around the altar, the vision I was caught in, was a trap?"

The warm breeze in his mind whispered across him again.

"Right, got it." An icy shiver trickled down his spine. "And it wasn't any old vision, was it? What I saw could become reality if we don't stop it."

The breeze came again, this time icy and sharp.

"Got it. And thank you. Thank fuck for you."

Nate eased back from the door to the storeroom and almost touched the bench—caught himself at the last moment. His instinct for police work kicked in, and he backtracked as close to his original steps as possible. This was a crime scene, and supernatural or not, it needed to be preserved.

And it had been a trap. Why?

Twice now he'd been called to the florist shop—and this time a magic snare had tried to trap him here. Why?

The pieces came together, and he whirled, heedless of the scene, and raced for the ute.

The trap had done its job. Had already drawn him away.

Nate used the voice command on his mobile phone to call Sim, but her line went straight to voicemail.

"Fuck."

He slapped the steering wheel, shoved the ute into gear, and took off, wheels screeching, toward the hotel.

He redirected his call to Thrane as he raced through the near-empty streets. With clipped words, he explained what had happened, what he'd found, and what he thought was going on. Thrane agreed to meet at the hotel, and then Nate disconnected.

But, for fuck's sake, do not let him be right. Do not let him be too late.

Nate's heart pounded hard, fast in his chest. In his ears. All he could hear was the pound, pound, pound of every beat that it took to cross over the streets, pull his ute into the curbside of the hotel.

The front door was closed. He rattled the handle. It didn't budge. He launched himself at the door shoulder first, throwing a spell of power before him. He hit it in a rush of physical and magical force. The old jam fell away, splinters of timber flying in all directions.

A crash echoed in the back of the building, and Nate ran inside—but after one step in, something in the public bar caught his peripheral vision.

The universe stopped.

Sim lay on her back, arms askew, blood at her mouth, on her chest. Her jacket was parted, the shirt beneath ripped.

Behind her, Frank lay crumpled on the ground. The rest of the room, utter disarray.

"*Sim.*" He dropped to his knees beside Sim, reached out shaking hands to touch her. Her skin was cold. Ice shoved its biting claws into his heart. He tapped her cheek. "Sim. *Come on, baby, come on.*"

No response.

He tapped her harder. "Sim!"

No response. *Come on!*

Nate tried to find a beat at her neck. But the only thud was the shuddering beat of his own heart.

Something moved at the back of the room. A giant of a man, knife in hand, hulking toward him.

Fuck. He had to get medics here now. He needed to start

a healing spell. And he needed to put the bastard coming at him down. Now.

But he couldn't do anything if he was fucking dead.

Nate called up the healing spell. Instinct made him want to close his eyes, pour all his energy into the magic. But there was no time, so he called out a fast, short incantation, sent white-hot healing magic into Sim.

A fountain of pain erupted inside him.

Nate reeled, barely caught himself as the shock of the pain took his breath. Fucking hell—he grabbed at his chest —right where the pain hit him, but there wasn't anything there.

He eyed Sim's wound. Was he feeling what she did? Holy fuck, it hurt. But pain meant life. That was the only thing that mattered.

Fucking hell, let his healing spell be enough. It had to be because the muscleman had reached him.

The muscleman was bigger, but Nate was fast, and he shot up, darted to the right. Muscleman swiveled too late, and Nate cleared him easily.

"Stop! Police," Nate yelled. "Drop the knife. Now!"

Muscleman froze. His thick eyebrows squished together.

Right—he wasn't dealing with the sharpest mind. Nate took the time his words bought him and stepped back. Tried to draw the muscleman away from Sim and Frank.

"We need to get the medics. Why don't we just take this outside—"

The muscleman's brows smoothed out, and his gaze flattened before he switched his grip on the knife—it looked like one from the kitchen—and lunged.

Nate stepped in, pressed all his strength into his left

hand and, with an open palm, knocked the muscleman's knife arm in and back across his meaty torso.

The muscleman swung wide with his other hand, but Nate expected the move, and he shifted his balance. And then punched the muscleman with a hard, fast uppercut beneath the chin.

The muscleman grunted, his eyes rolled back, and he toppled, knife clattering to the floor as he flopped to the ground.

Nate swore, kicked the knife far away. He called up a dampening spell to keep the muscleman on the ground, just enough that he didn't risk the power already feeding into Sim's healing spell. It was risky because the dampening spell needed continuous energy, and he was close to exhausted. But he did it—and held both incantations.

As he took a step to Sim, the fire in his chest burned even harder, made him stagger, gasp in a breath.

Fucking hell, how could she stand being in so much pain? He went to drop back to her side. A whispering touch entered his mind. The World Tree. Thank Christ because right then he didn't know how on earth Sim was even alive —the World Tree might be the only thing that could save her.

But the whisper didn't stay. It swept out of him, drew his attention with it back over his shoulder just in time to see the swinging blond hair of Anna Johnson. A silver-hilted dagger—not unlike the one his family used when they practiced their magic—twirled expertly through her fingers.

Her blue eyes were lit with an unearthly fire. Recalled him to the magic trap he'd been drawn into.

"Fuck." This, right here, was the real danger. The giant

on the floor maybe had the brawn, but this female was the real threat.

Nate briefly eyed the dagger and drew the probe spell automatically to assess her magic. He whispered the words beneath his breath, shoved his will into the tendril of energy, and instantly the other two spells tugged on his magic.

Fuck. Those spells *had* to hold. But he didn't have a choice. He also had to know what he was up against. He sent the spell flying toward Anna, then spread his hands wide.

"Anna, what's going on?"

She stepped farther into the foyer; her steps light, sure. Precise. She flicked a glance at the giant on the floor. Her lips curled. "Worthless," she spat in the muscleman's direction.

Anna paused mid-stride, flicked her gaze back to Nate just as his probe met her. And the result of his probe almost singed him with its depth and darkness. She was one hundred percent witch.

She must've been suppressing it the last two times he'd been around her, otherwise he'd have noticed it earlier.

And if she could suppress her magic, she was strong. He mentally cursed but couldn't let on that he'd read her—he needed every advantage he could get.

One golden brow raised in a perfect arc, and her eyes rested on his. No amusement, no malice, just pure ice. The sweet-faced façade he'd dealt with back at her shop had dropped away.

"You're going to tell me where the child is. The child of that one." Anna's chilled gaze dropped to Sim.

Nate's gut tightened. *This* was the danger to Tara. And he

fully understood why Tara had been removed. They could never let this woman with her dark magic near their girl. Thank Christ, Tara was up at the farm. It was up to him to stop this woman from getting close to her.

Sim's pain and the pump and flow of her heart and blood still pulsed through him. With every breath she took, he was right here with her. There was no way he could risk removing the healing spell that was keeping her alive.

And Nate was seriously tired. He'd used his magic over and over, and the absolute worst thing of all would be to flame out.

Anna stepped closer again, the knife still dancing between her fingers.

He recalled the wound in Sim's chest. That's where Anna would aim.

He could remove the spell from the muscleman, but then he'd be facing two fighters, not one. That would be insane. Unless he could get rid of muscleman ...

But he had to be closer to the giant on the ground before Anna threw the knife.

"Why?" Nate asked as he took a step backward. Another. "Why the child? And why did you pretend to be a shopkeeper?"

Anna tilted her head to one side.

"You mortal witches think you're so smart, but I had you fooled. How did you like my snare?"

"Well, your trap didn't work that well, did it?"

Nate needed to check how close he was to musclemen. He risked a fast glance over his shoulder. *Yes, he'd made it.*

"Stop stalling, witch. You have no weapons; your magic will never be as strong as mine. All you do is stave the inevitable, and I do not have time. Now, tell me where the witchling is."

Nate held his breath. The time had to be now, and one look at the pale, icy blue eyes before him told him it was.

He let the dampening spell go—and poured energy into the muscleman.

"No. Go fuck yourself." He shoved his hand on his hips.

Anna's eyes narrowed. The knife blade danced between her fingers, spun under her hand, twisting so the metal hilt fit into her palm. And then she threw it at him.

Light caught the tip, and he had the briefest moment to appreciate the true, swift throw as the blade cut through the air. He stepped to the left. The muscleman, released from the dampening spell and filled with energy, sprang up. Nate grabbed his arm, pulled him into the space where he'd been standing.

Nate blew out a breath. He'd never moved so fast.

Anna screamed. Her face contorted.

The muscleman's eyes widened before he dropped again, this time to his side. The knife sticking out of his chest.

Nate sprang toward Sim, though he kept his eyes fully on Anna. With his magic, he searched for Sim's pain, the ebb and flow of her blood. Heaved in a breath when he found it.

He never thought he'd be so happy to feel such bloody pain. But pain was life. He took what reassurance it gave, then made sure his healing spell was still intact.

It was there—small but fighting still to keep Sim alive.

"That was a terrible move, witch," Anna growled.

"I'm not just a witch."

Anna—or whoever she was—raised both hands, her fingers curled into talons and spat a curse at him.

"The knife would have been the easy way. But I'm going to enjoy this now." Her lips drew back from her teeth; the skin high on her cheeks was taut. And she whispered a word, just one.

The force of magic that erupted from her parted the air currents as it raced through the foyer.

Nate dove to the side. But as fast as he was, the wave of heat, a fire spell, seared and burned him as it blasted past. Singed the skin on his cheek, on his arm. Fiery pain tore a gasp from him. The acrid stench of char filled the air.

Holy fuck. She was a fire witch.

Tingling gathered beneath the burns, and he patted the skin along his cheek. It was smoothing out already.

"Keeper? *You* are a Keeper?" Anna's face contorted again.

Nate hissed as the pain ebbed through him; for all that his body was healing, it still hurt like fuck. But he needed to stay close to Sim. His healing spell wouldn't last without proximity.

"I told you," he panted. "I'm not just a witch."

"That will make this even more special. I've killed dozens of Keepers. You'll just be the next. I'll work out where the witchling is, and once I've gotten rid of her, then it's time for your Tree. Bye-bye, now."

Nate didn't wait. He called on his energy, everything he could tap into without risking the healing spell. Fast, clean words tumbled from his lips, and he threw a blast of ice, dagger sharp and diamond hard, straight for Anna.

Her fire met his ice right in the middle of the foyer. The searing burn of her magic raced along his nerve endings.

But he also sensed when some of his ice—the coldest, hardest diamond heart of the spell—slipped through her incoming spell and rammed through Anna's shoulder.

She cried out.

But then a tremendous pain punched into Nate. The burn lanced his side, the pain, a horrendous funnel of white heat, racked him. He fell to the ground, and the need to scream and somehow stop the invisible flames tore through him. Nate heaved in a breath, almost lost his vision as the pain sent his mind into darkness—right there alongside Sim's.

And still, the ebb and flow of her heart echoed inside him. But the beat was slower, lighter. Fear helped calm him, bring him back out of the dark. Nate couldn't lose Sim. Couldn't lose Tara. His family.

He had to fight.

Somehow, through the absolute fatigue, the pain, the rage, the urge to lay down and close his eyes, he kept both eyes open. Nate shook his head, cleared the darts of dark away from his vision. He didn't bother looking down at his body—could imagine the mangled skin and char he'd see. Instead, he struggled to lift his head, his muscles strained and at the end of their endurance, and looked at Anna.

Thank Christ, she'd sunk to the ground. Fresh blood was running down one side of her body, and a massive pick of ice stuck out of her shoulder.

But her eyes were open too, and as they locked on Nate, hatred welled from their depths. She placed one shaking hand on the ice, murmured a spell, and it melted away.

Oh fuck.

34

Thump. Thump. Thump. The thrum of Nate's heart echoed in his ears to the pulses of pain that radiated through his body from his fingertips to his head.

Nate glanced over his shoulder. Anna's eyes were closed now, but she held a hand to her wound, and the ice wasn't just melting—the gash in her shoulder was sealing around it.

One more hit by the fire witch and he was a goner. He knew it. And if he was a goner, so were Sim and Tara. The image of the red boot crushing millions and millions of souls played through his mind. If this woman, this witch, got to the Tree, everything he loved would be a goner.

Thump. Thump. Thump. The healing spell connecting him to Sim still pulsed in the very back of his mind, a link to his heart that, even through his pain, let him sense Sim's life hanging by a thread.

A fresh chill flew through him, followed by the icy certainty of one thing—Thrane and India needed to know about Anna.

But the only way Nate could communicate with them would be through the Tree. He tried to drag enough energy to mentally push out a message, but fatigue clawed him back, kept him grounded. The healing spell winked out.

No beat. No pulse of life. The thread of his spell snipped.

Nate shuffled to Sim, reached out with his good hand to touch shaking fingers to her wrist.

His world spun to a halt. The only beats thundering in his ears were those of his own blood and heart.

And then ... there ... a pulse against his fingers. The faintest of resistance. He swore, pressed harder. Felt it again. Thank fuck. Her pulse was there, but light. So very fucking light.

Nate called up his magic, dragged in every scrap of energy he could find, and called up the little healing spell once more. He tried to push the magic out of his body, shoved with everything he had, but it wouldn't go.

No matter how hard he strained, he had no energy left. Nate went to brace himself on one arm, but it gave out beneath him, and he half toppled onto Sim. Maybe if he touched her fingers, he might push the spell through.

Except he couldn't do it—the Tree, this world, needed to know about Annalise Johnson. And he knew with total, dead certainty that he could either use his very last heartbeat of energy to get a message out or try to keep Sim alive for that bit longer.

He had moments, maybe less, before Anna would be free of his ice and ready to throw another burst of magic at him. At them.

He leaned up, used his good hand to stroke Sim's hair back from her face. Drank in the sweep of her cheek, the scattered freckles, the curve of her lower lip. A pulse of love shifted in him.

Followed by the deepest sadness he'd ever known.

But even as anger surged, fueling one last flicker of energy deep, deep inside, a scraping sound echoed behind him.

Anna staggered to her feet.

Nate swallowed hard. Rested his forehead to Sim's, took that last scrap of energy and sent a message to the Tree.

A faint, far-away murmur echoed in his mind—the World Tree had heard him. And with that, his magic stopped. Nothing. He had nothing left.

"How touching. But now it's time to die. Say bye-bye to your magic. I'll take that too." Anna sneered, then spat out her spell.

Nate didn't turn as the words rolled over his skin. He knew what was coming. Instead, he touched his lips to Sim's. Gave her every single ounce of his heart—mortal or otherwise. Breathed in her essence.

Sorrow. Longing for what could've been. Hope that at least his last effort would not be in vain. Love. It all crashed through him.

But his love—that was his last thought—because he wanted nothing other in his mind when his end came. Nate wrapped his good hand in Sim's hair, drew her lips up to meet his, and he held them together. Where one began and the other ended didn't matter. Sim was his world. His everything.

He was never letting go. Not for the moment they had left, nor for the eternity he could've wished for.

"I love you, Sim Morris, forever," he whispered the

words onto her lips, refused to be parted even for one second. "See you in the next life."

And then Sim's eyes opened. They were ablaze with a fire that burned more brightly, more deeply, than anything he'd ever seen. Known. And right there, shining clear in those depths, he swore her love shone, too.

She kissed him back.

A howl rented the air behind him. He didn't care.

The fire witch spat out her spell. Verbal daggers that sent a funnel of searing magic to fly into Nate and Sim. To send them to their afterlife together.

But instead of the slam of fire and the singe of flesh, a burst of golden light erupted from within Sim. It exploded through her where their lips touched. Grew to flow over him. Blew out in a shock wave that sent everything around them flying.

Knives of agony roared through Nate. His body jack-knifed, and his last thought before the world went dark was that he was bloody well damned sure Sim loved him too, the bloody stubborn witch.

Sim shielded her eyes against a blast of light. It was so filled with glimmering shards erupting all around, its brilliance blinded her.

As soon as her vision cleared, instinct demanded she get up off the floor. She tried to stand, but pain tore through the middle of her chest. She gasped, dropped back to the ground. Through the pain, she drew in a shaky breath.

Tears blurred her vision, and with shaking hands, she felt over her chest.

Found sticky, wet open skin.

A cry burst from her.

What in the hell was that?

Oh God, it hurt. Every inhale and exhale sent a wall of pain through her.

Through her tears, Sim gingerly looked around. Cried out as more pain rammed through her. She rolled onto her side. A body was beside her.

Nate. Dear God. Nate.

And everything came crashing back.

Nate, kissing her, his blue eyes wide on hers. Nate, whispering his love, even after everything she'd said and done to him. Nate, right there with her, even when she'd been lying on the floor, swimming in a sea of pain and haze. Somehow a part of her.

Sim rolled again, crying and gasping at the effort. But she had to know. Frank was still there—eyes closed, body unmoved. A sob worked its way up her throat, and she shifted as even the sob caused more tremors of pain.

And then another body came into focus, upended against the wall. A woman. The blond woman. Her arms and legs were at wrong angles; her head slumped forward.

But suddenly her eyes opened, and they focused on one person. Nate.

Hatred shone through her gaze, and her lips curled back. She hissed, and her head jerked like a marionette on strings.

Gasping, breath shuddering, Sim pushed herself

forward, cried as more pain lanced through her, but somehow, she shuffled over to Nate. No way was she letting this woman—thing—hurt him.

Panting through the pain, Sim placed her blood-covered hand on Nate's chest. Almost cried in relief when it rose, deeply and surely.

"Nate, Nate. Wake up ... we've got to ..."

An inhumane sound, a wrenching cry and scream, shattered the air, and Sim tried to roll over Nate, tried to cover him.

She looked back at the woman, only to watch as a fountain of blood erupted from her mouth, her nostrils—even the corners of her eyes.

Sim shook Nate harder, cried as even that motion sent shards of fire across her. "Nate! You need to wake up now."

And then another motion caught her attention. Right above the woman, a tiny bead of darkness appeared. Spinning around and around, growing larger and larger.

A deep foreboding hit Sim. Her chime, right where the bloody tear in her chest was, rang inside her, hard and long.

She whacked Nate. It hurt her way more than him. But thank the stars. He groaned and opened his eyes.

Instantly, he sat up. She blinked at how fluid, how fast he moved.

"Sim. What the fuck happened—"

She just shook her head, pointed at the woman and at the spinning ball of dark that had grown significantly in size. "That. That's happening."

Nate looked at her chest swiftly. Then back to her face, but he blinked hard. "Are you okay? How are you okay?"

"No, I'm not okay. It hurts. And I've got a bloody big tear in my chest. But, Nate, that's not important."

She glanced back, the sense of seriously wrong clanging harder inside her. Just in time to see the spinning circle bulge inward, then outward, and suddenly Sim was looking into a hole, like a goddamn portal into another world.

She screamed as four shining black talons curved over the edge, and then another four. They reached out and into the hotel, grasped the head of the woman, her face a painting of red already. Now more fresh blood poured as the talons gouged her skin, drew across one eye, one cheek, one side of her lips.

Nate leaped to his feet, shouted three words, and a shaft of heat flew from his hands. So hot it warmed Sim before it blasted into the talons and into the witch as they dragged her through the spinning black hole.

India and Thrane burst through the front door of the hotel just as a thundering crack shook the room, and the portal disappeared.

The witch, the talons, all gone.

Only the smell of char and a faint rippling in the air remained.

Nate dropped back to his knees at Sim's side. His face, normally so cool, blazed with distress. And in his eyes, the love that he'd whispered.

Man, how he still loved her was a mystery, after all she'd done. But it was right there. Clear for her to see.

"Sim, here, let me lay you down. I need to see your wound." Nate shot a glance at the others. "Call an ambulance, now. Sim's hurt; tell the ambos it's a puncture wound to the chest. And Frank's injured too, not sure how bad."

Thrane and India ran over to Frank, but Sim couldn't see anymore as Nate leaned over her and eased her back down onto the ground. The pain came again, but this time it wasn't so bad.

"Nate, we need to talk. I have to tell you—"

"Sh, not now, Sim. Save your energy. I'm going to call up a healing spell until the ambos get here."

She tried to shift again and see around India and Thrane.

"Is Frank ... Is he ... ?"

India turned around, tears brimming in her eyes.

No, not Frank. Gentle, wonderful, kind Frank.

"Are there anymore?" Thrane asked from where he knelt at Frank's head.

"Not out here," Nate said. "But can you check the rest of the building for the staff and guests?"

"On it."

Sobbing, Sim pushed herself back to a sitting position. The movement caused another wave of pain. But she was alive, somehow. Poor Frank. Just helping her out, like he always did.

Except ... these were witches.

"Don't worry about me, Nate. Get your spell to Frank. Please, please save him."

Sorrow tightened Nate's eyes. His hands were so gentle as he stroked the hair back from her temple.

"Honey, I'm so sorry, but we can't defy the laws of nature. We can't bring him back."

A wave of cold swept through Sim, and she couldn't contain a sob. And another. And with each one, more pain arced through her.

"Sh," Nate whispered, tears welling in his eyes too. "Sh, Sim. Stay still, come on. Please, baby."

The tears in his eyes fell over his cheeks. She tried to stop her sobs and got control. But Nate, good God, Nate was crying.

Oh God, she had to talk to him. Now. "Nate, I can't wait. I need to tell you—"

"Hush. Seriously, Sim. You need to save your energy."

"I can help too, Sim," India said, kneeling opposite Nate.

"There's no need for that," Luc's liquid voice called out from the doorway.

Sim frowned. Luc strolled into the hotel bar, hands in his jeans pockets, creamy knit sweater perfectly settled around his waist. He had a look of faint interest in his eyes as he surveyed them all.

Nate growled. Bared his teeth. Sim did a double take as a flare of energy poured off Nate, the invisible force powerful enough that it swept over her skin like a gust of wind.

"What the fuck are you doing here?" Nate said to Luc.

Sim eyed Nate as more power swept off him. "Nate, what's going on?"

"There's no need for any magic, witch." Luc held his hands up. "I will not hurt you or Simone."

"Then stay right there and out of our way. I need to focus on Sim."

"As you wish. But I can help." Luc rocked back on his heels.

"Nate, maybe we should listen to him?"

"If he says one more thing before I get you settled, I'm going to fucking kill him."

Luc sighed, shrugged. But he said nothing.

And then a small orb of light, a core of red at its heart, spun to life in Nate's hands. Sim had seen nothing like it before.

"What's that?" India asked.

Apparently, neither had India.

"My healing spell. But it's never been red before."

"Maybe we don't need that spell, then. And really, I'm feeling much better. Maybe I'm okay."

"You were stabbed in the chest, Sim. Here, I'm going to lay you back down. Now stay still and don't say another word."

India's drawn face suddenly lightened, and she rocked back on her knees, shot a hand to Nate's arm.

"No, Nate. Look," India said. "Sim's right. Look."

Sim raised her head. The raw, split flesh of her wound was mending, fiber by fiber. Chunk by chunk.

Her inner chime rang lightly, long, over and over.

"What the hell is happening?"

Nate suddenly leaned over her. "Sim, your wound is knitting."

"I can see that. I mean—*how* the hell is that happening?"

"I don't know. I don't sense any spell."

"May I speak now?" Luc raised a hand.

Nate growled, the sound reverberating through his chest. Sim was about to tell him to calm down when Thrane ran back into the bar and skidded to a halt.

"Lucifer? What are you doing here?" Thrane said.

Sim's gaze flew to Luc. What—who—had Thrane called him?

"First," Luc said silkily. "We of the Old World have a covenant—no portal between worlds can ever be opened. I am here to ensure that covenant is upheld. Second, of course, Simone is healing. She is the child of an elder Angel. She is immortal."

35

Walking through the brush and scrub of the forest, Sim breathed in the soothing tang of the evening air. Nate was at her back, and Luc, India, and Thrane were ahead of her. Tara was at the farmhouse being pampered by June, Liz and Nate's family—much to Tara's delight.

Sim's little hotel would be closed down for some time. Which she was okay with. She had a lot to process.

Had it really been less than eight hours since the attack?

Poor Frank. How could he be gone—it seemed impossible? Her heart hurt, a raw, open wound that would take a long time to close over. At least Stu was in the hospital. He'd been alive, and the combined powers of all the witches had been enough to stabilize him until he'd gotten the full medical help he'd needed.

The police had come, and Nate had allowed them to do their job. The man with the knife was a known criminal, and the police had accepted the explanation that he alone had been behind the fight at the hotel, along with the gruesome find in the florist. Although Nate had said there would be an investigation and they would all just have to ride it out.

Tears stung her eyes, and she wiped them away—like she'd been doing all day.

Ahead of them, Luc navigated the brush of the forest expertly. She'd barely spoken to him since the morning, but now apparently, he had to head back to wherever he came from, and she had some important questions before he left.

Focus, Sim. She wiped the last of the tears away and forced herself to tune into the surrounding conversation.

"Luc," Nate said from behind her. "When you ran into the hotel this morning, you said you were there to stop the portal. What did you mean?"

Luc glanced back at them, and she swore Nate tensed up, even though she couldn't see him. But it had been like that all day. Sim was so attuned to Nate, she could sense his location, his feelings, even when they weren't in contact.

Which was oddly reassuring.

"As you now know, I am not of this world," Luc replied. "I do, however, spend time here, under the covenant of the World Tree."

"Covenant?"

"Breaking into the Mortalworld through a portal that anyone ... anything ... can access is an absolute taboo. I sensed a portal in your hotel, so I came to close it. Only there was no need. You did it for me."

"I threw a spell at it," Nate said. "But I thought the portal closed on its own."

"No, that's not possible. A true portal rips open a tear into the fabric of the worlds, and that tear has to be mended." Luc dropped his gaze to Nate's hands and then kept walking.

Sim dropped back to walk side by side with Nate. Between his palms, he was shaping and turning a red-gold orb of light, and Sim sensed his unease, mingled with curiosity, to see what it meant.

Though Sim and Nate had been in the same space for most of the day, they'd had no time alone. She was growing antsy with her need to tell him how she felt.

She glanced around. Luc had caught up with Thrane, and India had dropped back to follow them all.

"Hey, how are you doing?"

He gave the little orb one last look before he closed his palm, and the dancing ball of red and gold disappeared. "I should ask you that."

"Don't try to divert me. I'm serious. Are you okay? When I came to this morning in the hotel, and you were on the floor, I ... I thought you were dead. Just for a moment."

Nate sighed, but while they kept walking, he took her hand in his, absently rubbed his thumb over her palm. The simple caress sent a lick of warmth through Sim.

"Sim, I thought I had to choose between ..." Nate swallowed hard, and while his eyes were on the surrounding forest, his struggle, the pain, the horror of that choice was clear on his face. "Between you and me. Or Tara, the Tree, and the millions of lives protected by it."

"Nate, I'm so sorry you had to face that choice, but I can tell you, you made the right call." Bloody hell, if she'd had to make the same call ... Sim squeezed his hand. "You did."

His lips curved in a sad smile.

"But I still don't know how we survived that last spell?"

"It's time we found out. I hate to rely on your Luc for anything, but it seems he might be the only one who can give us the answers we need right now."

"He's not my Luc." Sim wrinkled her nose. "But I agree. And I've got some other questions of my own."

Sim and Nate were still holding hands when the clearing widened up farther, and then the World Tree was straight ahead. Sim would've known it even if she was blind. There was something about the very air as if it were more precious, more energized, than anywhere else in the world.

And then there was Nate. She was still so attuned to him she even sensed when he reacted to the Tree. His commitment, his connection, was visceral. He must've been experiencing close to a physical tug toward the Tree.

"Luc," Sim said, "we have just a couple of questions. Do you know how Nate and I survived?"

Luc considered them both for a moment, then sighed and rested his hands in his pockets. "From what Nate told us about the surge of energy that happened when the spell hit you, Sim, I am certain that your Angel blood extended you the one protection afforded to your sire's people. Magic can't harm you. In fact, any attempt to wield magic to harm you will rebound."

"So, I'm immortal and magic can't hurt me. Hold on, my father is dead. How's that possible?"

Luc nodded, although a guarded look entered his eyes. "Immortality does not mean being unable to be killed. It just makes it very difficult. And with an Angel, even more so. The only way is to harm them so badly they can never regenerate from their wounds."

"So, stay away from sharp objects?" Nate squeezed Sim's

hand, although Luc didn't even smile. "So that explains me, but what about Nate?"

"Nathaniel was, according to you, directly in contact with you at the time the witch launched her spell?"

"Yeah, I kissed her," Nate said.

"Then, through that connection, Sim's protection extended to you. That makes sense."

"What do you mean?" Nate asked.

"You have been curious as to the change in your magic all day, correct?"

"Yes, to that too."

"And prior to the spell being launched, you said you'd exhausted your magic. You had no ability to protect either yourself or Simone. Yet, you launched a spell of such force you closed a portal from this world. Something I have never seen before in a Mortalworld witch."

"What do you think it means?" Nate asked, still rubbing Sim's palm.

"I believe it means that the witch, this Anna, used a spell that would steal your magic. Something we know the Order do often. But as Simone is an Angel, instead of Anna stealing your magic, Simone stole hers. And because of your connection, the rebound of the spell ended up with you, Nate."

"Holy hell," Nate breathed. He let go of Sim's hand and stared down at his.

"Was Anna a fire witch?" Luc nodded at Nate's hands.

"And ever since the fight, my magic's had a red core that was never there before. And my wounds healed immediately. Anna got me with a blast of her fire early on, yet when I came to, the burns had healed."

"Your magic caused your wounds. It makes sense that your magic, your new magic, healed the same injury it caused." Luc looked around them all before his gaze settled on Sim. "Now, I have one more task. Tara is very special, Simone. No, don't bristle. I am telling you because there is the possibility others will come for her. You need to be ready. They will come for the Tree, and they will come for her."

"I'm not letting anyone take her," Sim growled. "Ever again."

"And neither will we," Nate said. "We'll fight with everything we have to keep Tara safe."

"Thank you, Nate." A lump tightened Sim's throat. "Thank you."

Luc eyed their clasped hands. "I get the sense you'll be strong enough together to do that. Now, I am going to find out who dared try to hunt for your daughter, my offspring." He withdrew his hands from his pockets and moved past them all to the Tree."

"Wait." Sim grabbed Luc's arm. "You said you planned on being around for Tara. Is that still the case?"

"Of course. Tara will need to learn about her heritage."

Holy hell. Her baby's daddy was *Lucifer*. And then a thought struck. "Do you know why my magic triggered suddenly?"

"Yes, I do." Luc shrugged. "I needed to ensure your magic was powerful enough to tackle any danger to your child. I suspected Tara was coming into her power, and that as she did, her heritage might draw unwelcome attention.

"Tara will need those around her who can fight for her with all their powers. Your father's spirit visited me—he had been trying to contact you but feared you were subconsciously repressing your power. Benedict suggested I could trigger your craft with a surge of power."

"Damn it all, Luc. Was that you I saw ... when this all started in my backyard? Was that you standing above me?"

"Yes. I needed to make sure it had worked."

"You have a gall, don't you? How about you just come over and say hey, *Sim*, you might want to know this important fact about your daughter, and here's how I can help you?" Luc didn't say a word, and that steamed her even further. "So, what, Tara is some kind of heir of yours now? Don't you have any other kids?"

"I have other offspring. Few and all females. I had hoped that perhaps a child of the Mortalworld might prove to be a male. I was wrong."

Sim gasped. Bloody hell! "Luc ... Lucifer ... whoever you are, did you target me specifically? I mean, target a half witch, half angel to have a child with?"

"I did."

"And the rest ... all that talk of being attracted to me? Was that bullshit?"

"Simone, you are a very attractive woman. That was no lie. I am a single male. Why would we not enjoy ourselves when I'm here to see Tara?"

"Yeah, well, you might be single, but I'm not." Sim grabbed Nate's hand.

"Pity." Luc shrugged. "See you soon." And then he touched the Tree and disappeared.

The clearing went silent, and Sim stared at the World Tree. The only good thing she could honestly say about Luc right then was that he'd given her Tara.

"Wow. He is such an asshole," she said into the silence.

"So you're not interested in being with him?" Nate said.

"Luc? The man who slept with Marlee after propositioning me? Eew. No way. And even if he wasn't a complete dick, he's not the man I want to be with."

"But he's Tara's dad, and I know you put Tara first."

"He's her biological dad. And he may make an okay dad in his own fashion. But he's not the man who gave up his entire world to find Tara. He's not the man who takes her to see the horses, who makes her hot Milo. Nate, you've been more of a father to Tara in the last year than I think Luc will ever be. And you're the man Tara adores."

"Really? Me?"

Sim laughed, and tears stung her eyes at the wonder in Nate's gaze.

Nate stared at her, and then he laughed, and the joy in that sound made her heart leap.

And so she leaped, too. Into his arms. He folded her close, and the rumbles of his laughter vibrated through his chest.

A smile spread across Sim's face that she couldn't have stopped for anything. "Nate, I need to tell you one thing. And I don't care who else is here. I'm not waiting for another moment. This morning in the hotel, when we were on the floor and you kissed me, I heard you. Heard your whisper. You said you loved me still. And I have to tell you ... need you to know ... I love you too."

"Sim, I—" Nate's eyes blazed fiercely down at her.

"No, please, let me get this out." She covered Nate's mouth. "Because before that, when you dropped me off, I was angry and scared. You had that right all along, Nate.

Because if I let you in, let you get close, one day you'd walk away, and I couldn't bear that.

"So when I got mad at you, and yeah, I was mad, I used that as the reason to get in first. Leave you before you could ever leave me. But I also realized something more important. That's not who I want to be. I don't want fear stopping me from having the life I want to have. I know you and I will disagree. And we'll have arguments. But I'd rather take that, with you, than have a life without you."

She took a deep breath. Searched his eyes. Let everything she felt for him shine through her gaze. And then she had an idea. "I know I'm risky too, and I haven't given you any reason to trust that I won't run or push you away. But I feel you,"—she tapped her chest—"here. You're already part of my world, and I never want to lose that. Can I touch your heart, try to show you?"

Nate swallowed, and though he looked like he was going to say something, he just nodded.

Sim moved her hand beneath his sweater and lightly ran her fingers along the ridges of his stomach. His muscles contracted beneath her touch, and then she reached his chest—right where her chin rested.

She let all her love, all her determination, all her desire to have a life with him flow through her fingers and into Nate.

Nate groaned. "Sim, I feel you too. And yeah, I love you. Let me say that fully, loudly, for everyone to hear. I. Love. You. And I was angry too. But I had my own realization back at the hotel. Whether we have one minute or a lifetime together, I'm going to be here. And yeah, I have this drive to protect you. Hell, everyone. But I'll do my best to include you along the way. You'll just have to hold me to account. Because I don't want to lie. I'll try but might not always get it right." Nate searched her face as if looking for her understanding.

She snorted. "You're such a protector, of course you're going to get it wrong." His expression fell, and she laughed and pressed a kiss to his lips. "And yeah, I'm going to tell you, every time."

"Sim, you're amazing. After all that you've been through, you're standing here, and I know we can make this work. Because I feel you too." He smiled, but then his eyes turned serious. He smoothed her hair back once more from her face. "I've been falling in love with you a little more every day since you moved to town. It started with these freckles. And then your smile. Your eyes. Your heart. Your courage."

That bubble of happiness inside Sim grew and grew, and this time when she pressed her lips to his, his tongue swept in, and he hauled her up, fitting her against his body.

"Uh, guys," India called out from where she and Thrane had tactfully moved out of the clearing. "This is great and all, but it's cold out here. Can we do this later?"

Sim somehow pushed back from Nate's hard, hot chest. His lips were red, his breathing short, and then they both laughed.

"Always with the interruptions."

"Come on, Sim. Apparently, those two are cold. Let's head home."

EPILOGUE

Ri'Anit could lift her neck now, though her legs remained useless. But she didn't move. Wouldn't have, even if she had the ability. She had failed and would pay the price her god demanded in every way required.

The pain was inconsequential. What mattered was that Irrika had sent her minions to bring Ri'Anit home and not left her to be killed in the Mortalworld. So she lay where they'd dropped her at the foot of her god's altar, surrounded by those seconds and thirds who thought they could take her place as Irrika's first.

But she'd show them. She'd come back. Would be the first who delivered the Mortalworld to Irrika.

The End

ALSO BY HM HODGSON

The Immortal Keepers

Book 1 The Last Keeper

Book 3 Keeper Of My Desire

Relics and Legends

A Wreath Of Thorns

Anthologies

Mermaid Kisses

Guarded Hearts

Thank you for reading Keeper Of My Heart and joining me on another adventure into the world of *The Immortal Keepers.*

If you enjoyed Sim and Nate's story, I would be very grateful if you would leave me a review. As a new author, every review helps me pursue my dream of a career in writing.

Thank you!

FREE EBOOK GIVEAWAY

Can a cursed Merprince blackmail his way out of a fairytale nightmare?

Read now to enjoy this Beauty and the Beast retelling!

Get your free ebook now by joining my reader group.

ACKNOWLEDGMENTS

First, to my family. My hubby, kids, and the entire extended crew. Once more, our family message chat has lit up with character names, cover pics, questions and suggestions.

Next, to my writing crew, the Romantics With Attitude. From plot to character to cover, you've helped my book baby take shape.

And an extra shout out to Jacqueline Hayley, whose mad cover skills helped to create this cover—my favourite so far —along with Marina Farcic for her photoshop prowess.

To my friends, whose beautiful, funny and wicked personalities helped inspire these characters.

To editors Sarah and Jo, your wisdom, honesty and belief in my story and these characters have made my words shine. To Sandra Greenhalgh, beta reader extraordinaire, for your encouragement and feedback.

To the Romance Writers of Australia and their competition teams—this story has gone through several writing comps and each time has come out a better product for it. Thank you to the judges and the contest team who volunteer their time to make these competitions happen.

And finally, to everyone who has read The Immortal Keepers stories so far. Your love of this world motivates me to make the next book (and the next) even better.

Thank you, all.

ABOUT THE AUTHOR

HM HODGSON

Brisbane author, HM Hodgson, has always loved stories. Creating her own is the natural evolution of a passion for reading, a love for what makes people tick, and the fantastic places that can be imagined.

Today, she writes about romance (steamy scenes a must!) and magic. Magic that moves worlds and takes her to another place. When not writing or reading or reluctantly cleaning up after her children, she loves looking after her veggie patch and a little flock of chickens.

Keep in touch with HM Hodgson at:
www.hmhodgson.com

www.ingramcontent.com/pod-product-compliance
Lightning Source LLC
Chambersburg PA
CBHW010513100726

47903CB00009B/2728